LOOK WHAT YOU MADE ME DO

AMY ANDREWS

Boldwood

First published in 2013 as *Holding Out For A Hero*. This edition first published in Great Britain in 2024 by Boldwood Books Ltd.

Copyright © Amy Andrews, 2013

Cover Design by Rachel Lawston

Cover Illustration by Rachel Lawston

The moral right of Amy Andrews to be identified as the author of this work has been asserted in accordance with the Copyright, Designs and Patents Act 1988.

Every effort has been made to obtain the necessary permissions with reference to copyright material, both illustrative and quoted. We apologise for any omissions in this respect and will be pleased to make the appropriate acknowledgements in any future edition.

A CIP catalogue record for this book is available from the British Library.

Paperback ISBN 978-1-83617-932-0

Large Print ISBN 978-1-83617-933-7

Hardback ISBN 978-1-83617-931-3

Ebook ISBN 978-1-83617-934-4

Kindle ISBN 978-1-83617-935-1

Audio CD ISBN 978-1-83617-926-9

MP3 CD ISBN 978-1-83617-927-6

Digital audio download ISBN 978-1-83617-929-0

Boldwood Books Ltd
23 Bowerdean Street
London SW6 3TN
www.boldwoodbooks.com

To second chances, old flames and found family.

1

MIDDLE OF NOWHERE KANSAS – POPULATION
5,238

It had been two years, eight months and twenty-three days since Ella Lucas had last done the horizontal rumba. And even then, it hadn't been very good.

With the powerful Harley throbbing between her legs, she was acutely aware of every asexual minute. The machine pulsed against her, taunting barren places, reminding Ella of her depressingly sexless existence. Was it possible to orgasm on the seat of a Harley?

Alone?

She revved the engine. *Lock up your husbands, Trently, Rachel's daughter is back in town.*

Her red lips twisted in a bitter smile. Seventeen years she'd spent in this speck on the map trying to do the right thing, trying to be her mother's opposite, playing the good girl. Until she'd cracked under the pressure of it all and just walked away.

Almost two decades later it had taken them all of forty-eight hours to make her feel like that powerless and frustrated teenager again. So today she was determined to give them what they'd always wanted.

Proof. Actual proof.

Something real to gossip about once she'd hightailed it out of this one-horse town. Something to truly damn her. Something for them all to nod sagely over and say, *See, we were right, the apple never falls too far from the tree.*

And she intended having a damn fine time doing so too.

The sun beat down on her shoulders as she thundered into Trently's main street, rising off the pock-marked road in a shimmering haze. It could have been any of a hundred main streets in rural Kansas – wide, bordered by barren cracked pavements and brick store fronts that hadn't changed in decades.

The bank, the pharmacy, the beige austerity of S. J. Levy's law practice, the realtor, the meat market and the Trently diner – with the same blue-and-white striped awning from her childhood – stood exactly as they always had. It was like entering a time warp. Not even the advent of two-dollar shops had infected the Trently streetscape.

People stopped abruptly on the sidewalk as she passed, their heads turning to track the noisy motorcycle. Business owners stared askance through their shop windows, craning their necks to see if a marauding bikie gang had moved into town.

Ella ignored them all. She was a successful career woman who had long ago cast off the shackles of Trently.

And she was on a mission.

Blood thrummed through her veins as she parked the bike outside The Rusty Nail. Cutting the engine, she kicked down the stand, her reckless mood ratcheting a notch as she dismounted.

The townsfolk still hadn't moved as Ella took off her helmet and hung the sleek black dome on the handlebars. She shook out her untethered hair and it fell in careless disorder around her shoulders, just like in a shampoo commercial.

She'd always wanted to do that.

Sadly, biker bitch was as far removed from her ponytailed high-school-math-teacher existence as was possible. She was as nerdy today as she'd always been.

But Trently didn't know that.

Squaring her shoulders, Ella stepped resolutely toward her target. The rasp of her denim-clad thighs brushing together was almost gunshot loud in the preternaturally silent town.

Good. She had their attention.

Scandalized whispers to her right permeated Ella's focus. Two old ladies she recognized instantly were sitting on a bench that had been located outside the town's favorite dive bar for as long as anyone could remember.

"Afternoon, Miss Simmons, Miss Aberfoyle," she said, not bothering to wait for an acknowledgment.

Crossing the sidewalk, she yanked open the bar door, wishing for a second it was one of those old-fashioned swinging doors from the days of the Wild West. She had, after all, ridden into town for a showdown, of sorts.

It took a few seconds for her eyes to adjust from the bright, summer day to the cool, dim interior of Trently's oldest liquor establishment. The patrons inside stopped mid-conversation to stare at Ella. Only Johnny Cash crooning about not taking your guns to town broke the charged silence.

Ironic.

Ella didn't bother to look around. She knew he was in town – she'd seen him at the funeral yesterday, standing in the distance under the canopy of the giant old cottonwood – and she knew exactly where he'd be. Like his father before him, Jake Prince was behind the bar.

She didn't know why the famed tight end – known to football fans as *The Prince* – with two Super Bowl rings to his name was back home in far eastern buttfuck Kansas pulling beers. Ella vaguely recalled seeing or hearing something about an injury a few months back but still, Trently seemed like an odd place to recuperate.

Not that she cared. He was here and – hopefully – a means to an end.

If she could pull it off.

Ella strode the short distance to the bar, placing her elbows on the aged wooden top, as pock-marked as the road into town. He'd changed and yet he hadn't. Physically he'd matured. Grown into those good looks he'd wielded so indiscriminately back in the day. And there was a *polish* to him now she didn't recognize.

Yet he still *felt* like the Jake Prince of her past.

A beat or two passed as Ella held Jake's gaze. Despite their situational similarities growing up, she'd barely ever spoken to him. He'd been two years ahead of her at school and already refining his bad-boy rep. The last thing she'd needed was an association with him tainting the good-girl persona she'd tried so hard to inhabit.

And now here she was, about to proposition him.

Publicly.

Neither of them said anything but everyone in the place inched slightly closer, including the gum-chewing, peroxide blonde pulling a beer at the taps.

"Jake."

Regarding her for a moment, he picked up a glass. "Ella," he murmured, drawing her gaze to the scruff of whiskers smattering his jawline which seemed more lazy than designer. "I'm so sorry about your mother's passing."

Ella nodded, swallowing a sudden lump in her throat. He'd be about the only one. She wasn't entirely sure she was sorry herself and the harshness of the realization almost sucked her breath away. What kind of a daughter was she?

What kind of *human being*?

Disgust with herself intensified her grief and strengthened her purpose. And yet, as her gaze flicked to the side, her conviction wavered. Perched primly on the closest stool, decked out in her standard attire of twin set and pearls, was Mrs. Coleman, Trently's retired school librarian.

Ella's plan had seemed simple when she'd come up with it back in her mother's house, with its memories and a hostile teenage brother goading her into action. But she hadn't counted on doing this in front of the elegant octogenarian who had taught her how to use the Dewey Decimal System.

Taking a deep, fortifying breath, Ella gathered the simmering anger around her like an armor.

She wasn't seventeen anymore.

"Your dad still have an apartment upstairs?"

It came out steady and clear and she was proud of that, even more so because of how it had surprised him. Not obviously – she doubted anyone else picked up the slight falter as he dried the glass or the *what the hell* widening his eyes.

But she had. She who had spent many teenage moments furtively studying his carefully maintained *screw everybody* demeanor.

"Yes, ma'am," he confirmed, barely dropping a beat.

"What do you say? Wanna give everyone round here something real to talk about?"

Ella ignored the gasp from a rapt Mrs. Coleman as her heartbeat thundered through her head. She felt thirteen years old again, as awkward beneath Jake's scrutiny now as she'd been the night he'd asked her to dance with him at the only homecoming she'd ever attended.

She couldn't tell what he was thinking. His rugged expression was completely inscrutable now as time seemed to slow. As the silence stretched.

Damn it, say something!

After what felt like an eternity, he put the glass down and, without looking at the blonde said, "Mind the bar, Kel." Then he gestured toward the door marked private on the far wall and said to Ella, "Ladies first."

The irritating noise of the barmaid's gum chewing was suddenly silenced and Ella knew in that moment that every Trently resident inside The Rusty Nail was judging them.

But, when hadn't they?

Ella's legs were shaking as she passed the jukebox to one side of the door before she opened it and turned left to head up the stairs. Trently's reaction vaporized into nothingness as Jake's gaze seared liked a brand on her ass.

Were things jiggling too much back there? Damn it, why hadn't she ever used that ridiculously expensive Thigh Master?

The stairs terminated at a door and Jake overtook her at the top, inserting a key into the lock. He pushed it open and stepped into the large open-plan room. Ella briefly noted the two windows that overlooked the street below, a small kitchen area and an unmade Murphy bed pulled out of its cupboard.

"You sure know how to make an entrance," he said as he turned, shoving his big hands on narrow hips, drawing her gaze to the way his jeans hugged his powerful thighs.

Seeing no point in wasting time on pleasantries, Ella kicked the door shut and launched herself at the wall of his chest, ignoring his slight indrawn breath at her impact. The man was a star football player – he could certainly handle her.

"Ella."

The pity in his voice was too much to bear as she twisted the fingers of one hand in the soft cotton of his button down and snaked the other around his neck. Lifting on her tippy toes, Ella dragged him down awkwardly, mashing her lips to his. Her fingers moved to his hair, the velvety fuzz of his number-two cut as decadently delicious as the scrape of his whiskers.

With a groan he pulled out of the kiss, holding her at arm's length. "Don't let them get to you, Ella," he muttered, his breath falling harshly between them. "You were always too classy for this town."

Ella growled in frustration, struggling against his hands, straining to get closer. "Damn it. I'm not a kid, Jake. I know what I want."

"No, you don't."

"Yes, I do." She pushed against his bonds. "I'm thirty-four years old. I've been making up my mind for a long time now."

"Doing this as some kind of FU because you're sad about your mom, isn't very smart."

He was right, it was a whole lot of dumb, but she was a big girl. "I'm offering you sex. Since when did you give a shit about a woman's motivation?"

Jake's playboy jock reputation was a thing of legend – both here *and* nationally. The man was the definition of a sure thing.

"It's okay. No one has to know it didn't happen," he continued, ignoring her question in his best placatory voice. "We'll just hang here for a bit then go on down."

Ella blinked. She could see he was determined to be *honorable* Jake and couldn't believe he'd chosen to develop some morals on the one day she needed him to be the one-and-done Jake of tabloid fame.

She gritted her teeth. "I don't want to *hang*." His gentle restraint on her arms was both aggravating *and* stimulating. "I want you to screw me. Quick and hard."

Ever the good girl, Ella wasn't big on crude language, but she wasn't above using it either, if the situation required.

"And when you're done with that, I want it long and slow."

He met her bald statement with a lazy eyebrow quirk. "Little Ella Lucas." He tutted. "Science geek, math nerd, teacher's pet. If I'd only known you had such a filthy mouth, we could have been friends all those years ago."

Ella snorted. As if she could ever have risked that.

"What's the matter?" she taunted, determined not to be derailed. "Is *The Prince* too big time for some small-town action? Or is your injury more extensive than first thought? Can you not perform?"

Ella suddenly remembered his injury had been *groin* related. For a man whose groin (according to the tabloids) seemed to rest very little, it must be a frustrating experience.

Ignoring her first jab, he homed in on the second with a sardonic smile. "I can perform just fine."

Ella smiled back. "Excellent."

Sighing, he said, "You're gonna hate yourself later."

The absolute certainty in his words brought Ella up short and she stopped struggling. Of course she'd hate herself – she just didn't *do* casual sex.

Ella knew he was right.

Hell, she had three university degrees in *right*. But she wasn't here for his fortune-cookie advice. She was here for the sex. And from what she'd heard, Jake had a few degrees in that.

"Listen, in the last twenty-four hours, I've buried my mother, inherited a teenage brother I never knew existed and discovered that the entire town thinks I ran off with the school principal at the age of seventeen. If I'm going to be damned for my loose ways then you better believe I want to at least reap the benefits."

"That's a lot." His hands fell to his sides. "You're allowed to be angry."

"Gee, *thanks*," she said waspishly.

So nice to have *permission* from the guy who'd been given a get-out-of-jail-free card thanks to a football scholarship. Kick a pointy ball around a piece of grass and the world was your oyster. Work your butt off at school and people accused you of sleeping with the principal.

Another hot surge of rage rose in her chest, swelling to tsunami-like proportions, besieging Ella with the very unreasonable urge to pummel her fists against the solid wall of his chest. She didn't, but they were close enough for her to put her hands on him so she did that instead, laying her palms flat against his pecs.

"They *knew* me, Jake. This town. These people." She bunched the fabric tight, rage still simmering beneath her skin. "They knew me better than that."

His top button was at her eye level and suddenly her frustration found a more constructive outlet.

"I was a valedictorian," she muttered, her thumb brushing across the stitching.

Jake placed a hand against hers but she batted it away, a red mist fogging her vision. Focusing all her pent-up hostility, she concentrated on the little plastic disk. "I was top of every class for five years straight."

Her hands shook as she set about undoing it, fumbling like a two-year-old who hadn't yet learned the art of undressing. When it finally popped, Ella made a triumphant noise in the back of her throat.

"I tutored kids for free," she told the next button, having as much trouble as the first.

"Ella."

He placed his hand on hers again but she shook it off and took a deep, calming breath. "I volunteered at the old folks' home." The button popped. "I sponsored a child in Africa." The last disk fell victim to her steadier fingers. "I still do."

She eyed him squarely. "I was a girl scout."

"You think I don't know what it's like to grow up in a place that ostracizes you for the sins of a parent?" His gaze bored into hers. "How unfair it is? How crazy it can make you?"

Ella knew he knew. Perhaps that was why she was here – because *he* more than anyone else in this shitty town understood.

"It doesn't matter what they think, Ella."

She laughed then. "That's easy for you to say. You got to become a big famous football star. You can do no wrong around here. I'm still" – she leaned in and whispered in that disparaging tone of voice townsfolk had always used when uttering her mother's name – "*Rachel's* daughter."

Overwhelmed by the emotion that'd been building since the funeral, she pressed her forehead against his chest, while she battled for control. His skin was warm and smooth and she inhaled deeply. He smelled like beer.

"Ella."

His voice was husky and sounded a little strained and she shut her eyes at his hesitation. "You don't want to have sex with me?" She wasn't sure she could take that kind of rejection today.

He took a shuddery breath. "That's not what I said."

Pulling her forehead off his chest, she peered into his face, trying to read his eyes. "So you... *do* want to?"

"Ella," he murmured. "It won't help."

"Wanna bet?"

"I think doing this the day after you buried your mother is maybe not the wisest way to cope."

Ella stared at him. Since when had he become so damn smart? "Why don't you let me decide what's the healthiest way to cope with my grief?"

* * *

Jake was running out of reasons why he shouldn't just throw caution to the wind like she obviously had. He was trying really hard to do the right thing but Ella's mood was heady with seething sexuality. Her anger, frustration and grief had morphed into a raw, sexual cocktail.

She needed to burn off some heat. And he was her explosive choice.

It was a stark contrast to her quiet dignity at the funeral yesterday. The townsfolk had been there in full force, their ghoulish delight at Rachel's demise barely disguised, but she'd weathered it all with a mellow poise that had called every faux mourner to account.

She wasn't so poised now, though, her troubled blue gaze still clawing at his gut. How often in the years they'd all but silently co-existed had he related to her torment?

Understood her caged misery?

Not one of the people downstairs understood the demons that drove her. But he did.

Which was why this was a bad idea. Because Ella was different. He didn't know why. She just was. She always had been. The only girl in his fifteen miserable years in this town that had barely looked at him.

Apart from that one time.

But she'd come a long way since the sweetness of that brief shy press of lips she'd granted him at the end of their particularly memorable dance at homecoming. Hell, she'd graduated with honors in the kissing stakes.

There'd been nothing shy or sweet about Ella's kiss just now. It'd been hot and hungry. The same with that look in her eyes. Even in the cute little gingham shirt she was wearing showing *zero* cleavage, there was a directness in her gaze that left him in no doubt what she wanted.

"*Please*," she whispered.

Sweet Jesus. How was he supposed to resist that streak of raw desperation?

"I... don't have any condoms."

Without missing a beat, she reached into her back pocket and pulled out a strip of five. They concertinaed down like a pack of magic cards before she threw them at him. They bounced off his chest and fell to the floor.

"That should do us."

Jake looked at the little packets of temptation. *Five?* He swallowed as his gaze returned to hers. "Kel's off shift in an hour."

"Then why are you wasting time?"

He wished he knew as his gaze returned to the condoms, feeling their lure almost like a physical force.

She gave a frustrated growl low in her throat. "You know, Jake, this wasn't how I pictured it."

He laughed. "Oh yeah? How'd you picture it?"

Glaring at him, she grasped the knot at her navel where the tails of her shirt had been tied. In one quick movement she unknotted it then ripped the shirt open. Buttons flew in all directions, pinging on the wooden floorboards as she shrugged out of the garment, flinging it down beside the condoms.

"You weren't talking, for a start."

Jake's laughter cut out. A gentleman may not have looked but there wasn't one person in Trently who would ever accuse Jake of being a gentleman. So he looked. In fact, he barely stopped himself from licking his lips.

He'd seen a bra like that hanging on the Lucas clothesline when he'd been fourteen. Red lace. D cup. He'd known it was Ella's – Rachel was smaller and hadn't ever been big on underwear anyway.

There was a point at which resistance became futile and God help him, he'd reached that point. Lifting his fingers to his mouth, he mimed zipping them closed and throwing away the key.

Then he slid a finger through her belt loop and yanked.

2

DELUCA, SOUTHSIDE SUBURB OF INVERBORO,
WISCONSIN, POPULATION 2 MILLION

Two years later

Ella groped her way through the crowd to meet Rosie at their usual booth. Except it wasn't their usual booth. Nothing about the mom-and-pop neighborhood bar was usual anymore.

It had been destroyed, the new owner making no attempt at retaining any of the kitschy honky-tonk charm.

The death knell had sounded a few months ago when Ed and Phyllis, owners for the last thirty years, had announced they were selling up and buying an RV. The entire time it had been shut down for refurbishment there'd been an awful feeling in the pit of Ella's stomach.

The sign going up last week had confirmed her worst nightmares. The Touchdown was a *sports bar*.

Gone were the slightly shabby, chipped linoleum tables and worn red leather bench seats and the endearing faux flaming torches that balanced on the walls, throwing a comforting blanket of warm yellow light. In their place was horrible retina-detaching neon and big-screen TVs in every direction.

The display of beer cans from around the world had been sacrificed as well. As had the comfortable, wide wooden bar stools that actually supported her ass, replaced by trendy metallic structures that looked like they'd crumple beneath Ariana Grande's svelte frame.

The cheesy Coolidge prints of dogs playing poker and snooker above the pool tables were gone, too. In their place were framed footy jerseys and other sporting paraphernalia.

And it was dark. Black-hole dark.

The neon may have been bright enough to induce epilepsy but it barely threw the light of a firefly. Ella winced at the slick, shiny surface of the metallic booth table, cold beneath her elbows. An equally metallic song with a heavy bass beat and no discernible lyrics throbbed around the room.

"This is horrible," Ella bitched.

"Yup," Rosie agreed, handing Ella a glass of white wine. "I think we're gonna have to find a new TGIF watering hole, babe. This is more Holy Shit it's Friday."

"But I liked it here," Ella whined then hated herself for whining when it was the epitome of a first world problem. Still, today was going from bad to worse. "And it's ten minutes from home."

Rosie quirked an eyebrow. "What's up?"

Ella took a sip of her drink. "The letter came today." They'd only just started the new school year for crying out loud. Way to take the shine off.

"Bastards!"

"Uh huh."

"Pen pushing, bureaucratic, assholes."

Ella nodded, her friend's insults music to her ears. Real music, not the techno-crap that was currently vibrating around them. "What you said."

"That lot couldn't organize a fuck in a brothel. Screw them. Screw them all."

Ella smiled despite the heaviness that had settled around her since opening the ominous yellow envelope at 8 a.m.

Her bestie's colorful language was the perfect counterbalance to Ella's more judicious use of profanity. Growing up around the quirk and color of the midway had well and truly rubbed off and Rosie's unique way with words was just one of the things Ella loved about her.

Combine that with dramatically dyed black hair, chunky combat-style boots, blood-red lips and eyebrow piercings, and Gypsy-Rose Forsythe was a sight to behold.

Raising her glass, Ella clinked it against Rosie's. It was good to have such an ardent supporter in her corner. "Amen."

Ella's self-appointed champion since the age of seventeen, Rosie had been exactly what tightly wound Ella had needed. People who knew them often wondered what two women of such complete opposites had in common. But Ella didn't – she knew she owed Rosie everything.

That fateful day when the carnival had driven in to Trently had been a major turning point in her life and she thanked her lucky stars for it, for *Rosie*, every day.

Two misfits against the world.

"How long have district given you?"

"Till the end of the year," Ella said gloomily. "If my enrollments haven't picked up and my truancy record improved, they're going to shut us down."

"What?" Rosie shook her head in disgust. "Fuckwits."

Ella swirled the contents of her glass gloomily. "I never wanted this damn job. I never wanted to be principal."

"I know."

She threw a desperate look at Rosie. "I'm a math teacher."

Rosie squeezed Ella's hand. "And a damn good one."

Ella gave her friend a lopsided smile. "How were any of us to know that Kelvin was going to crack under the pressure? This position was only meant to be temporary."

"It's not your fault no one wants to work there."

Ella sighed. "They're not bad kids. Not most of them. They're just living really tough lives." Something that had been further exacerbated by the current cost of living crisis.

"I know," Rosie murmured again.

And she did know. They both knew how rough it was to grow up standing on the outside, looking in.

To be one of the have-nots.

"But they need Deluca High. The whole community does. Even if they don't realize it."

Sure, a small public school in the lower socio-economic suburbs of southside Inverboro, faced its share of challenges but Ella believed passionately that every kid, no matter their circumstances, deserved a good education. The problem for Deluca High was the proximity of two other public high schools and a district office looking to pinch pennies.

"I can't turn my back on that," she continued. "Not like Kelvin."

"What are you going to do, babe?"

"I don't know. I just don't know. But I've got five months to come up with something."

"You will." Rosie squeezed Ella's hand again. "We will."

Ella smiled. This was the Rosie she knew and loved. Behind the don't-fuck-with-me facade, Rosie was a bona fide pussy cat. She gave to buskers – even the terrible ones – she helped in the local soup kitchen, she wrote letters of protest for Amnesty International.

And she collected strays. Including Ella.

"Enough of me," Ella dismissed, so sick of herself and her constant woes. "How's it going with preppy boy?"

"He kissed me today."

"*What*?" Ella's eyes widened. "How old is he again?"

"Twenty-eight."

"God, Rosie. He's a baby."

"I know. I'm a bad, bad person." She sighed dramatically. "I'm probably going to hell."

Ella rolled her eyes. Like the thought of a fiery afterlife wasn't a turn-on for a semi-Goth chick. "What happened?"

"I dragged him into the stationery cupboard and suggested that we should do something about the chemistry burning between the two of us and that he should take full advantage of my appalling lack of morals and kiss me already."

"Oh my God." Ella laughed. Rosie, in complete contradiction to her appearance, worked as a systems analyst at city hall. Preppy guy worked in the same building in the mayor's office. "So he kissed you?"

"Well, at first he said it was highly inappropriate and broke the rules of workplace conduct from 11a through to 19b."

Ella gasped. "He did not!"

Rosie grinned. "I swear to God he did. And then I said in my opinion workplace rules were the most fun to break and he should give it a go."

"And?"

"Let's just say that man follows directions to the letter."

Shaking her head, Ella said, "Isn't he a little... strait-laced for you?"

In Rosie's quest for *the one*, Ella had seen a procession of men through her life and none of them would ever be described as preppy. Her men were edgier. They rode motorbikes and got into bar fights. None of them would have given one fuck about the rules of workplace conduct.

"Yeah, but there's something so endearing about him. He's so neat and prim. I just want to... mess him up a bit."

Ella shook her head, wishing for the thousandth time she could have just an ounce of her friend's faith that Mr. Right was out there somewhere. If Rosie's life was a song it'd be 'I Get Knocked Down (But I Get Up Again)'.

Ella's would be '(I Can't Get No) Satisfaction'.

"They're not toys," she tutted.

"Well, this one certainly isn't. His great-grandfather was governor of the state back before World War I. His grandfather was a senator. His father is a fancy lobbyist for the DNC and his mother is some hobnobbing charity queen. He still lives at home *with his parents*. In Warrington Fields."

Ella raised an eyebrow at the mention of the exclusive outer suburb known for its mansions and acreage. Rosie getting involved with a wealthy political dynasty? That didn't compute.

"He doesn't even *cuss*."

Smiling at Rosie's horrified admission, Ella cut to the chase. "So, he's a challenge?"

"Well." Rosie grinned. "I do love me a challenge."

Yes, she did. But for the first time ever since she'd known Rosie, Ella saw a brief hesitation before the confident grin. Something told her Rosie wasn't as sure of herself as usual.

"Hey." Rosie brightened. "Maybe Simon can use his connections to help with the school thing?"

Ella shrugged. "Maybe." She was willing to take any help on that front.

"I haven't seen Curtis at the house all week," Rosie said, changing the subject.

"We decided it was best to stop seeing each other."

"Oh, babe." Rosie reached across the table and squeezed Ella's hand. "I'm sorry."

Ella sighed. "Don't be. I think it was possibly the dreariest relationship I've had to date."

"That's saying something."

Ella didn't bother to protest her friend's statement. It was depressingly accurate. In the last two years, in her effort to exorcise the ghost of the best sex she'd ever had with the one man on earth she shouldn't have had it with, she'd decided to only date Jake opposites.

Men who had proper jobs and didn't give a damn about sport. Arty men. Intellectuals. Bookish.

"Don't get me wrong, he was great. But in the bedroom department, he was a bit..."

"Dull?"

Ella shook her head. "Too..."

"Boring?"

Frustrated, Ella searched around for the right word that didn't make her sound like an ingrate. "Nice."

Feigning horror, Rosie suppressed a smile. "That's terrible."

She shot her friend a quelling look. "You know what I mean. Is there something wrong with wanting a man to take the lead for once? A little bit of masterfulness?"

"So you want to be dominated?"

"No!" Well... maybe a bit of friendly bondage would be okay but no red room stuff. "I want... I don't know what I want."

Rosie looked at her patiently. "I do. You want head-banging sex without the emotional vulnerability. The *nice* get too close and, thanks to Rachel, you've spent your entire life keeping men at a distance."

Sometimes Ella hated how well Rosie knew her. She placed her wine glass down. "Do you know what I found myself thinking about when we were doing it last time? Pythagoras."

Rosie laughed. "Because A squared plus B squared equals C squared is some kind of math nerd turn on?"

Ella groaned and *thunked* her forehead on the table. "No. But he was being so... considerate. You know, touching all the places in the correct order as if he was ticking them off a list. It was like... sex-by-numbers."

Lifting her head, Ella took a drink, propping an elbow on the table and slipping a hand under her head for support.

"And he kept talking," she continued. "Asking if I was okay. Did I like it? Was there anything I needed? Tell him to stop if I wasn't comfortable. I mean, I know we're supposed to want that these days and intellectually, I *really* appreciate it. But... whatever happened to talking dirty? My mind just drifted."

"To *Pythagoras*?"

"Yup." Typical that instead of conjuring up some filthy fantasy like sex with a boat load of marauding pirates, her mind had drifted to a dead Greek mathematician. "In my defense, I had been trying to explain it to Cam a couple of hours beforehand. And... Pythagoras was apparently a bit of a hottie."

Dubiousness quirked Rosie's eyebrow. "Oh yeah?"

"It's true, I've seen busts."

Rosie pressed her lips together. "Uh huh."

"God." She shook her head. "What's the matter with me? If I have to fake another orgasm, I think I'm going to join a convent." Ella stopped and frowned at Rosie. "Wait... are nuns allowed to masturbate?"

"I would have thought it a prerequisite."

"Right?"

"Look. Babe." Rosie eyed Ella over the top of her glass. "It sounds to me like you need hot jock sex again."

Ella opened her mouth to protest. Hot jock sex was exactly what she *didn't* need. What she'd been trying to *purge* from her system. But hell, at least Jake Prince had made her come three times in forty minutes.

That was three times more than any other man had made her come over the last two years.

And he hadn't stopped to ask her what she did or didn't like, he'd just thrown her on the bed and taken charge. Told her what he was going to do to her in the most smutty, explicit terms possible.

Even now her toes curled at the memory.

"I certainly wasn't thinking about Pythagoras when I was with Jake."

"I like Jake."

Ella rolled her eyes. "You've never met him."

"He made you come, right?"

"A lot."

"Then I like Jake *a lot*." Rosie grinned as she raised her glass. "To multiple orgasms."

Ella clinked her glass against Rosie's. "Amen." But honestly, right now, she'd settle for just one.

Throwing back the contents of her glass, Ella was done with this music. "If I have to listen to one more minute of this techno-crap garbage I'm gonna burst a blood vessel." She stood. "I'll get us another round and put something decent on."

Ella groped her way carefully into the darkened environment, more than a little pleased to find the jukebox was in its original position. Even if it was a different model. It was still old fashioned though, reminding her a little of the one in The Rusty Nail, and she felt curiously comforted by its presence.

Maybe the new owner had a heart after all.

As another synthesized musical monstrosity assaulted her ears, she eagerly scanned the list of songs, quickly growing dismayed. All her favorites were gone. All the country hits were gone as was all the great seventies and eighties rock. All the good music was gone!

The antique shell held a cold neon heart.

Instead there was a who's who of gangster rap, dance music, hip-hop and electronica. The sort of stuff Cam and half the students at her school listened to incessantly, blaring from their ear buds at eardrum-piercing volumes while *vaping*.

They didn't even have Taylor Swift.

Ella shuddered. This had to be a joke! After the day she'd had, messing with her jukebox was unforgiveable. The absolute last straw.

Whoever this new owner was, he was about to get a piece of her mind. She could forgive him the neon and the big-screen televisions but the jukebox?

That was going too far.

* * *

Jake ignored the rough bite of bricks at his back as he leaned against the alley wall and downed half of his Corona.

He was drinking too much.

Perhaps buying a bar hadn't been such a swell idea, but what else did washed-up sports stars do? If it was good enough for Sam Malone it was good enough for him.

Still, there'd been plenty of commentary from friends and colleagues over his choice of bar location. They'd all urged him to buy a hip place in the swankier northern suburbs where people with money – him included – lived. But there'd been something *familiar* about the suburban, southside honky-tonk that had appealed.

That had spoken to him.

Sure, he'd erased all that kitschy shit during the renovation but, according to his father, it was the people that made a bar what it was and, although this neighborhood was a far cry from his current lakeside digs, he felt at home here.

Raising the bottle to his mouth again, Jake took a long pull, savoring the cold bitter taste. As a young rookie, he'd learned the perils of alcohol the hard way and had been practically teetotal for the rest of his career. But with that in the toilet and his father's genes tightening their grip, his fondness for the amber liquid had returned with a vengeance.

A clatter further down the alley disturbed the peace and Jake turned to locate the cause. A sad-looking excuse of a mutt backed guiltily away from some upended wooden crates, eyeing Jake warily. It was some kind of Jack Russell cross, painfully skinny, its ribs well defined beneath mangy fur that was probably mostly white beneath all the ingrained filth.

"Hey, boy." Jake slid down the wall, the bricks snagging at his black T-shirt. He reached out a hand and waited patiently for the neglected animal to come closer. "You lost?" he murmured as the dog approached tentatively, a slight limp making his countenance even more pathetic.

The poor animal looked like he'd been kicked when he was down one too many times and Jake could relate. The mutt's steps grew even more hesitant the closer he got and, in the end, it was Jake who gently bridged the distance between them.

"I'm not going to hurt you," he crooned, scratching the soft spot under the dog's ear. "What's your name, buddy?"

Jake looked for a collar, not surprised when he didn't find one. "Are you a runaway, boy? Are you homeless?"

He cupped the dog's head, noting the gray muzzle as he looked into those sad, mistrustful eyes. Old and down on his luck. "Yeah, life's a bitch, ain't it?"

The dog whined and Jake petted the length of his coat, feeling each dip of his ribcage. "You hungry, boy?"

The door beside him opened abruptly and the bass throbbed into the sultry ripeness of the alley. The dog pushed himself closer to Jake as a low whistle emanated from the doorway.

"That's one ugly dog."

The dog moved closer again and Jake petted him reassuringly. "It's okay, this is Pete. He's an annoying pain in my ass but he won't hurt you."

Pete crouched beside Jake letting the dog sniff his hand. "Some woman's at the bar bitching about the jukebox and demanding to see the heartless asshole who's ripped the soul out of her honky tonk."

Jake sighed as he fondled the dog's head. Running a bar in Inverboro wasn't like back home. It wasn't like TV either.

Draining the last mouthful of beer, he stood. "Well, I guess that's me."

Pete stood too, clapping him on the shoulder. "That's why you're paid the big bucks," he quipped before heading back inside.

Jake looked at the dog, who gazed up at him with don't-leave-me eyes and gave the most pathetic tremble Jake had ever witnessed. "It's okay, boy. I'll send Petey out with some food soon."

3

The monotonous beat vibrated through Jake's chest as he entered and even he winced at the soullessness. Give him Bruce Springsteen screaming 'Born in the USA' any day.

God, he was tired.

He walked past his office and through the back area of the bar, stopping to snag another Corona from the fridge. He cracked the top and took a long drag, not caring how long he made the dissatisfied customer wait.

She could always go find somewhere else to drink.

He frowned as he rounded into the front area. The complaining woman's raised voice was eerily familiar and his pulse kicked up a notch as he laid eyes on her. Two years since she'd swaggered into Trently and dragged him upstairs and yet the memory was as vivid for him as if it had happened yesterday.

She was different, of course, dressed more conservatively in a white blouse with her shoulder-length hair, the color of his on-tap stout, pulled back into a loose ponytail.

He'd always had a thing for ponytails.

"I mean, just how old are you?" she demanded of Pete. "Obviously not old enough to appreciate a classic. You ever heard of the Stones, the Eagles, Johnny goddamn Cash?"

Jake smiled at the imperious index finger pointing in Pete's face. He was the picture of *the-customer-is-always-right* patience. Ella, on the other hand, somehow managed to make *goddamn* sound exactly the way it would coming from a high school teacher with a stick jammed up her ass.

He knew she lived in Inverboro – or had two years ago anyway. But in a city of over two million people, he'd never expected their paths to cross.

"The Chicks?" she asked in desperation. "You know, something with a lyric and more than one note?"

"Well, well, well," Jake drawled as he strolled unhurriedly in their direction. "Looks like you can take the girl out of Trently, but you can't take Trently out of the girl."

She swiveled toward him so fast, he was unprepared for the impact of her gaze after all this time. "*Jake*?"

He took another slug of Mexican nectar. "Ella."

They stared for a while. A long while. Then she glanced at Pete. "This is the boss?" Not waiting for an answer, she flicked her gaze back to him. "*You're* the boss? You *own* this place?"

The astonishment in her voice rankled. He raised his bottle to her. "Surprise."

"I didn't know you lived in Inverboro."

"I moved back here almost two years ago."

She was clearly blindsided. But even so, there was none of the anger, sadness or frustration from their last meeting. No, she looked as cool and detached as the Ella he had known as a kid and, for some reason – maybe it was her incredulity, maybe it was the beer, maybe it was that ponytail – it irritated the crap out of him.

"If you're after a repeat of last time, I have to let you know that *this* establishment doesn't have a room upstairs."

Her hasty glance at Pete and the red flushing her cheeks didn't give him the level of satisfaction he'd hoped.

"Don't flatter yourself, Jake," she said as Pete wisely moved away. "It wasn't that good."

He chuckled. There were two things Jake knew how to do. The first was how to block. The second was how to make a woman *come to Jesus* between his sheets. And Ella Lucas had *definitely* undergone a total religious conversion in his bed.

"Ella..." He tutted. "I wouldn't mind betting that I'm the best you ever had."

Her mouth tightened. "You're mighty sure of yourself."

"What can I say?" He took a swig of beer. "I'm gifted."

Drawing herself up, she gave him that distant haughty look he'd seen often back home in Trently. "I faked it."

Jake threw back his head and laughed. "All three times?"

Looking him directly in the eye, she nodded. "All three."

"Well then, you deserve an Oscar. Meg Ryan could learn a thing or two from you."

"What can I say?" she said, her smile saccharine sweet. "I'm gifted."

"Lots of practice, huh?"

If looks could kill, her glare would have driven him six feet under. But he was damned if he was going to back down now as he drained his beer and slapped it down on the bar top.

She narrowed her gaze. "Are you drunk?"

Reaching into the fridge behind him, he grabbed another Corona, cracked the lid and took a deep swallow. "Not yet."

"Drinking the profits, Jake?"

It was a low blow but he guessed he deserved it. "My father gambled the profits, Ella. He didn't drink them." Although his father's top shelf habit definitely helped lubricate his gambling woes.

"Hey babe, a girl could die of thirst waiting for you."

The intrusion dragged Jake's attention from Ella to the woman at her elbow. Dark hair, eyebrow piercing, blood-red lips. She looked at him as she asked, "This the owner?"

"Jake," he said, holding out his hand, not waiting for Ella to do the honors.

"Rosie." Her grip was firm, her tone polite. Then she glanced at Ella, speculation in her eyes. "Jake? *The* Jake?"

"*The* Jake?" He cocked an eyebrow at Ella.

"The Jake who made you come—"

"Comes from Trently?" Ella interrupted quickly, her eyes bugging at her friend. "Yes, that's right. The arrogant jock."

Unperturbed, Jake chuckled. "Pleased to meet you, Rosie."

"Likewise." She grinned. "I've heard so much about you."

"Well now, I'll just *bet* you have. I was just explaining to Ella, I am gifted."

"She was referring to your career," Ella said acidly.

Jake didn't believe *that* for a moment. Ella had never been a football groupie. In fact, when other girls had smiled and batted their eyelashes at him in his uniform, she'd always looked at him with disdain.

"Ah, well, I'm gifted there as well."

"Hmm." She glanced at Ella. "His ego's healthy."

"That's one word for it," she agreed.

"So Jake," Rosie said, eyeing him frankly. "You're going to be in the neighborhood a lot by the looks of it. You should drop by one day. We live just a few streets away."

The *hell no* expression on Ella's face was comical. Jake took a swig of his beer to hide his smile. "I may just do that, Miss Rosie."

Rosie turned to Ella. "Have you asked him about this God-awful noise yet?"

She shook her head. "Haven't gotten around to it."

Rosie faced him. "I don't know if this had escaped your attention but this music is utter crap."

He laughed. "Yes, it is."

"We can't come to a place every Friday night to unwind from the week's stresses and listen to synthesized whales on crack. You wouldn't make us find somewhere else to ponder the meaning of life, would you?"

"No, ma'am. I'll get a wider range of music put in first thing tomorrow. Will that be more to your liking, ladies?"

Rosie whooped and punched the air. "Damn straight."

"Thank you, Jake," Ella said politely. "Much appreciated."

The words hit Jake like a sledgehammer. She'd said the same thing two years ago as she'd sauntered out of the apartment above The Rusty Nail.

Thank you, Jake, much appreciated.

Although they'd been said with a low, husky vibrato that day. Not cool and distant like now.

Had she remembered? Was her word choice deliberate?

"I aim to please," he replied, just as he had back then.

Her eyes widened slightly before she turned away and Jake had his answer.

* * *

The following Friday, Ella arrived at Jake's bar too late to grab the usual booth and with Rosie cooking dinner for Simon at home, it didn't make sense to take up an entire table.

She just wanted a couple of quiet drinks and a chance to think before meeting the new man in her friend's life. This place might not be the quiet, laid-back bolt hold of old and, she was running the risk of coming face-to-face with Jake again, but it was close to home and old habits died hard.

So, she'd chosen a bar stool and was consequently balancing precariously on an inadequate piece of chrome and plastic while her butt cheeks fought and lost the battle with gravity. She felt like an elephant sitting on a pogo stick.

How the hell she was going to get off was a total mystery.

She'd fought with Cam today. *Again.* He'd skipped school.

Again. How was she supposed to be the authority around Deluca High when she couldn't even control her own brother?

And damn it all – why wouldn't he let her in?

"Hi."

Ella looked up from her wine to find a tall, nice-looking guy about her age standing next to her. He was wearing a suit, his tie pulled loose.

"Haven't I seen you some place before?"

Ella groaned inwardly. Just what she needed right now – a pick-up line. She could see a group of guys watching them and nudging each other in her peripheral vision and had no desire to be part of some horrible dare.

"Yes," she said unsmilingly. "That's why I don't go there anymore."

The guy's confident smile slipped and for a moment Ella felt a twinge of guilt but the loud guffawing in the background hardened her heart. She watched him slink back to his friends, who slapped him vigorously on the back.

Ella returned to her wine and realized Jake had appeared behind the bar.

Topping up her almost empty wine glass, he murmured, "Are you torturing my customers?"

She spied the nearly empty beer bottle he held in his hand. Noticed his hands, period. Magic hands. Hands that knew their way around a woman's body. She'd relived those three orgasms he'd given her obsessively this past week and her abdominal muscles contracted in primal recognition.

Which made her seriously cranky. She had more important things to think about than Jake's freakish ability between the sheets.

"I try not to feed the animals."

Jake gave a faux horrified gasp. "That's not a very nice thing to say."

The group of men broke into a chorus of loud cheers as they watched some football replay on the closest big-screen. They punched the air and grunted like a pack of gorillas.

She raised an eyebrow at Jake. "I rest my case."

He grinned then downed the dregs of his Corona. "Now, now, Ella. They've been working hard all week. All they want is to sit around with their friends, watch the game and maybe even get laid if they're lucky."

Three giggling women came to the bar and called to Jake. They were blonde and big-boobed and impossibly young. Smiling at them, he said to her, "Don't go anywhere," before sauntering off.

His imperious command was irritating but not enough to shift Ella's ass off the pogo stick. No way was she going to execute a move with such a degree of difficulty in front of the Barbie triplets who were currently presenting their forearms for Jake to sign.

Ella rolled her eyes as they giggled and waggled their fingers at him as they left. "Looks like you're the only one getting laid around here tonight," she said as he sauntered back.

Jake inserted a slice of lime into the neck of his next Corona. "They just wanted my autograph."

"Oh please. I saw the way they were batting their eyelids at you. You could have had all three of them at once."

He laughed. "Ménages aren't as fun as they used to be."

Ella's mind went blank. Ménages? *Plural?* "Poor baby," she said derisively.

He leaned forward on his elbows. "I prefer to devote all my energy to one woman at a time."

Before she could lecture herself on not, *under any circumstances,* thinking about how good Jake was at devoting all his energy to one woman, Ella was already there.

Which made her super pissy. She was supposed to be thinking about *Cam,* goddamn it.

"Well, I'm sure they'd all take a number, Jake."

Her deliberate insult slipped off him as he hooted with laughter. "Where's Miss Rosie tonight?"

"She's cooking her sure-thing curry for this guy she's trying to woo."

He raised an eyebrow. "Woo? How old fashioned."

Ella shrugged. Maybe it *was* old fashioned but it sounded better than *debauch.*

"Sure thing because it works every time?"

She nodded, marveling anew at her bestie's healthy libido. "*Every* time."

He narrowed his eyes. "We're not talking about curry now, are we?"

"Nope."

"Does she add some secret aphrodisiac potion to it?"

"No, she just makes it so hot they have to go lie down."

Jake's laughter was drowned out by another round of loud hooting erupting around the bar and Ella gritted her teeth.

"Who do you root for?" he asked, his eyes flicking to the nearest screen.

"Oh please." She snorted. "I'd rather stick a red-hot poker in my eye."

He laughed. "Not a fan?"

Not a fan? Man, was *that* an understatement. Lifting her wine glass to him in salute, Ella said, "I hate it with a passion that consumes my entire being."

"Whoa. What did football ever do to you?"

A familiar sense of impotence clawed at Ella's throat. How could she say *it took you away* without sounding... ridiculous? How could he understand that although they'd rarely spoken she'd felt a desperate kind of affinity for him?

Jake's mere existence had made things more bearable in Trently. Someone else in their dive of a town who truly understood what it felt like to be *tolerated.*

And then he'd left. To play *football.* And it was far easier to hate it than to hate him for taking his chance at getting the hell out of Dodge. Although tonight, after her day with Cam and her emotions in a complete tangle, she was more than happy to hate on him a little, too.

"Nothing. I just... hate the... slavish devotion we have in this country for a bunch of guys who just throw a dumb pointy ball around a stupid bit of grass."

He laughed. "It's not quite as easy as that."

Yeah, maybe. But right now, Ella was too riled up to care about the intricacies of the game. She slapped her hand down on the bar. He was missing the point.

"It's not rocket science, Jake. I mean the NFL's not trying to find a cure for cancer. All they're doing is taking a bunch of young guys fresh out of college, stuffing their pockets full of money, plying them with gifts, telling them their poop doesn't stink all so they can make a shit ton of money."

He nodded. "That's one way of looking at it."

"Jesus, Jake, there are children all around the world and right here that live in poverty but we don't have the money for that. We have kids in America who can't read or write or add up but we don't have the money for that. They're trying to close my school down, for crying out loud. But never mind, there's always money for football."

Ella ran out of steam, slumping over her glass and staring morosely at the contents.

"Finished now?" he asked quietly.

She sighed. She wished she felt better for getting it all off her chest but she didn't. They were still shutting her school down and her brother still hated her. "Finished."

"Jake," Pete interrupted as he entered the bar area, "your damn dog's howling."

"You have a dog?" Ella asked, straightening.

"Kind of."

She blinked, wondering if she'd consumed more alcohol than she thought. "You *kind of* have a dog?"

"He's a stray who's been hanging around. I don't suppose you know anyone in the neighborhood who could take him do you?"

As a matter of fact, she did. She lived at stray central. She opened her mouth to say as much then shut it again. She didn't feel like doing him any favors tonight. Which was irritable and bitchy but she just didn't care.

"Why don't *you* take him home?"

"No pets allowed in my building."

Of course not. She supposed he lived in some posh penthouse somewhere. A place where everything was marble and leather and designer pooches that fit in handbags were fine but dirty strays did not belong.

As if he knew she was prevaricating, he leaned in a little. "Come on, Ella." He waggled his eyebrows. "You owe me one."

She blinked as his meaning. Since when had their down and dirty liaison in The Rusty Nail been transactional?

Since he had a stray dog to offload, apparently.

"He'd be a great watch dog," he cajoled. "Protect two vulnerable women living by themselves. He's got a helluva bark and a menacing personality."

Ella held his gaze for a moment, ready to make some quip about his assumptions but there was little point. Daisy and Iris would never forgive her if she didn't volunteer to take the dog in so that was that.

Resigned, she drained her glass in two swallows and said, "Show me."

4

"Cerberus?" Ella looked from the dog to Jake to the dog.

"Uh huh," he confirmed, squatting to give him a pat.

The dog looked up at her, wagging his tail in apology, as if even he knew the name was rather ambitious. She may not have been expecting three heads but she'd been expecting more than a skinny Jack Russell cross.

She couldn't have been more surprised had it been a Chihuahua called Satan.

"This is the watchdog with the menacing personality?"

Cerberus gave a well-timed pathetic tremble as Jake nodded again. "Underneath this flea-bitten exterior lurks the dark heart of a ninja dog."

Crouching beside Jake, she scratched behind a soft, floppy ear. "Ninja dog, huh?" Cerberus angled his head to allow Ella more access and gave a shudder of ecstasy which made her smile. "What do you say, boy? Want to come live at my house?"

Cerberus whined his agreement and Ella sighed as she ran her hands down the length of his body. "Okay, then."

"Thank you."

The soft words were heartfelt and Ella glanced at Jake. Which was a *big* mistake. Their heads were close and, out of the neon gloom, his features were sharp and defined.

As a teenager Jake had been good-looking. But as an adult, with that care-less smatter of face scruff, his broadly angled face and a set of acre-wide shoulders, his attraction had matured into a lethal weapon.

He was a man now.

A man who, two years ago, had taken her to his bed and systematically reduced her to a pile of quivering goo.

Of its own accord, her gaze dropped to his mouth and her breath hitched as she remembered how masterfully he'd kissed her that day. The thrill of it tingled through her lips even now and the air in the alley became heavy with anticipation.

Ella shut her eyes on a shuddery breath, trying to block him out, but she was close enough to feel the warm puff of his breath, to smell beer and lime. Close enough to just lean in and *take*. If she wanted. But she didn't... right?

Oh God. *This was bad.*

Hastily, she stood, her trembling legs barely holding her upright. "Come on, Cerberus." She cleared her throat. "Let's go home."

Without a backward glance, Ella headed out of the alley assuming, like most strays she knew, the dog would happily follow. The last thing she expected was Jake falling into step beside her. "What are you doing?" she asked, stopping abruptly.

Jake also stopped. "I'm walking you home."

Oh hell, no. "It's only a few blocks. I'll be fine."

"I'm not going to let you walk home alone in the dark."

"It's not dark yet," Ella quibbled. Not really. "And anyway, I'm not alone, am I? I have the hound from hell, ninja dog with me."

They both looked at Cerberus, who wagged his tail and trembled at the same time. Rolling his eyes at the pathetic combination, Jake said, "I insist," and started walking again.

Ella refused to move. She didn't want him to accompany her. She didn't want to spend time with him. Frankly after two years of mediocre sex, a week of hot dreams and whatever the hell *that* was just now, she was so horny she didn't trust that she wouldn't try to jump him before they even left the alley.

"I'm a big girl, Jake. I don't need a chaperone." If anyone needed a chap-erone it was him.

He stopped, walked back to her, grabbed her arm and pulled. "Just come on."

Ella resisted the tug, her skin buzzing where he'd touched her. "What about the bar?"

"I'll text Pete and let him know I'll be gone for a bit."

Ella dug her heels in. "He's kind of young to have that sort of responsibility, isn't he?"

"Don't worry about Pete. He can handle himself."

Reluctantly, Ella let herself be dragged along, shaking her arm free as soon as they exited the alley. She took some deep, steadying breaths of the warm August air and mentally congratulated herself on not slamming Jake against the bricks and having her way with him.

They ambled along the sidewalk, Cerberus trotting perkily between them, the techno beat from the bar gradually fading. "So what do you want to talk about?" he asked.

Ella, who was pretending she wasn't walking beside God's gift to the female anatomy, was grateful for the silence. "Talk is overrated."

He laughed. "You sound like my kind of woman."

"Yeah. I figured you for wham, bam type."

More laughter. "Well, you'd know, sweetheart."

Muscles deep inside her performed a wild tango at his ungentlemanly reminder. They walked in silence for a moment or two, Cerberus trotting between them, Ella concentrating on the rumble of commuter traffic.

"So what's the story with you and Rosie?"

Ella didn't answer for a while. Where did she start? How did she put almost two decades of friendship into words?

"It seems like you've known each other for a long time."

"Nineteen years."

"She was in Trently?" He frowned. "I'm sure I'd have remembered her."

"She came halfway through twelfth grade." He'd moved to Kansas City to further his football career by then.

"Has she always been... alternative?"

Ella grinned. "Always. She grew up in a circus. Like... a literal circus. Her family have been circus people for generations. So she was never going to be beige."

He laughed. "I bet Trently wasn't ready for that."

His laugh was delicious. Rich and warm, oozing over her like warm toffee. It gave her goosebumps despite the sultry evening and those muscles did their thing again. The way they were going she'd have the tightest pelvic floor around.

At least she'd be able to get a job as an exotic dancer firing ping pong balls out of her business if they shut her school down.

"Trently most definitely disapproved."

He looked at her speculatively. "So you befriended her?"

"Yes." Actually, Rosie, recognizing a fellow misfit, had invaded her personal space and refused to leave. "Is that so hard to believe?"

"You were always such a..." He shrugged. "A loner."

Ella snorted. "Do you think that was through choice?" She stopped walking and Cerberus glanced at both of them, giving a low whine. "None of the good moms of Trently wanted their precious little girls playing with Rachel's daughter."

And loneliness had been far preferable to rejection.

"None of them wanted their daughters playing with Jake Prince either. Fortunately for me," he grinned, "teenage girls and their mothers often don't see eye to eye."

Yeah, she hadn't forgotten just how popular Jake had been back then. Ella huffed out a laugh but it rang with hollowness.

"Ella," he murmured. "The mothers of Trently were a mob of prissy, small-town, narrow-minded bitches."

She knew he was right but, oh, how she had longed to go to Sarah Charlton's eighth birthday party along with all the other girls in her class.

Or any of the other birthday parties.

Cerberus whined again as if he could sense Ella's mood.

"I know that. Now." She reached down and patted the dog's head. "But as a kid, I just wanted to fit in. To be like the others."

"That's what I liked about you. You were different from the others."

Surprised, Ella glanced at him. He'd *liked* her? A bunch of silent distant acknowledgments, some brief, perfunctory exchanges and one dance that had culminated in the world's most chaste homecoming kiss? "We barely said boo to each other."

"Yeah, but you never judged me because my father was a drunk who blew our cash at the track every week."

"Well..." She frowned as she straightened. "That would have been completely hypocritical of me, wouldn't it?"

He shrugged. "Trently thrived on hypocrisy."

Yup. Truer words had never been spoken. She forced herself to walk again, and Jake and Cerberus fell into step.

"For what it's worth," he murmured after several beats, "I really liked your mother, too."

She slid him the side eye. "You knew Rachel?"

He just nodded and she silently berated herself. *Of course* he knew her mother. *Everyone* knew Rachel.

Ella remembered the first time she realized what her mother did and why they were ostracized. She'd been in fifth grade and overheard some teachers talking. She remembered the shock as if it was yesterday, trying to comprehend how the woman who danced with her to 'Blue Moon' every morning and had home-made, choc-chip muffins waiting for her after school, was the same person these adults were talking about.

She'd always known her mother wasn't like the other moms but she'd liked that. Rachel had been the prettiest mom at the school and Ella had been secretly proud. She used to sit and watch her put on her make-up every morning, totally entranced, longing for the day when she would be old enough for red lipstick and pink cheeks.

Of course, the fact that Rachel was always in her silky dressing gown, day and night, should have been a clue. As a kid, Ella had just loved the cool slippery feel of it against her face and the way it smelled of perfume and powder. It had seemed so sophisticated. So adult.

Later she'd grown to hate it and all it represented.

"Yeah, well," she said derisively, shaking off the memories, "she tended to have that effect on anyone with a Y chromosome."

"No." Jake shook his head. "She always had the time of day for my dad. A lot of people didn't. It meant something."

They paused at a traffic light and Ella was struck by the sincerity blazing in his eyes. It was startling to hear someone defending Rachel and she felt like a child again, desperately wanting Trently to know her mom the way *she* knew her.

The light changed and the moment passed. When they got to the other side, Ella turned right, away from the main road and into the quiet suburban back streets of Deluca. She hadn't known where she'd end up all those years ago daydreaming about escape from Trently but the rich, cultural tapestry and sheer anonymity of Inverboro, sprawled along the shore of Lake Michigan, had been a balm to her soul.

She couldn't imagine living anywhere else.

"So you and Rosie have been friends since twelfth grade?"

Ella nodded as Jake expertly steered the conversation back on track. "We hitched out of Trently together the night of the prom, ended up here, at her aunt's place. Rosie always jokes she's probably the only kid in the world who ran away from the circus to join home."

He laughed. It filled the warm air around her and cocooned her in a comforting embrace. "So, you didn't flee with the principal that night?"

"No. Contrary to popular opinion, Mr. Edmonstone and I were not having an illicit affair."

"He liked you though."

"Yes. He did. He was the most inspirational person I had ever met. He told me about all the places he'd been and the people he'd met. He encouraged me to aim high. To get out of Trently and make something of myself. Go to college. Travel. Expand my horizons. He was a good teacher. The kind of teacher every student should have. I owe him a lot."

"He was a pretty decent guy," Jake agreed. "I wasn't much of a scholar but he never gave up on me."

As Jake had spent more time outside Mr. Edmonstone's office than he'd spent inside a classroom, Ella figured he spoke from experience.

"He sure as shit didn't seem like some creeper who'd run off with a student."

Anger simmered in Ella's belly; she was still pissed at the rumor. "How were we to know he'd choose exactly the same night we were high tailing it out of Trently to pull a disappearing act too?"

And that Trently would put two and two together and come up with five. Because *Rachel*.

Ella slowed as they approached the old 1930's brick bungalow sitting cheek by jowl to the ones either side, lights ablaze. It had been her and Rosie's refuge when they'd first arrived from Trently and been their beloved home ever since.

It sat in a street of similar buildings; the vast majority having undergone renovation as this area of Deluca had become more and more gentrified. Theirs had not, but it had good bones even if it could do with a lick of paint. It did stand out, however, being the only one with a fence.

With so many strays to contain, it had been a necessity.

Clearly already picking up on the furry occupants of the house, Cerberus sniffed at the gatepost with great interest.

"That's a lot of house for two," Jake said.

Ella smiled. "Two of us, Rosie's two eccentric great aunts – Daisy and Iris – several stray animals *and* a teenage boy."

"Oh yes. How is Cameron?"

Ella's hand tightened on the gate. "He's fine," she dismissed maybe a little too quickly.

"He's what, fifteen?" Jake grimaced. "I remember what I was like at fifteen. Full of hormones and rage. That's a tough age."

"He's... it's... challenging at times."

Now there was the world's greatest understatement. Ella felt like she'd been beating her head against a wall for the last two years. She was somewhere between concussed and popping a blood vessel. Even the thought of having to confront him over his latest episode of truancy was bringing on a headache.

A warm hand slid over hers. "Hey," Jake murmured. "Don't forget he also grew up in Trently."

Ella looked at his hand, surprised at how much strength it loaned her. She was trying hard, really hard, to remember. God knew she'd cut him enough poor-kid-grew-up-Rachel's-kid-too slack to last a lifetime.

But she was nearly at the end of her rope.

Her brother was so hostile and she didn't understand how blowing off his education – his one true chance at leaving his upbringing behind for good – was going to make anything better.

"Do you want to come in?"

The husky invitation was out before she had a chance to fully consider the wisdom of it. Which spoke volumes about her reluctance to be the *big sister* right now. She might have been snippy and irritable with him at the bar and he came burdened with their own complicated history she'd rather not think about but, standing here contemplating the fraught conversation in her future, she'd take whatever delaying tactic she could get.

Even if it was Jake.

He didn't say anything for long beats which, perversely, only made her more desperate for him to agree. "It's usually utter chaos around here," she admitted with a nervous half-laugh, "but if you're game..."

Cerberus yipped an encouraging bark and they both glanced at him as he gave an enthusiastic tail wag/whole body wiggle.

Jake petted the dog. "I'm always game."

Relief flowed cool as Lake Michigan in December through Ella's system and she pushed the squeaky gate open. "Virgin sacrifices first."

He grinned. "Should I be afraid?"

"Very. Daisy loves fresh blood."

5

Suddenly there was a rumble of barking and a flash of fur and Jake found himself surrounded by four canines, all in various stages of excitement. A large Golden Retriever leaped up onto Jake's chest.

"Genghis!" Ella chided. "Down, boy!"

But Jake didn't mind, ruffling the dog's head affectionately before crouching to pat the other dogs who were taking it in turns to sniff Cerberus's butt. When Ella shooed them all into the house the pack seemed perfectly okay with the new dog on the block tagging along.

"Sorry about that," she apologized. "They're a lot."

"Nah." Jake pushed to his feet. "I miss having a dog."

They'd always had some mangy mutt or other his father had managed to pick up from God knew where so Jake felt right at home here. In Ella's house. Ella Lucas from Trently.

No matter how he tried, he still couldn't wrap his head around how two misfits from the same tiny town in Kansas had ended up reconnecting in the same Inverboro burb.

Life was one weird son of a bitch.

He'd been drafted to the Inverboro Sentries for his rookie year and had lived here for a couple of years before being traded to the Broncos, then on to the Oregon Founders. But it was fair to say, his memories of Inverboro were not fond.

Stuff had gone down here that had been directly linked to the ignominious ending of his career. Still, when choosing where to settle after his retirement, it had been a no brainer – Trish lived here, so he'd moved back.

"Come on, I'll take you through."

Jake nodded even though he had no idea why he'd agreed to this at all. It was cozy, family crap which was stuff he usually avoided – even with Trish. But Ella had seemed so desperate and something else, something bigger, had wrapped his resistance in a giant tentacle and yanked.

They climbed up the four steps to the porch and entered via the front door which was wide open. Not particularly safe given the area they lived in but then anyone entering the house would have to brave the dogs and he supposed they probably could be fierce if called upon.

The house was best described as *lived in*. There were signs of some wear and tear and the furniture was cozy rather than fancy, but it was well proportioned and solidly constructed.

Jake stopped at a framed black-and-white portrait-style photograph hanging on the wall near the doorway that separated the dining room and kitchen. It was of two women, very beautiful although quite young.

Twins, he realized. Same dark hair, same wide-set eyes.

One was sitting at a table, her wrists laden with thin bangles, big hoops hanging from her earlobes. Her beringed fingers cradled what he could only describe as a crystal ball. And there was a faraway look in her eyes, like she knew something no one else did.

A secret.

The other woman stood behind, her hands resting on her sister's shoulders. She wore a sleeveless dress with a modest neckline, leaving her thin arms bare. Except they weren't bare. They were covered in tattoos from wrist to shoulder. This one's gaze was more... Frank. Piercing, even.

As though she could sum a person up in an instant.

The background was one of those innocuous backdrops from an old photographic studio but there was something special about the portrait. As if the person behind the camera had known the subjects and managed to capture the essence of the sisters – the similarities as well as the differences.

"I like this," Jake murmured.

Standing beside him, Ella smiled softly at the picture. "That's Daisy and Iris. Back in the day."

Jake glanced at her. "You weren't kidding about the circus thing, then?"

"Nope. They got out a decade before we turned up on their doorstep. Come on." She gestured to the back door. "Come and meet them."

He followed Ella out to the porch where the aroma of cigarette smoke hung in the air. Two frumpy gray-haired women sat at an old-fashioned table. There were bowls and cutlery in the center along with a large pitcher of water and several glasses.

Two tumblers half-filled with amber-colored liquid were placed in front of each aunt. A bottle of bourbon and an overflowing ashtray sat between. One shuffled a pack of tarot cards. The other held what appeared to be a large iPad.

Two pairs of eyes fell on him. Age had grayed and frizzed their long dark locks, there were wrinkles around eyes and mouths, their bosoms were ample and their laps generous. But they were unmistakably the same women from the portrait.

The one with the cards gave him a dreamy smile while the other one, her tattoos still vibrantly colored and on full display, looked at him shrewdly.

Several dogs – not Cerberus – who were lolling on the floorboards, lifted their heads and thumped their tails against the boards. At the far end of the table sat Rosie who leaped up and gave him an enthusiastic hug. "Jake! I'm so pleased Ella invited you back for curry. Simon will be here soon and I'll dish up."

Jake glanced at Ella, who gave him an almost imperceptible shake of her head. "Er, thanks, but I can't stay for long. I have to get back to the bar."

"I take it we have you to thank for the dog?" said the tattooed one in her two-pack-a-day voice, indicating the back yard where Cerberus was making himself at home by methodically lifting his leg on every tree, bush, rock and blade of grass.

Genghis followed after the smaller dog, peeing over the top of the newcomer's wet spots.

"Yes." He smiled at the older woman. "That's Cerberus."

She nodded. "And you're Jake."

Ella introduced him to Daisy and Jake felt an instant rapport. There was an astuteness to her that reminded him of his own great aunt – Thelma – who'd raised him for many years after his mother's desertion.

She'd died of a heart attack when he'd been twelve and he'd missed her every damn day since.

"You know what an eight-letter word for storm is?" Daisy asked. "Starts with a B."

"Oh…" Jake drew a blank. "Sorry, no."

Daisy *hmphed* as she returned her attention to the device. If it was a test, Jake had definitely failed but he didn't have any time to ponder that as Ella introduced him to Iris.

"You're a Sagittarius, aren't you?" she asked as they shook hands, her fingers devoid of the rings from the portrait but her wrists still sporting dozens of fine silver bangles.

Jake smiled at the woman with the dreamy voice. "Yep."

Just then, the dogs leaped up and started barking in unison. "That'll be Simon," Rosie announced giving a little jiggle as she departed quickly, a pack of excitable dogs on her heel – Cerberus included.

Rosie was back quickly with a guy in tow. He looked a little younger than her and reeked of old money from his preppy haircut to his expensive threads which were currently covered in dog hair. In his hand he clutched a bottle of wine and a bunch of flowers and was clearly nervous.

He didn't look like he'd ever ventured this far south.

"So this is Simon?" Daisy said, eyeing tonight's second virgin sacrifice. "Come here. Give me a proper look at you."

Simon walked closer and Rosie introduced them.

"Bit young for you isn't he, Gypsy-Rose?" Daisy commented, looking him up and down.

Simon shot a glance at Rosie, who was grinning affectionately at her curmudgeonly aunt. "I believe age is irrelevant," he said politely.

"Hmph!" Daisy grunted. "Speak to me when you're seventy-two. You know an eight-letter word for storm? Starts with a B?"

"Oh… um." Simon shot a quick glance at Jake who gave him a *don't-ask-me* look. "Um…" He returned his attention to Daisy. "Is it… brouhaha?"

Frowning, Daisy consulted the screen. "Yes!" Tapping it in, she smiled approvingly at Simon.

"You're a goat, aren't you?"

"A... goat?" Simon asked as he darted a bewildered glance at Iris.

"Capricorn," Rosie said, rescuing him. "Your star sign."

"Oh, right." He gave a laugh which sounded as weirded out as he looked. "Yes actually, I am."

"And this is my bestie, Ella," Rosie continued.

"Ah." Simon smiled. "I've heard so much about you."

Ella returned the smile with a huge one of her own, which annoyed the crap out of Jake. She'd *never* smiled at him like that. Not even after three goddamn orgasms!

"Don't believe half of it," she said.

And then it was Jake's turn, but Rosie barely got a word out before Simon interrupted. "Good God. You're *Jake Prince*." He extended his hand and pumped Jake's vigorously. "I'm a big fan. *Big* fan. It was a tragedy to see you go."

"Thanks, man," Jake said as he withdrew his hand, aware everyone was looking at him. The aunts clearly had no clue who he was, Rosie was beaming and Ella looked genuinely surprised that he'd been recognized.

Which was also seriously fucking annoying. He may never have deliberately courted attention and not be playing anymore but he was *The Prince*.

"Do you miss it?" Simon asked.

A great well of emptiness opened inside Jake at the question. *Only every moment of every day.* Football had been the only thing he'd ever been any good at and the way it had ended still churned in his gut. But he wasn't about to open that can of worms.

"Sure."

"What do you think the Founders' chances are this season?"

Before Jake could answer, Ella interrupted. And hell, if he could have kissed her for it. "Must be curry time?" she said.

"Yes, yes." Rosie clapped her hands. "Everyone sit. You too, Jake, I insist."

"Oh no," Ella said dismissively, "I think Jake has to get back."

Her gaze met his, her eyes bugging slightly, a little movement of her head indicating it was time for him to go.

Which was bad fucking luck because, grateful or not for her interruption, he was in a *mood* now.

And she'd started it.

She'd invited him inside for whatever in hell reason and now he'd fulfilled some purpose he wasn't aware of, he could just walk his ass out of here?

Nope. He'd leave when he was good and ready.

"Thanks, I think I will." He held Ella's gaze as he grabbed a seat. The tightening of her lips was exceptionally satisfying.

"Can I help?" Simon offered.

"Nope." Rosie dazzled a smile in his direction. "You're a guest. Sit that cutie patootie down, mister."

The three women blinked at Rosie as she departed, clearly surprised at the saccharine language. Jake was surprised, too. He hadn't known Rosie for very long, but he'd seen enough to know *patootie* probably wasn't in her normal vocabulary.

Daisy eyed Simon once Rosie had left. "Just so you know, this is your first test."

"Oh?" He raised an eyebrow. "I thought that was you?"

Daisy hooted out a laugh and Jake gave him props for not only recovering from the culture shock of the introductions but not being intimated by the older woman.

"You survive your first curry, then we'll worry about me."

"Deal."

"Cam grabbed some curry and took it upstairs," Rosie said as she placed the large heavy pot in the center of the table and started dishing it into bowls. "He wants to watch the football."

"That kid watches too much TV," Daisy griped.

Jake, who was sitting next to Ella, noticed her pale a little at the comment. But that could have been the curry which was, as advertised, hot enough to melt his face off. It didn't even start warm and build. It just went straight for the throat.

Simon coughed after his first mouthful and Daisy poured two glasses of water, passing them to the curry virgins.

"Some girl called him earlier," Daisy said as she tucked into her curry with wild abandon. "Marissa...? Miri? Something like that."

"*Really*?" Ella gaped. "How'd that go?"

"Kind of silent this end. He did a lot of nodding."

She laughed. "Yeah. I bet."

"Any more thoughts on a plan of attack, dear?" Iris asked Ella, changing the subject.

"Not really."

"Problem?" Simon asked.

"Bureaucratic bastards at district are trying to shut Ella's school down," Rosie explained.

Simon pursed his lips. "Can they do that?"

"They sure can." Ella grimaced as she worried a linen napkin between her fingers.

Had it been paper it'd be in shreds. She was clearly stressed about the situation given she'd mentioned it to him earlier. Maybe that's why she'd been in such a *mood* at the bar?

"I still can't believe they will," she continued. "For a lot of the kids in this area the school is a refuge, a place where they're seen and free from the everyday struggles of life for a while."

Jake liked that Ella had become a teacher and it was apparent that it was more than just a job. The school and its students obviously meant the world to her. And not just to her if the wacky ideas for saving the school that were being thrown around – winning the lottery, having it declared an historic site – were any indication.

Simon, who'd been slowly making his way through his bowl, suddenly locked eyes with Jake. "I've got it," he announced with a snap of his fingers.

Everyone turned to face him. Everyone except Cerberus, who was already looking at him adoringly, waiting eagerly for the next spoonful of smuggled curry. The other dogs, lounging far away from the table, appeared to know better.

"Does the school have a football team?" Simon asked, absently patting Cerberus's head.

An itch shot up Jake's spine. He *did not* like where this was going.

Ella frowned. "No. There's a field so it must have at some point but there's no money for extracurricular things like that. We don't even have enough in the budget for the mandatory one lesson a week of PE."

"How about getting a football team together and entering the high school football championships? You get to the playoffs and no way would they shut down a school that got that far."

She gaped at Simon. "What?"

Jake, who'd been mentally preparing for the wackiest idea of all since Simon had eyeballed him, relaxed tense shoulders. Ella looked like she was about to have a stroke. Or at the very least ask Simon if he'd been dropped on the head as a baby.

He thanked God for her pathological dislike of football.

"Just like that," she asked incredulously. "Just win a bunch of football games?"

"Look... I'm not saying it'll be easy. But you do have a secret weapon sitting right at this table."

Ella turned and looked at Jake. "He means you, right?"

Ignoring her, Jake glared at Simon. "No."

Jesus. The last thing he needed was this kind of hassle. He was *retired*. It might have been forced on him, he might not have been ready for it, but he was *done*. He didn't need to stir up a bunch of media interest now it had finally all died down.

He had a bar. He was drinking beer. Life was one long happy hour.

"You could coach them," Simon pressed.

"Ohmigod, yes." Rosie clapped, bouncing in her seat. "It's perfect."

"No," Jake said at the same time Ella did. He shot her some side eye before returning his attention to Simon. "I'm retired."

"He's retired," Ella repeated.

"Every year Chiswick Academy invites another high school football team that has done well in the competition to play a nonconference game at their campus," Simon continued. "It's *very* prestigious to even be asked. There'd be a lot of eyes across that game. Win that and you'd be untouchable."

"Yeah, even I've heard of that," Ella admitted. "But... we'd have to win, right? A lot. As a new team? We'd need more than Jake. We'd need God's gift to football."

Simon cocked an eyebrow. "Jake is one of the best tight ends this game has ever seen. He *is* God's gift to football."

Jake accepted the accolade without any false modesty as her eyes flashed over him. Eyes that had turned contemplative. Like maybe she was... *considering* the hare-brained suggestion?

"The cards are favorable," Iris said with pursed lips, snagging Jake's attention.

Her almost empty bowl had been pushed to one side and she was staring down at several cards laid out in front of her in some kind of pattern. Nodding at them, she added, "They're indicating it could be very good for Cameron."

Jake sensed Ella, who'd been holding herself rigid, deflate a little, a sigh escaping her mouth. "Well that's it then," she said to Rosie.

His head swiveled between the two of them. What was *it*?

Rosie nodded. "The cards are never wrong."

"Do they say we'll win?" Ella asked.

Iris gave a faraway smile. "You know they don't deal in absolutes."

Ella turned her gaze on him then, determination turning them steely. Jake shook his head. "No."

She gave him a reproving look which didn't move him one iota. "I'm retired," he said, exasperation in his voice.

Everyone stared at him.

"So you have plenty of time on your hands."

What the fuck? What was happening right now? A minute ago she was on *his* side. "I run a *bar*."

She faltered for a moment, and Jake thought she was going to change her mind. But then her gaze slid momentarily to Iris, who nodded and Ella straightened her shoulders. "Challenge too big for you, Jake?" she goaded. "Not up to it? Prefer to fritter away life drinking beer and signing women's body parts?"

Was that even a proper question? "Hell, yeah."

Ella rolled her eyes. "This is important. More important than beer and women."

"Nothing's more important than beer and women." Certainly not this stupid, hare-brained... *whim*.

"Margaritaville every day for you, huh?"

"Yes, ma'am."

She regarded him for a long moment. It was clear she was suddenly, desperately invested in this ridiculous plan. "*Please.*"

Oh God... the way she said please. Like she had that day two years ago and *man* if it didn't tug at him just as hard.

He sighed. "A public school has *never* won against Chiswick Academy since they started doing it ninety years ago."

Ella started. "Is that true?" she asked Simon.

He nodded. "Doesn't mean yours won't be the first."

"Right?" She turned to Jake. "We could be the ones."

"You told me, not even an hour ago, that you despise football."

"I'm prepared to tolerate it."

Jake huffed out an exasperated breath. "Don't you... have a plan B?"

"Sure, sleep with the entire education review panel."

"There you go, then." He nodded. "Problem solved."

"You want me to do a dozen sexual favors for a bunch of men who look like they come from the pre *g-spot* era?"

Cameron chose that moment to appear. Considering he was a big kid, he looked surprisingly like his petite mother. Ignoring everybody, he snatched up a handheld game console that had been sitting discarded in the middle of the table.

"Hey, Cam," Ella called as he turned to leave.

Cameron came to an abrupt stop, clearly aggrieved by the intrusion. "What?"

"Can you let me know when the game's over, please? I need to talk to you."

He blasted a hostile glare at his sister. "Talk, talk, talk. That's all you ever do." Then he stormed off in the direction of the door.

"Cam," she called after him.

"Fuck *off*," he threw over his shoulder as he yanked open the door and slammed it behind him for good measure.

Jake blinked as an uncomfortable silence descended. Ella sat deathly still, her knuckles blanching white against the back of the chair. No wonder she'd looked so strained earlier. If he'd spoken to an adult like that at fifteen, he would have been knocked sideways.

Cameron Lucas needed a serious attitude adjustment.

But, amid the heat simmering inside him, a primal kind of recognition glowed. Ella's brother was a product of Trently. As he had been.

Cameron Lucas was him – before football.

"Okay." He stood abruptly, driven by something deeper than he could explain. "I'll be there Monday at three o'clock. You got yourself a coach."

Then he excused himself and left before he changed his mind.

6

Jake's cell phone jangled in the dark, quiet room like hell's doorbell. He woke with a start, groping around blindly for the offensive item, the noise like a hot needle in his temple.

"This better be good," he growled as he punched the answer button.

"Good, you're awake." Pete's chipper voice grated along nerve endings that already felt like they'd spent the entire night on the rack.

"What the hell time is it?"

"Two."

Jake turned his head toward the sliver of light he could see through a gap in the heavy black-out curtains covering the window. "Two p.m.?"

Where the hell was he? A bunker? A dungeon? A coffin?

As much as it hurt to think, he searched back into the abyss that was last night. There was poker. And drinking. And a girl. He reached out a hand and came in to contact with a warm naked thigh. The woman attached murmured something and rolled toward him, draping herself across his chest, her hand sliding down to the flat of his belly.

Crap!

"Uh huh. You have to be at the school in an hour."

Jake groaned. He wanted to crawl into a corner somewhere and die. He did not want to run around a football field with a bunch of rag-tag high school amateurs. At the moment, getting out of bed seemed way too big an effort.

But then a picture of Ella's strained face at Cameron's insult the other night floated through the ninety-proof quagmire of his brain and he sighed. "Okay. I'll be there."

"Cool."

Jake squinted into the darkness. "Er, Pete? I don't suppose you happen to know where I am?"

Pete laughed. "Sure, I dropped you and fan-girl back at her place last night. Would you like me to come pick you up?"

Fan-girl's hand moved lower and he grabbed it before it reached ground zero. "Hurry."

* * *

Jake winced as he climbed into the passenger seat of his car and was greeted by an unbearable blare of noise that was the musical equivalent of fingernails down a blackboard.

He reached for the dial and turned it down. "Jesus, Pete."

Pete grinned. "I hope we practiced safe sex?"

Jake glared at him. "What are you, my pimp?"

"Actually." He laughed. "I think I am."

Jake contemplated murder as Pete's laughter ricocheted like jackhammers inside his head. "I should have left you on the streets," he muttered.

Pete laughed even harder. "We're late. Ella's going to be ticked."

Well, Ella could get in line. He was pretty annoyed at himself. He couldn't remember the last time he'd written himself off enough to cause *amnesia*.

Maybe two years ago when the Founders had given him his marching orders?

Had he practiced safe sex? Hell, had he even *had* sex? He'd woken up with his clothes on and somehow, he seriously doubted he'd have been capable...

Christ, he'd *never* not been capable.

Jake shut his eyes, his head throbbing double-time the harder he tried to remember. Unfortunately, not even the combination of closed lids, an ultra-dark window tint and his aviator sunglasses was able to block the stab of harsh afternoon sunlight filtering through the smoky glass into his eyeballs.

They felt as if they'd been ripped out, stood on, rolled in shell grit then stuffed in back to front.

His head sank back gratefully into the spongy luxury of the leather interior as the powerful engine of his BMW surged forward. Thankfully, Pete didn't try to communicate any further and the construction crew in his head downed tools for a while.

He wasn't sure how much time had elapsed when the car glided to a halt, but he knew he was going to need a hell of a lot more to even begin feeling human again. He peered out the window at a poorly maintained field. The grass was patchy and mostly weeds. Large areas were totally bare. The posts had rust stains and the score board was peeling and listed to one side.

He was a long way from the Super Bowl.

A large crowd sat on derelict wooden bleachers as he turned to Pete. "How do I look?" he asked, taking his glasses off.

"Like crap. And you stink of booze. Here." He rifled around in a backpack and passed over a can of deodorant.

Jake lifted his shirt, the action turning the bolts in his temples a little tighter, and sprayed. The car filled with a truly sickly smell, like Old Spice and Brut had a fight to the death and they'd bottled the festering remains.

"Jesus! What the hell do you call this?"

Pete dropped his voice an octave. "Metrosexual Mojo."

Jake half-laughed, half-snorted both at the name and the delivery and then instantly regretted it.

"Laugh away, boss, but the ladies go crazy for it."

"This? This gets you laid?"

"Never fails."

Jake pushed his sunglasses back on, wondering what the hell was wrong with women these days. "Were the women of your generation born with malfunctioning olfactory centers?"

Pete laughed and sprayed some more deodorant in Jake's general direction, ignoring his boss's protest. "It sure as hell beats your Eau du Alcohol Poisoning."

Jake wasn't entirely sure about that as the sickly aroma intensified in the close confines of the car. "Let's just get this thing done."

* * *

"You're late," Ella hissed as he approached.

Jake winced, her tone just the right frequency to twang his already fragile neurons. And frankly, it irritated the crap out of him. He was here, feeling like death warmed up, doing her a favor, saving *her* ass.

A little gratitude wouldn't go astray.

Squinting at his watch through bleary eyes, he said, "Ten minutes."

"These kids don't give you ten minutes."

Jake looked over her shoulder at the motley collection of students. They were watching him curiously but there was a wariness to their gazes he wasn't used to seeing. Usually, crowds surged forward, smiling and talking all at once. They slapped him on the back, shook his hand, shoved bits and pieces of paraphernalia at him to autograph.

These kids looked at him with a guardedness that was beyond their years. Jake rubbed his temple. "Tough crowd."

"You have no idea," she muttered.

Even through the pounding at his temples, Jake couldn't mistake the dejection and disappointment in Ella's voice and his self-loathing raised another notch. "Hey," he said, lifting a hand to cup her face. "I'm sorry. It won't happen again."

For a moment she seemed to soften, lean into him before recoiling. "Jake!" She stepped quickly back and his hand fell away. "You stink."

Her raised voice slammed into his brain and Jake reached for his temples. "Ella. Do you think you could keep it down?"

She stared at him like he'd grown another head. "Oh my God!" she hissed, snatching at his glasses, whipping them off. "You're hungover!"

"Ella." He snatched them back and shoved them on his face.

"How could you?" She stepped closer, her voice noticeably lower. "What kind of example are you setting for these kids?"

"They won't know."

She snorted. "You smell like a collision between a brewery and a cheap perfume factory."

"Hey," Pete protested.

Ignoring Pete, she eyed Jake with a level of disgust that made him feel lower than a snake's belly. "Trust me. They'll know." She shook her head. "Shit Jake, I didn't think I'd have to give you a code of conduct. I mean really—"

Unable to stand one more hissed syllable, Jake placed two fingers against her mouth. "Shh. Please. Just shh." His head felt like it was going to explode and her low, angry whisper was throwing petrol at the fuse.

Even hungover as he was, Jake felt the transient pulse of awareness as the softness of her mouth and the sigh of her breath against his fingertips streaked straight to his groin. He wanted to press harder, use his finger to smear the gloss off. But it didn't take a genius to figure out she'd probably bite him if he tried right now.

Dropping his hand, he used it to rub a temple that was bitching at him instead. "Just go and introduce me, Ella."

She looked like she was about to argue but decided against it, turning on her heel and walking toward the crowd.

"Okay, everyone." She raised her voice to hush the few murmurs that hadn't stopped as she'd approached. "I'm sure to many of you, he will need no introduction, but I'd like you all to meet Jake Prince."

She gestured vaguely in his direction and Jake took the cue, smiling and waving beside her.

"Jake apologizes for being late, he's... been unwell and dragged himself out of his sick bed to make this first session."

Jake grimaced at the paltry claps and cheers, realizing that his tight-end rep alone would not be enough to win these kids over. They were clearly not easily impressed and his tardiness had ruined any idolizing he'd come to expect as his due.

Today he definitely had feet of clay.

But he just didn't have the patience for niceties today. So he was late. So they were pissed at him. He had a few months to win their respect. Today was not the time for pleasantries. Today just had to be endured.

"Can I have—" Jake stopped as the effort to raise his voice caused a stabbing pain at the back of his head. He continued, his voice quieter. "Those students interested in trying out for the team head over to the end zone."

There were a few moments of shuffling and low murmurs before a couple of boys peeled hesitantly off followed by more and then more. "If the rest of you want to watch on the sidelines, you're most welcome. We'll be here every afternoon at three."

Jake headed toward the boys who were waiting for him, Pete trailing behind. Every step reverberated through his brain, kicking his headache up another notch. If he stood very still for the next hour maybe his head would still be on his shoulders by the end of it.

"We need between twenty and thirty guys," Jake announced to the assembled boys. Professional teams had a roster of fifty-three and most high school teams had around thirty. The final number would depend on how much raw talent was standing in front of him.

He turned to Pete. "How many here?" The realm of counting was beyond him.

"Fifty."

Jake nodded, the action jarring through his temples and he wondered again how the hell he'd been roped into this. Then he spotted Cameron among the hopefuls and side-eyed Ella.

Well... hell.

"Right. This week is the selection process. Pete here" – Jake slapped Pete's back – "is going to put you through your paces and next Monday I'll announce the team."

Pete looked at Jake with startled eyes and turned his back to the assembled students. "Err, Jake?"

"You got this," Jake assured. "You live, eat and breathe this stuff and have been to every public Founders training session since you were twelve years old."

Pete stared at him for a long moment before nodding. "Okay."

"Good," Jake murmured. "Run them into the ground."

Pete smiled. "Yes, sir."

"That's it?" Ella demanded as Pete rallied the troops.

Jake grimaced. "Yup."

"What? No pep talk? No encouraging words from *The Prince*?"

"Nope."

She glared at him and Jake felt it all the way down to his balls. "As much as I enjoy monosyllabic conversations, would you care to elaborate on your game plan here?"

Jake would rather give up one of his Super Bowl rings than admit he had zero game plan right now. "I've got to cut fifty to twenty something."

"And is there some sort of criteria for that?"

"Run their asses off for an hour and keep the ones still standing at the end of each day."

She blinked. "Is this strategy from the hungover school of coaching? Don't you need kids with specific skills?"

"Skills can be taught, practiced. Stamina is paramount."

"But aren't—"

"Ella." Jake cursed under his breath as he massaged his temples. "Please *shut up.*"

"Hey, it's not my fault you're hungover. I'm just trying to help—"

"Ella," he interrupted again with a wince. "If you want to help you'll go find me something, *anything*, to ease the sledgehammer pounding in my brain."

"I thought jocks could hold their booze?"

"It's been a lot of years since I mainlined tequila."

"What on earth possessed you?" She shook her head. "Did coming here today scare you that much?"

Jake gritted his teeth at her insight. He'd deliberately gone out last night to get wrecked enough to forget about this hare-brained scheme. Sure, it had been under the guise of a poker game but deep down he hadn't wanted to be alone in his apartment with nothing but thoughts of today.

"Yes."

He didn't know why it did, it just did. Whether it was Ella or returning to football or the ghosts of two years ago or even further back to Trently – he didn't know. But at least it was enough to halt Ella's relentless questions.

"Fine," she muttered. "I'll go find some Tylenol."

Jake watched her walk away, her hips swaying in her long brown skirt, that ponytail of hers swinging. She was wearing a cream shirt of thin cotton that sat wide on her shoulders and through which he suddenly realized he could see her bra strap,

Goddamn! He must be hungover to the point of near death to have missed that when she was closer and facing him.

He returned his attention to the field in time to see a couple of boys run into each other as they checked out their hottie principal rather than watching where they were going and he smiled for the first time since waking up with a splitting headache in a strange woman's bed.

Maybe this day wasn't all bad.

* * *

Minutes later, Ella was back, Tylenol in hand, exceptionally conscious of Jake tracking her progress across the field despite the dark tint of his aviators. He was looking better than any man – let alone a hungover one – had a right to in tight blue jeans, tight black T-shirt and a growth of overnight stubble that'd surely leave one hell of a beard burn.

Which was definitely *not* an appropriate thought to be having in the middle of a high school. Especially about a guy who'd shown up late *and* hungover.

She'd been torn between kissing him for showing up and throwing the stupid football at his stupid head when he'd finally arrived. This morning at assembly the student body had greeted her announcement with the kind of skepticism only those who had been let down by life could perfect and she'd spent all day assuring her students that yes, they were fielding a team in the comp and yes, *The Prince* was going to be the coach.

The weight of utter depression as each minute had slipped by without Jake's presence had been hard to bear.

Hell, did he think he was the only one who was scared? Being around him scared her, too. Jake who knew her. Who knew *all* about her. Her mother, the smears, the humiliations, her loneliness, her isolation.

Not even Rosie knew her as well as Jake.

And here she was betting all her chips on him. The one person from Trently – from her past – who knew all her dirty little secrets.

"Nice blouse," he commented, his voice heavy with appreciation as Ella reached him and wordlessly passed him the pills and a bottle of water.

She looked at him for a long moment, hating that she couldn't see his eyes behind the tint of his glasses, itching to remove them from his face. The fact he could see her but she couldn't see him made her feel even more vulnerable.

"Thought you were hungover," she said, drily.

"Hungover. Not dead."

Ella felt a funny pull down low. What was she supposed to say to that? Thankfully, she didn't need to say anything as an excited squeal came from behind.

"Jake! Jake!"

Ella turned surprised to find fifteen-year-old Miranda Jones hurling herself at Jake, clinging to his neck and jumping up and down, chattering excitedly about the team and the comp.

She'd taught Miranda math in eighth grade. She was a nice kid, well brought up, smart and motivated. Not really the football groupie type.

Ella frowned as the hug continued. Clearly, they knew each other, but it was hardly appropriate behavior for a schoolgirl with an adult male and she was annoyed that Jake didn't seem to get that. Although to give him his due, he did seem to be trying to settle her, if only to stop the incessant squealing that must be playing havoc with his headache.

Uncharitably, Ella hoped the noise was a particularly virulent form of torture.

"That's enough, Miranda."

A familiar woman, blonde and petite and about Ella's age approached and Ella searched her memory banks to place her.

Trish Jones, Miranda's mother.

The similarities between the two were amazing. Miranda was a tiny blonde, like her mother. Cute as a button with a perky smile and a personality to match.

"Hey, Jake."

Jake set aside Miranda more than a little gratefully, Ella thought, as he wrapped Trish up in a hug.

"Oh God, Jake." Trish pulled away, clearly alarmed. "You stink. Are you hungover?"

"*Mom!*"

Ella laughed at the look of horror on the teenager's face as the other woman turned and said, "Hi. Trish Jones." She held out her hand. "I think we've met once before."

Miranda's mother had an easy smile and an open, friendly face. "Yes, we have." Ella shook the proffered hand. "At a parent–teacher night. Ella Lucas."

"Don't mind Miranda. Jake and I go way back – she's known him since she was born. She was so excited when she called me earlier to tell me she had to come back to school straight after her dentist's appointment to watch Cameron try out and that Jake was going to be here."

Cameron? Ella blinked. *Her* Cameron? Could this be the Miri from the phone the other night? Mature, articulate, Miranda Jones? The straight-A student?

Ella didn't get a chance to process the information before Jake butted in. "This is Deluca High?"

"Yes..." Ella frowned. "I assumed you knew. You got here, didn't you?"

But he didn't get a chance to answer. "This is a great thing you're doing, Jake," Trish said. "Really amazing. Haven't I been saying you should coach?"

Rather than intrude on a private conversation, Ella forced herself to concentrate on Pete putting the students through their paces. Searching for Cam, she prayed he wasn't among the boys who had already fallen by the wayside. He was beefy, all muscle, built like a tank. Built for endurance, not speed.

But, thankfully, he hadn't faltered.

Trish laughed and Ella's attention was drawn back to her and Jake. What exactly was their relationship? Trish had said they went way back and their familiarity was palpable.

Had they been lovers? Were they still?

And why did that make the sad, lonely, Trently girl that still existed deep down inside, want to curl up in a ball and cry?

7

_____

The following Monday there was a knock on Ella's door after lunch. "Come in."

Holding up her hand, she quickly finished the paragraph she was reading then looked up. Her smile faltered as she saw her brother standing in the doorway.

Ella sighed. "Oh, Cam, what have you done now?"

Normally she received a phone call as a bit of a heads-up before one of Cam's teachers sent him down to see her.

"Jesus Christ, Ella. Nothing. Just _forget it._"

Cam turned away and Ella wished a sharp knife had been handy to cut her tongue out. She stood abruptly. "No, wait."

He was seeking her out? _Voluntarily?_ Her pulse picked up at the thought. "I'm sorry, Cam. Please come and sit down."

Cameron glared at her and the chair and then back at her before sullenly acquiescing, slumping himself down with as much teenage surliness as was possible.

"You wanted to see me about something?"

Cameron nodded and she waited patiently for him to start. He sat staring morosely at the ground, his shaggy overgrown hair obscuring his eyes from her gaze. Ella detested the latest mullet craze the male students had all embraced so heartily. Her mind wandered to Jake's uber-short cut and she wished she had the power to line all the boys up and shave every single head.

"Cam?"

"Do you know who Jake's chosen yet?" The question was fired at her with his usual hostile edge, as though everything bad in the world was her fault.

"No."

Cameron snorted. "He hasn't given *you* a peek at the list?"

Ella ignored his belligerent tone. "No."

"But... you're the principal. Doesn't he have to check with you about it?"

She'd not spoken to Jake all week. She'd seen him a couple of times when she'd gone to the field on her regular vape-confiscating rounds but had deliberately kept away from him, including avoiding the bar on Friday night. He was here in her school performing a necessary evil and she was grateful, but she was acutely aware of both their baggage *and* her attraction and she wasn't about to put herself in the path of that truck.

"No, he doesn't. He's the expert. It's his team. We'll all know in a couple of hours."

"Has he hinted at all, maybe, that I'm in?"

The desperation in his voice vibrated through the air like a tuning fork. She'd never seen Cameron so gung-ho about anything. So motivated. Ever since she'd dragged him from Trently, he'd lived with a permanent scowl, so this interest was heartening. "I haven't spoken to him all week."

She regarded the boy/man who just wouldn't let her in. He was so big, already a foot taller than her and growing out of his shoes at a rate of knots. "You really want this, don't you?"

Cameron looked up from the floor. "Yes, I do."

Ella swallowed as emotion welled in her throat. This was only the second time in two years he'd looked her straight in the eye. The other time had been after their mother's funeral, when he had told her he hated Rachel, despite the tears streaming down his face. She'd tried to reach out, to gloss over what their mother was but he'd just turned away.

"Well, you've practiced hard. You've stayed standing. I think you're in for a good chance."

Cameron shook his head. "But what if I'm not? Can't you... can't you use your influence with him?"

A hot prickle burrowed into the base of Ella's spine. "My influence?"

Cameron looked at the ground again. "You know him from Trently. And... I see the way he looks at you. Maybe a... favor might help convince him."

Time whirred to a halt. A pain sliced through Ella's chest as if Cameron had picked up a knife and rammed it straight through her heart. She could barely breathe as the full implications of his suggestion twisted the knife.

"You want me to use *sex* to get you in the team?"

Ella felt as if she was watching the scene from a great height. She couldn't believe how calm she sounded, how composed, when her heart was breaking.

He shrugged. "It worked for Rachel."

His words fell like stones into the silence and Ella drew in a shaky breath. It was like he truly didn't know that he'd insulted her more deeply than she'd ever been before.

"I hope you're not comparing, Cam."

"What?" He snorted. "Compare the saintly Ella to Rachel? No, no, no, I wouldn't dare."

Ella dragged in a swift breath at the pure scorn in his voice. There was a whole minefield of emotions behind his words, stuff from Trently that he never talked about no matter what she tried to get him to open up. "I'm not the enemy, Cam."

"Then prove it." He was looking her in the eye again. Talking about stuff he had no idea about. Speaking with the confidence of youth – fifteen going on fifty.

"You know," she said quietly, disappointment and hurt warring for top billing, "it's been a lot of years since a boy made me feel so cheap. I guess you Trently guys know how to do that really well."

Ella took no pleasure from the stain that spread across her brother's cheeks as her rebuke hit its mark and he looked to the ground again. She hoped he was ashamed, that he felt as dirty about making his comment as she did on its receiving end.

"I know you think that I owe you, Cam. That I left you behind in Trently and didn't care about you. Even though you know I wasn't aware of your existence."

Cameron's mouth tightened. "All you had to do was pick up the phone and call her."

Ella swallowed, the deep-seated guilt she'd always felt about cutting herself off from Rachel returning. She'd called her mom only once after she'd left and that was to let her know she was in Inverboro and safe and she wasn't coming back.

Something she'd regretted heavily since finding out about Cam. The underlying ache in his sneered reprimand stuck like barbs in her flesh because he was right. If only she'd made the effort, there wouldn't be this great gulf yawning between them.

"I think you know that I'm sorry about that."

She looked at the set of Cameron's jaw, the bitterness glittering in his gaze. He'd never given her an inch and it looked like he wasn't about to start.

"Forget it. Just forget it," he dismissed. "I did alright without you for thirteen years. I don't need your help now."

Ella watched as his chest puffed out, looking like the boy of two years ago who'd told her he didn't need a sister. He didn't need anyone. To go back to Inverboro and leave him alone. It hurt that after all this time he still felt he had to hide behind that facade. To pretend he didn't need her.

But for once she wasn't going to be guilted into backing down. What he'd said was unacceptable.

"I think you're wrong. I think you do need me. But just for the record, I'm not going to assuage my guilt by getting you something you haven't earned. And you can hate me for that if you want, that's fine, but it's just not the way I operate. You need to achieve things on your own merit."

She reached across the desk to touch his hand and felt his rejection as a body blow when he snatched it away. "Have a little faith in your abilities, Cam."

Cameron rolled his eyes. "Well, I'm sure that works out real well in Ellaland but IRL, things aren't always so fucking peachy." He pushed up out of his chair and stalked to the door. "Thanks for nothing, *sis*," he threw over his shoulder as he yanked it open.

Ella braced herself for the bang as Cameron made his disgruntled exit. He didn't disappoint, the window rattling from the force.

She sat for a moment, her elbows on the table, her head in her hands, her whole body shaking at the confrontation. She wondered if she was going to lose her lunch as his suggestion that she do a Rachel to secure a spot on the team for him appalled and sickened her all over again.

"Can I come in?"

Ella looked up, startled, to see Jake standing in the doorway, a clipboard in his hands. "Oh. Sorry." She gestured for him to enter. "I'm sorry, I didn't hear you."

"I noticed Cam leaving here pretty steamed," he said as he shut the door and sauntered toward her. "Are you okay?"

Ella gave a mirthless laugh and rubbed the back of her neck. "Not really, no."

He perched on her desk. "Did you argue?"

She regarded him for a long moment, the muscles in his denim-encased thigh moving interestingly in her peripheral vision as his leg swung at the knee. He was wearing another T-shirt that fit snugly over well-defined biceps. His jaw was scruffy as usual, his green eyes probing her with a frankness and intensity that was compelling.

They knew her, those eyes.

"We didn't yell at each other, if that's what you mean."

"But he upset you," Jake persisted. "What did he say?"

Ella felt absurdly like bursting into tears and wished Rosie was here. She blinked hard, not wanting to cry in front of Jake. She focused on the swing of his knee instead as Cam's words made her feel dirty all over again.

"He suggested that I sleep with you to secure a place for him on the team." She braved a look at him. "After all, that's what Rachel would have done. Like mother, like daughter, right?"

The angle of his jaw tightened and his knuckles whitened as he gripped the clipboard tighter. "You're not your mother."

His soft rebuttal was more powerful than an outraged rejection and Ella swallowed hard. She was ashamed to admit there'd been a time when she'd wanted to be exactly like Rachel. When she'd been little and her mother had just been this beautiful creature with yellow-blonde hair and a laugh that could light up a room.

"*I* know that, Jake. You know it. But does he? I mean, half of the boys back home thought I was tarred with the same brush, didn't they?"

"They were jerks. And Cam's just yanking your chain."

Ella nodded, pleased to hear Jake's quick dismissal of the boys who had contributed to her Trently hell. "But why wouldn't he think that, growing up in Trently under Rachel's roof? Why wouldn't he think that all women use their bodies for favors?"

"He knows right from wrong, Ella. You shouldn't cut him so much slack."

Where had she heard that before? "You sound like Daisy."

Daisy had her own tough-love opinions on how Cam should be raised which were in stark contrast to Ella's softly-softly approach. But there were so many years to make up for and Ella was trying to get by as best she could.

And a large part of her sympathized with the kid. Cam was exactly what she'd wanted to be all those years in Trently – tough and not afraid to take anyone's crap.

Just like Jake.

He grinned. "I like Daisy."

Ella knew full well that the feeling had been 100 per cent mutual. The phone on her desk rang and she was pleased for the reprieve from the irresistible humor in his green eyes.

"Yes, Bernie?"

"I have Gwen for you."

Ella nodded, as her administrative assistant put Cameron's biology teacher through. "Hi, Gwen."

"Hi, Ella. Have you finished with Cameron?"

"Yes. About ten minutes ago. Hasn't he returned to class?"

"No."

Ella appreciated the gentleness of the reply. Unfortunately it didn't make the situation any better. "Okay, thanks Gwen. Write him up."

"Cam taking some time out?"

"That's one way of putting it," she said as she hung up.

Standing, Ella walked to the window, her impotence with the situation making her restless. A train had pulled into the Metra station across the street and she'd like nothing more right now than to walk out the gates, get on the train and never come back.

"Does he cut class very much?"

Ella placed her forehead against the glass. "Cam's truancy record puts yours to shame."

He whistled. "Impressive."

"Yep." She stared for a beat longer before turning back to face him, her gaze falling on the clipboard. "Is that the list?"

Jake eased off her desk and walked toward her, extending the clipboard. "Rest easy, you don't have to sleep with me."

Ella took it from him as he leaned his hip against the windowsill. She ran her finger down the list, stilling when she spotted *Cameron Lucas* neatly printed among the twenty-five names. Relief made her dizzy and she shut her eyes for a moment to compose herself.

When she opened them, she was steadier but a question nagged at her. Glancing at him, she asked, "Are you doing this as a favor to me?"

"*Every* kid on that list" – he tapped it for emphasis, his eyes bright with sincerity – "deserves their spot."

A flood of pent-up emotion clogged in her throat and prickled at her nose. Ella's teeth dug into her bottom lip to prevent it from spewing out. She looked down, blinking rapidly to clear the hot shimmer of tears.

"Thank you," she whispered, her voice scratching like sandpaper in her throat.

"Ella?"

When she didn't answer, he lifted her chin with his thumb and forefinger. "Ella," he repeated.

She shook her head, avoiding eye contact, looking at his neck, his ear, the round outline of his shoulder. "I'm sorry. It's been... He just doesn't have any confidence in himself... but he's smart, you know?" She swiped at a tear that had managed to avoid her blinking and spilled over. "All his teachers say so, he just doesn't apply himself... He's too angry – with me and Rachel – and I know how much he wanted this..."

"Hey," Jake said, his thumb drying another tear. "Don't cry."

She gave a gurgle of embarrassment, dodging his touch as every cell in her body screamed at her to *lean in*. "I'm sorry. I don't know what's the matter with me. I'm not usually this emotional."

Despite often extreme provocation, Ella had learned early to shelter behind an aloofness she wore like armor. Where no one could touch her.

Hell, she'd not even cried at her mother's funeral.

"It's just... It's been a tough couple of years and... I never thought I'd *suck* this badly at being a big sister."

He nodded, his expression full of compassion, his eyes full of *knowing*. Full of understanding – as only Jake could. On the back of Cam's insult, it was surprisingly comforting.

"I swear to God," she said, her voice perilously shaky. "If you don't stop looking at me like that then I'm going to be bawling like a baby."

He smiled as his thumb swept across the ridge of her cheekbone. "Like what?"

The caress was so gentle Ella's eyelids fluttered closed as she swayed a little. They opened again to find the look in his eyes had changed. His pupils had dilated, the green intensified. He was staring at her mouth.

Was he closer? Was she?

"Like what, Ella?"

Like he wanted to kiss her. "*Jake.*"

If he heard the warning note in her voice, he ignored it.

In fact, he took a step closer. She supposed she should back up, but all of her faculties deserted her as her gaze locked irresistibly on his mouth. The gallop of her pulse echoed in her ears as her belly looped-the-loop.

His head dipped at the same time she lifted on her tiptoes and when his lips settled on hers she sighed against his mouth. It was soft and gentle and she welcomed his lazy exploration, her blood pumping thick and warm and slow through her belly and breasts and thighs.

But then his tongue stroked against the seam of her lips and the slow heat roared to life like a struck match and she wanted *more*. She wanted to feel the full force of his kiss. She wanted open mouths and heavy breathing. Parting her lips, Ella's tongue sought his, bold and sure, deepening the kiss on a husky moan, gripping the front of his shirt, pulling him closer as pure, unadulterated lust coursed through her system.

The loud trill of the school bell was like the proverbial bucket of ice water and they both pulled back.

Ella's pulse leaped at the unexpected interruption and it took a second for her to grapple her thoughts back from the abyss of pleasure still swirling and sucking at every inch of her body.

But then the real world intruded as the sounds of students rushing by outside brought her back to the here and now.

They were standing *in her office*. In front of *the window*.

For the entire world to see.

Anyone could have caught them. A student. A parent. Donald Wiseman from the district education review board with the creepy smile and penchant for adjusting himself during his unannounced visits.

God knew the train full of passengers seemed to be inordinately interested in the goings on.

Just as well the bell had rung because who knew what kind of show they'd have witnessed had it not.

What the hell had she been thinking?

"Of course, if you want to sleep with me..." His deep, lazily amused voice rumbled around her. "I could always make Cameron team captain."

Ella rolled her eyes. *Very funny*. Garnering a strength she *did not* feel, Ella pushed away, walking to her desk on legs that weren't quite steady.

"I'm not going to sleep with you, Jake."

"What? Ever?"

She smiled at his mocking tone. "Now you're getting it."

"That's a long time."

Ella shrugged. "It's called self-control. Maybe you should try it some time."

He walked toward her desk, planting his fists on the edge. "You weren't big on self-control a couple of years ago."

Ella swallowed as the mention of that day rattled her further. Goddamn it! This was her office. *Her dominion*. He might have invaded it but it was still her turf and she wouldn't let him drag her into the past. Not when she'd worked so hard to leave it all behind.

"I'm not going backward, Jake."

He cocked an eyebrow. "I'm backward?"

"You're Trently, Jake. I left there a long time ago and I'm not going back."

"It felt like you wanted to go back when you stuck your tongue in my mouth just now."

A rush of heat threatened to swamp her at the memory but she beat it back. "You do know that abstinence doesn't kill people, right?"

God knew she'd have been dead a long time ago.

"It sure makes them mighty pissed though."

Right. Like *The Prince* knew about that. "And this you would know how?"

He grinned, pushing off the desk and picking up his clipboard. "See you at the field."

* * *

Ella watched Cameron's face as Pete read out the names. A lump rose in her throat at the play of his emotions. First stunned disbelief, then a slow dawning as a tentative smile grew into a grin as big as Lake Michigan.

The lump swelled to life-threatening proportions as his eyes sought hers and she saw tears shining in his tough-kid gaze. She gave him the thumbs up and he actually returned them.

Every kid whose name was called out stood an extra inch higher and Ella couldn't remember ever feeling such a charge of optimism in all her years at Deluca. A transformation was happening before her eyes. Kids who'd never had any expectations from life suddenly looked bulletproof.

Maybe this could actually work?

8

Jake turned to the shaggy-haired, inexperienced crew before him and wondered how the hell he was ever going to pull this off. Sure, there was some good raw talent, but he had to create in one season what other teams in the comp would have built up over years and years of playing and competing – unity, synergy, trust.

He glanced at Ella and then at Miranda, so like Trish, who was waving at him from the sidelines. He'd offered to pay for her to go to Fernbridge or St Erasmus or any of the uppity girls' schools in Inverboro but, no – Trish had wanted her daughter to stay grounded.

So now he not only had to do this for Ella but there was no way he could sit back and let anyone shut down Miranda's school.

"Okay, listen up," he called above the back slapping and high-fiving that was going on among the successful students. "There are a few ground rules before we begin. You want to be on the team, there are three non-negotiables."

He watched as smiles faded a little. "Pete?"

Pete dug around in his backpack and came out with a pair of hair clippers. He held them up and switched them on. They buzzed low and sure.

"No more mullets. Number twos for you all. Here, now, this afternoon."

There was a collective groan. "You don't want to? No problem. I have a reserve list and I'm not afraid to use it."

He didn't but he could make one.

"Training is every day," he continued. "*Every* day. Three o'clock sharp. Rain, hail, snow or shine. We have three weeks until the first game and a lot of ground to cover."

None of the boys were smiling now. Good. He finally had their complete attention.

"Lastly, one day off school, just *one*" – Jake held up a finger – "without a medical certificate... cut class just *once* and you're off the team. No exceptions."

Silence greeted him and he glanced at Ella. Even she looked slightly aghast. But Jake knew boys like this, like Cameron. He'd been one himself – disenfranchised. If it hadn't been for his Aunty Thelma getting him into football and setting impossibly high standards, God knew where he'd be today.

It was time to pay it forward.

"Those of you still keen, come join me."

The newly minted team members looked at each other. Then they looked from Jake to Pete, still holding the clippers, and back to Jake.

Cameron was the first to move and the rest followed.

Jake nodded. "Alright then. Go with Pete." The scruffy rabble shuffled off. "Cameron," Jake called. "Not you."

Cam frowned as he fell back. Ella approached, looking at them uncertainly. "Everything alright?"

"All good," Jake dismissed.

She glanced at a nervous Cam and opened her mouth to say something but was interrupted by an out-of-breath Trish lugging a large shoulder bag. "I just got your text," she said. "You want me to do what?"

Jake tipped his head to where Pete was standing with the new recruits. "Shave some heads."

The petite blonde eyed the boys in the distance and then glanced at Ella. Ella shrugged and Trish smiled. "It'd be my pleasure."

Jake laughed as Trish practically levitated her away across the oval. He turned back to Ella. "Why don't you join Trish?"

For a moment Jake thought she was going to stand her ground and demand to know what he wanted with her brother but she acquiesced with a nod. He and Cameron tracked her progress as she caught up with Trish.

"Did you want something, sir?"

Jake looked at the kid who could almost meet him eye to eye. He was big, stocky, and probably one of the few guys on the team with real talent.

But Cameron Lucas needed a damn good kick in the ass. And he was just the man to do it. Cam was going to be sorry he ever wanted on the team.

"I'm not your father, Cameron, nor am I a teacher. You can call me Jake or Coach."

Cameron swallowed. "Yes, Coach."

Jake regarded him seriously. "I understand you. Probably better than you understand yourself. I know Trently gave you a tough time. I know you probably spent your life with your fists up defending someone you didn't like very much in a shithole you didn't give a damn about."

Cameron remained silent but his jaw was set and hostility blazed in his eyes.

"Unfortunately for you, the next few months, your ass belongs to me and if you want on this team, then you've got to prove it to me – more than the others. Do you understand?"

Cameron nodded. "Yes, Coach."

"I don't know if you know this or not but I was at your place one night a few weeks ago when you told your sister to fuck off. If you ever talk to Ella like that again – ever – you're out. Got it?"

Cameron ground his teeth together so hard Jake thought he was going to break some. "But—"

"No buts, Cam. Men just don't talk to women like that. That's the number one rule, right there. Are you a man or a boy? This is where you decide."

"That's not—"

Jake held up his hand. "Ella's not the enemy. Maybe you should cut her some slack?"

"She's my sister," he muttered sullenly. "She was supposed to look out for me."

"No." Jake shook his head. "That was Rachel's job."

Cameron dropped his gaze to the ground, clearly wanting to tell Jake to also *fuck off* but not wanting to jeopardize his chances with the team.

"Got it?" Jake repeated.

Cameron's lifted his gaze, his jaw tight. "Got it."

He stalked away then and Jake re-joined Ella who was watching a sullen Cameron make his way to the team on the bleachers.

"Everything okay?" she asked, searching his face.

"Yep. Everything's fine."

He could tell she was curious about the conversation he'd had with her brother but she didn't go there. "Not that I don't appreciate it," she said, instead, "but what's the purpose of the haircuts?"

"Ahh, grasshopper." Jake smiled. "You have much to learn. The reasons are threefold."

Ella rolled her eyes. "Oh, this ought to be good."

He laughed. "Firstly, it's a test. I needed to know their level of commitment."

"Good test. Trust me, no one's more committed to the mullet than a teenage boy."

"Secondly, they can see the ball better when they don't have hair in their eyes."

"Excellent point."

"Lastly, it makes them look badass. And bluff is just as important in football as it is in any sport."

"They do look pretty mean," she admitted.

And they did. On these burly boys, caught halfway between adolescence and manhood, it looked mean as hell. Even the floral capes didn't detract from the don't-mess-with-us vibe.

Trish bounded over, grinning wildly, which made Jake laugh. She was obviously taking great pleasure in her work.

"They look hardcore, don't they?" she enthused.

"Amazing," Ella agreed. "I don't suppose you're free to do the rest of the school tomorrow?"

Trish eyed off the other boys who hadn't made the team. "It's tempting, isn't it?" she admitted.

"We need a photo to record this for posterity," Ella said with a grin. "Oh, actually..."

She paused and Jake could practically hear the gears in her brain kicking over. Which gave him a very bad feeling.

Snapping her fingers, she looked at them with a gleam in her eyes. Clearly, she had *a plan*. "We need the press in on this. Get ourselves a bit of a media profile which should hopefully spotlight the battle for the school and might get us some broader community support." She glanced at Jake. "Can I invite some local media to a practice session?"

Before Jake could say *over my dead body*, Ella continued. "Maybe we could re-create this scene? I mean, the kids might hate it, but these old bleachers turned into an impromptu hair salon would be an awesome photo." Ella turned speculative eyes on Trish. "Would you come back one day for a re-creation?"

Jake sensed Trish go very still beside him and he slid his hand into hers and gave it a squeeze. "No press," he intoned.

A small frown knitted Ella's brows together as she looked from him to Trish then back to him again. "Oh come on." She smiled. "A big hot-shot jock from the Founders isn't afraid of the *Deluca Daily* photographer, surely?"

Jake knew that the news of him coaching a high school football team would break soon enough. Everyone had a phone and a TikTok account these days. And he'd deal with that when it arose but he wouldn't go looking for trouble.

"No. Press."

"But..." She frowned. "It could be good for the school."

Jake locked his gaze on hers. "If there's so much as an organized photo op or I see a quote about the team attributed to you or *anyone* official from Deluca on any official news site, I'm out of here, Ella."

He couldn't control social media or snap-happy paparazzi but he could stop any official pandering to the media.

"That's number four and it's not negotiable. No. Press."

Then he walked away.

* * *

The setting sun was leaving behind tangerine clouds on the last Friday night in August but Ella didn't notice. Sitting in the bleachers with the small gathering of Deluca supporters, she was so nervous she couldn't decide whether she was going to throw up or have a full-blown panic attack.

The team were as ready as they could be after only three weeks but that didn't say much.

From her vantage point behind them, she watched Jake and Pete talking, or rather strategizing, if their hand gestures were remotely indicative. Jake wore a baseball cap tugged low on his forehead and a pair of dark sunglasses but still she could see people nudging and pointing at him, their phones out.

To be fair, most of them were women. And not just any women, but mothers. Ella had seen enough of them over the years to recognize that if any one group of women could use a bit of gratuitous eye candy from time to time, it was mothers.

And Jake certainly didn't disappoint.

He was like the Hershey's bar of eye candy. The Snickers. The Reese's Peanut Butter Cup. Ella could practically feel the fat cells on her ass multiplying as her mouth watered.

"Checking out the coach?" Rosie said, nudging Ella's arm.

Clearing her throat, Ella shook her head. "Absolutely not," she replied. Although she absolutely was.

Rose laughed. "Okay, sure. No one would blame you, you know? He's pretty damn fine and you are but a human woman."

Trying to deflect Rosie's attention, Ella tipped her chin at Simon who was walking toward them from the other side of the field. "Simon's looking very nice tonight, too."

He'd ditched the corporate look for chinos and a polo shirt which was about as casual as she suspected Simon could get.

"That he is," Rosie murmured, checking him out lasciviously.

"Things are going well with you two."

"Yeah." Rosie smiled, her eyes glued to Simon's progress. "I really like him."

Ella entwined her fingers with Rosie's. "He's good for you." Rosie was herself around Simon, which could not be said for many of her past relationships. And he was clearly smitten.

A shout from the field snagged Ella's attention to the boys warming up and she searched for Cameron. He was standing on one leg, stretching the other up behind, staring at the ground in fierce concentration.

The panic sensation returned. Yes, they needed this win for the school but Cameron needed it more.

"Don't the boys look amazing?"

Ella nodded. They did. They really did. In fact, she and Rosie were really going to have to stop thinking of them as boys. Today they looked exactly as Jake had hoped, in the red-and-black jersey he'd bought for them with Demons emblazoned on the front and their padded shoulders. They looked mature. A force to be reckoned with.

They were every inch the Deluca Demons.

Thanks to Jake the entire team had been kitted out in all the essentials – jerseys, helmets, cleats, pads, mouth guards. Ella had protested his generosity. She had no idea how much it had all cost but none of it had been bought at Walmart and she didn't want to be that indebted to him.

She was in deep enough.

But Jake had insisted that becoming a team involved projecting an identity. Ella had been dubious but damn if those boys – young men – weren't all standing a foot higher. They certainly looked the part next to the opposing team.

The Cats had been in the competition for twenty years and were looking at the Demons like they were mere bugs on the footpath. Their football field was immaculate, decked out in yellow-and-blue flags, making Deluca's oval look like a mosh pit the morning after a rock concert by comparison.

Simon joined them as Jake called the Demons together and Ella kept her eyes glued to him as they formed an eager huddle. He'd definitely made up for his tardy start. He only had to say jump now and the boys wanted to know how high.

"This is your cue," Simon said, interrupting her thoughts. "Go down and give your team a pep talk."

Say *what* now? "They're not my team," Ella demurred as Jake continued to gee them up. What could she possibly offer?

Rosie grabbed Ella's hand and looked her straight in the eye. "Of course they are," she said. "You're their principal. Without them, Deluca's going to be closed. They're the only team you've got, babe."

Ella searched Rosie's face then glanced at Simon. He nodded and gave her an encouraging smile. "What do I say?"

What did a bunch of high school students revved up on nerves and testosterone expect her to say to them? She'd spent the last two years with Cameron trying to figure out teenage boy speak to no avail.

Simon shrugged. "Tell them they'll get detention for a week if they don't win."

Rosie dug him in the ribs. "Not helping, Simon."

Simon half-laughed as he rubbed at his side. "Tell them to listen to Jake."

Ella nodded. That sounded like good advice. She stood and made her way down through the almost empty stand, ignoring the stab of disappointment she felt at the lack of Deluca supporters. Especially compared to the packed bleachers on the other side.

Sure, Deluca wasn't known for its community spirit and this was an away game, but she had *hoped*. So much was riding on today and home support could make a difference.

Ella caught the odd word of Jake's speech as she approached. She didn't understand any of it, but Jake seemed to know what he was doing and Pete and the team were nodding. She stood quietly, waiting for him to finish, feeling every inch the nerdy math teacher intruding on a male bonding ritual.

When he was done with his pep talk he turned away, practically running into Ella, his hands grabbing her arms to prevent a collision. "Oh," he said, clearly surprised to see her. "Everything okay?"

Up this close he was even sexier and his touch, no matter how impersonal, spread tendrils of warmth *everywhere*. "I was... wondering... hoping I could talk to the team?"

He hesitated and, for a moment, she thought he was going to tell her no. But then he nodded, his hands still firm on her arms as he leaned in a little.

"They're nervous," he murmured. "Keep it light."

Ella shivered as the low timbre of his voice slid into all her *good* places. She gave a small nod and his hands dropped away as he stepped aside. Clearing her throat, Ella took his place, super conscious of him hovering behind.

"Well, guys, this is not something I know a lot about but I just wanted to say that I'm proud of you." She caught Cameron's gaze and held it. "*Very* proud."

He looked nervous and, for a second, she cursed Rachel for keeping them apart for thirteen years. She wished she'd known him as a baby, bonded with him.

Surely things would be easier now?

"So, um... that's it I guess." She turned to Jake. "Do you say break a leg or something?"

Pete slapped his forehead in the background as Jake briefly shut his eyes. "No, Ella. Not under *any* circumstances."

The whistle blew and she was grateful for the interruption to her completely botched debut pep talk as the starters stomped past her in a cloud of testosterone. Pete and Jake took up position on the sidelines with the rest of the team all kitted up and ready to go.

She noticed Cerberus sitting by a long low bench seat set back a little from the sideline and she wandered over. Rosie, Simon, Daisy and Iris had turned up with the dog half an hour ago which had apparently been Simon's idea.

A football team needed a mascot according to him. A symbol of their potency. A representation of their strength. Something to strike fear into the hearts of their opponents.

Simon had been amazingly encouraging and supportive of the team but quite how a small, old, stray dog with an abandonment complex fit the bill, she wasn't sure.

He was hardly a spritely specimen of canine virility.

But Simon had just smiled and said, "He's Cerberus, the hound from hell. They're the Deluca Demons. It's symbolic."

Cerberus, hound of hell, whimpered in ecstasy as she sat and stroked his soft ears.

A few minutes after play started, Jake joined her on the bench. "I'm sorry," she said. "About the breaking a leg thing."

"It's fine," he dismissed, his gaze intent on the game.

Except it didn't seem fine. "I just wanted to be... succinct but I'm not au fait with football stuff."

Of course, it was hard not to have *some* knowledge of the game growing up in America. And with Cam the last two years, there'd been more football in her life than she cared for. But she'd never been sports inclined. *Any* sports. The sports segment on the news each night was her only regular consumption.

"Uh huh."

"But I want them to know I'm rooting for them and not just because of the school but for their individual growth, too. They've all been so committed so the least I can do is—"

"Ella." Jake's interruption cut her short as he dragged his gaze off the field. "*Must* you talk?"

Sick to her stomach with nerves, Jake's testiness was like nails down a chalkboard. Annoyed at his *tone*, Ella felt testy herself. "What?" she faux cooed. "Can't do two things at once?"

His eyebrow lifted. "I think we both know that's not true."

Ella blushed. Okay, yeah, she'd so picked the wrong man for that quip. *He'd multi-tasked his ass off two years ago.* "Sex doesn't count."

He snorted. "Sex always counts."

They stared at each other for a moment. "Don't you have a game to be watching?"

"Are you going to let me?"

She held his gaze for as long as she could, wondering if he was thinking about sex now too? Given the impatience bubbling in his eyes, probably not. "I won't say another word."

* * *

For the rest of the game, Ella sat on the edge of her seat. Rosie and Simon had joined her and she clung to Rosie's hand like the lifeline it had always been. Occasionally Jake would sit and explain things but more often than not he was wearing a path up the sideline, yelling encouragement and direction.

Pete also trekked endlessly up and down, video camera in hand. Jake explained that he'd use it to review the team's performance during the week. Cerberus shadowed Pete's every move, barking when things got exciting, whining when Jake's encouragement got particularly animated, and taking shameless advantage of spectators who threw the mangy-looking hellhound their hot dog leftovers.

Every successful throw, kick or pass from the Cats earned a massive roar from their supporters and triggered a peppy routine from their cheer squad. The squad was irritatingly perfect, with short blue skirts and tight yellow tees encasing all their youthful perkiness.

Blonde and bouncy, all twenty of them.

"Jeez, I didn't realize public high school science budgets ran into the millions," she murmured to Jake at one stage.

He frowned. "Huh?"

Ella nodded in the direction of the cheer squad. "Some genius at the Cats has managed to clone Barbie."

"You don't approve of cheerleaders?"

"Absolutely not." Ella shot him a disgusted look. "Talk about taking the women's movement back two hundred years."

Just then the Cats' quarterback made a break for the end zone so she was spared his response as he ran up the sideline, calling to his team, strategizing on his feet.

At half-time, the Cats were ahead by twelve and Deluca weren't even on the board. Ella watched with trepidation as the Demons walked off the field, all red-faced and sweaty, their shoulders slumped. Cameron didn't even look at her, his dejection arrowing straight through her soul. She sat on the bench, powerless, wanting to build the team up but not having a clue how to go about it.

Luckily Jake seemed to know. He talked non-stop in the fifteen-minute break,–reviving their spirits, praising them, encouraging them. Reiterating their goals, focusing them on the next half.

By the time the Demons ran back onto the field they were standing tall again.

And Ella was officially turned on.

Jake had been *magnificent*. He'd been articulate and passionate, his belief in his team and his passion for the game blazing from his eyes.

It was a potent combination.

The whistle blew and she dragged her attention away from Jake, forcing herself to concentrate on the game. And what an amazing half it was. The rejuvenated Demons left it all out on the field catching up until, two minutes out they ran one over the end zone, putting them one behind their opponents.

Then ten seconds before the whistle, Cameron kicked the ball toward the post. "He's going for the field goal," Simon said.

"How much is that worth?" Ella demanded.

"Three points."

Oh God. Ella couldn't bear to watch. If he botched this he might never recover. With her heart thundering in her chest, she buried her face in her hands and crossed her fingers.

Seconds later Rosie was screaming and Simon was yelling, "*He did it! He did it!*"

Amidst a cacophony of clapping, cheering and stomping from Deluca supporters in the bleachers behind, Ella was dragged to her feet by Rosie who hugged her and shouted, "He did it!"

Pulling out of Rosie's grasp, she turned in time to see Cam being picked up by his teammates and lifted high on their shoulders and Ella thought her heart was going to burst right out of her chest. She'd never seen such excitement and accomplishment on her students' faces before.

And she'd never seen Cam this... *happy.*

"We really won?" she shouted to Jake over the hubbub as the Deluca supporters surged onto the field, greeting their conquering heroes.

Miranda and Trish were in the crowd along with Cerberus, yapping excitedly as he ran between people's legs. Daisy and Iris were still clapping wildly from the bleachers.

Jake grinned. "We really won."

Hot tears pricked at Ella's eyes. She'd been waiting for someone to jump out and shout, *You've been punked*. Nothing much had gone right in the last two years – why should this be any different?

Suddenly, a huge weight had been lifted from her chest.

"Thank you," she mouthed to him as he was dragged into the maelstrom of jubilant, hyped-up teenagers. He touched two fingers to his forehead in a small salute to her before he was swallowed into a mass of sweaty bodies.

Her earlier state of arousal roared to life as she watched him laughing and joking, basking in the celebration.

Rosie sidled up to her. "Cam was awesome."

Ella stared at Cam who had not stopped smiling, a lump in her throat as big as the football field. "Yes."

"So was Jake," she murmured suggestively.

Shifting her gaze back to Jake, Ella watched as he shook hands with his players, clapping each of them on the back, laughing and smiling, making each kid *glow*.

And hell if that wasn't wildly sexy.

Rosie leaned in as she nudged Ella with her shoulder. "You want to do him, don't you?"

"Absolutely not." Although she absolutely did.

"Oh well." Rosie shrugged. "I doubt he'll be short of offers tonight. I'm pretty sure every woman here wants to jump his bones."

Ella sucked in a breath as the thought dug hot talons in her gut. *Over her dead body.*

9

A couple of hours later, at The Touchdown, Jake joined Rosie, Simon and Ella at their booth. He'd been caught up at the bar, helping Pete out with a rush, but had kept up a steady supply of drinks to their table.

Bringing another round with him, he handed the Piña Coladas to the women and passed over a beer to Simon. He claimed the last beer for himself as Ella scooched over for him to slide in beside her.

"You guys look deep in conversation over here," he said as he took a swallow of his Corona, trying to ignore the surge in his pulse and the hum in his veins as his thigh skimmed Ella's in the close confines. "What are we all talking about?"

"The game," Ella said, very matter of fact.

He chuckled. "And the walls are still standing?" he teased. "Who'd have thought: Ella Lucas *voluntarily* talking football."

Ella shrugged. "I'm pretty tipsy."

Jake laughed this time. She did look a little buzzed, her eyes bright, her cheeks pink. But, more than that, she looked... carefree. Not a state he'd ever associated with her.

"I suspect you're probably going to be getting a lot more Monday morning quarterbacking from me in your future."

As if finding that inordinately funny, Ella laughed, before plucking the bright red cherry off the rim of her glass and licking the creamy froth from its glazed skin.

"Where'd that term come from anyway?" she asked as she sucked the de-creamed cherry into her mouth with a moist, wet-sounding *ffft*, her lips glistening with sticky glaze.

Jake completely lost his ability to communicate as every ounce of blood he possessed rushed to his dick. Even when she looked at him, blinking clue-lessly, waiting for him to respond and then frowning at him in that impatient schoolteacher way she'd perfected, the blood refused to shift.

"Jake?"

He nodded, willing himself to speak. Nope. Blood still in pants. Not in brain.

"Jake!" She snapped her fingers in front of his face, which yanked him out of his glitch even if it did nothing for the blood situation.

"Right."

He flicked a glance at Rosie who'd been watching him watch Ella with a smile on her face before he returned his attention to the cherry sucker extra-ordinaire. "I'm not sure of the origins, I'm afraid. It goes back a ways though, I think."

She frowned. "What's the use of having a football legend in your camp if they don't know important stuff like this?"

Jake shook his head as her use of *legend* contributed to the major swelling action in his jeans. Even though he knew it hadn't been her intention to stroke his ego, his dick gave zero fucks. "The only thing that's important is winning."

She swished the creamy content of her drink around the glass with her straw. "You're such a jock."

"Lucky for you I'm a jock who knows how to win."

She rolled her eyes at Rosie. "There's that ego again."

Rosie shrugged. "It's kind of cute, doncha think?"

"No." Ella shook her head. "Puppies are cute. Fluffy yellow ducklings are cute. Little naked babies in pot plants are cute. Men with egos the size of Texas are not cute."

"Sure we are." Jake chuckled. "Maybe you just need another drink." He turned and gestured to Pete, holding up four fingers.

"Let me just" – Ella waved in the general direction of the restrooms – "go and relieve myself of the first few."

Jake scooted out of the booth, holding his breath as she brushed past him. She smelled like pineapple and was wearing one of those flowing skirts that moved with her body and almost brushed her ankles, elongating her shape.

The kind that made a man want to know what was underneath.

He sat as he tracked her progress and was relieved when she finally disappeared through the bathroom door. Hopefully, with the temptation of her well out of reach, he'd be able to coax some blood flow back to his brain.

Facing the table, he found Rosie and Simon watching him. "What?" he asked warily.

"Nothing," Rosie dismissed, waving her fingers in the air.

Jake wasn't falling for that. "What?" he demanded again.

She glanced at Simon who gave a barely perceptible shake of the head. Ignoring him, she asked, "Are you two going to step this up? Or are we going to have to keep watching it in slow motion?"

Jake grinned. He had to admit that, despite Ella's assertion that he was backward, there was an inevitability he felt whenever he was around Ella. Right now, his groin was hoping for the fast forward version but there wasn't enough beer in Mexico to make him think, even for a second, that Ella wouldn't take her own damn sweet time.

He regarded Rosie for a long moment, so different from Ella and yet somehow so right for her too. "Why don't you tell me? You know her better than I do. You met in twelfth grade, right?"

Yeah, he *was* changing the subject.

Rosie looked as if she wasn't going to roll with it for a beat before she acquiesced. "That's right. She was a conundrum. She looked perfectly normal and yet she was excluded from all of the cliques. I mean, I was used to it, but she took the prize."

Jake nodded. All the girls in Trently had hung around in groups or pairs. But Ella had always been alone.

"So you became friends?"

"Hell, yeah. If there's a bigger misfit around than me, I'm in. And besides, she didn't judge me, you know?"

"Yeah." *He knew.*

"Jake? *Jake Prince?* Is that you?"

Dragging his attention from Rosie, Jake saw a vaguely familiar guy greeting him like a long-lost brother.

"Roger Hillman." He stuck out a hand. "From Trently High. We were in the same year."

Jake smiled as he allowed his hand to be pumped, searching back through his memory banks.

"My sister Deidre had a major crush on you."

Ah. *Bingo!*

Roger Hillman, or *Rog* as he'd been called, had been a prize asshole, always keen to rub Jake's lack of social standing in his face. Deidre, on the other hand, hadn't been so fussy. In fact, she'd been downright accommodating that day she'd stripped off her top and let him touch her breasts.

It had been the first time he'd ever been allowed that far by a girl and he could still remember the total awe of the moment. He'd been a boob man ever since.

"Oh right, yes, great to see you again," Jake lied.

"I've followed your career. Man, you were dynamite." He looked pointedly at Jake's hands. "You don't wear your ring?"

"Well, it's..." *Ostentatious.* "Kinda heavy."

"Suppose it's in a safe somewhere, right?"

Jake nodded non-committally. His two were in his sock drawer.

"Man, you'd never get that bit of bling off my finger." He guffawed and Jake gritted his teeth. "Pity that piece of skirt ruined it there for you at the end." Roger gave him a playful punch on the shoulder. "You had another couple of seasons in you, I reckon."

Jake's fake smile slipped as the ugliness of that time revisited and he pulled his hand out of the other man's grasp. Rog was too stupid to notice the cool change.

"Why don't you go up to the bar and tell Pete your next one's on me?"

"Yeah? Cool man. I heard you'd bought a bar. Like father, like son, hey?" Rog gave a belly laugh, clutching his chest with one hand and patting Jake on the shoulder with the other before ambling off toward the bar.

Twenty years later, two Super Bowl rings and a kickass NFL career behind him, he was still Mick Prince's son. Jake turned bleak eyes back to his booth companions.

"That guy's a loser," Simon said.

"Complete fuckwit," Rosie agreed, shooting daggers at the retreating form of Roger Hillman.

Oblivious to what had just occurred, Ella arrived back and slipped in beside him. Drumming her hands on the table she announced, "I think I have room for that drink now."

"I like the way you think." Jake forced a grin as he yanked himself back from the quagmire of Roger Hillman's ugly words.

Pete appeared miraculously with a tray of drinks and Jake could have kissed him. Annoyingly, Ella did, landing a peck on his cheek. "You're the best, Pete."

"I know."

"Where on earth did Jake find you? Did he free you from a lamp or something?"

Pete laughed. "Something like that."

"Weren't our boys dynamite today?" she said to Pete as she took a sip of her cocktail.

Pete glanced at Jake. "It was great to see them get up."

Narrowing her eyes, Ella side-eyed Jake before turning her attention back to Pete. "What? Am I missing something?"

Pete shook his head. "No."

She quirked an eyebrow. "You think I don't know when someone is obfu... obfusca..." She blinked. "That's a hard word to say when you're tipsy. Being evasive," she substituted.

Jake traded anther look with Pete and Ella waved a finger between them. She looked at Rosie. "They just did a thing, didn't they?"

Rosie nodded. "Yep. There was a definite thing happening."

"What's going on?" Ella demanded.

Clearly, Ella wasn't going to let it rest so Jake nodded at Pete to spill the beans. Reluctantly, he obliged.

"We had a good result today but that's because we were lucky and the other team thought we'd be a walk over. They didn't try in the last half. They thought they had it in the bag. They were sloppy. We won on the back of their mistakes."

"Oh." Ella pulled her drink closer and took another hit.

Rosie shrugged. "Does it matter?"

"Yes," Jake said. "It matters. It's alright for now, for the first game, but it's going to get tougher and if we want to get anywhere near playoffs we have to be better. Counting on the other team being lazy or choking is not a strategy. We didn't win today. The other team lost."

"But... you were so good with them after," Ella said. "So full of praise."

Jake shrugged. "They deserved their moment in the sun. To feel ten feet tall and bulletproof for a couple of days. But Monday afternoon they'll be coming right back down to earth."

"Don't be too hard on them," she said, worrying her bottom lip. "You don't want to crush their spirit."

"Don't worry," he assured, "I'll tread carefully. We'll mainly be reviewing the tape with them so they can see their mistakes. It's often easier to show than tell, isn't it, Pete?"

"Absolutely. It's an invaluable tool."

"Or..." Ella smiled at Pete. "Maybe we can just rub our genie and make a wish?"

She gave Pete's arm a rub and he gave a wicked grin and said, "Lower."

Ella laughed which irritated the crap out of Jake. "I think you're needed at the bar," he growled.

Pete winked at Ella. "Can't blame a guy for trying."

Jake watched him go. "I should sack him," he muttered. The kid always had shown a distinct lack of respect.

"We can take him home with us," Rosie suggested.

"Just what your place needs," Simon remarked drily. "Another stray."

Ignoring Simon's keen observation, Rosie raised an eyebrow. "What's Pete's story anyway?"

Jake took a long pull of his beer, wondering where to start.

"Pete used to come and watch Founders practice sessions and he attended every home game religiously. He was this skinny fourteen-year-old with a quick wit and smart mouth who lived and breathed football. A super fan. He disappeared for a while then I saw him in his car one day in the stadium parking lot – he was seventeen at the time – and I realized he was living in it."

Even then Pete hadn't been downtrodden, confident that it was only temporary, but Jake had been appalled.

"His mom had passed and there was no one else and no money. Just her car. So, I..." He shrugged. "I hooked him up with a bunch of services. Got him a job." He took a sip of beer. "Haven't been able to get rid of him since."

"So," Rosie beamed at him, "you collect strays too, huh?"

"Nah. Just Pete."

"And dogs," Ella reminded him.

"And the Demons," Simon added.

"No wonder Daisy and Iris like you so much," Rosie said with a grin.

A prickle of unease at their unsolicited praise needled at the base of Jake's skull. It seemed, suddenly, he was a regular caped crusader. A tag he really didn't want. Or deserve.

Mother Theresa he wasn't.

Roger Hillman's piece of skirt crack earlier had focused his thoughts squarely on Trish. She knew better than anyone that his feet were most definitely made of clay. The night was turning into a real downer – first Rog and now this.

"You're actually a pretty decent guy, Jake," Ella said. "You know that, right? Very gallant."

Another time Jake might have laughed at the surprise in her voice. *Stop the press – Jake Prince is a good guy.* But his past sucked at him as a surge of anger and regret filled his chest.

Would she think the same if she knew the truth? And what kind of rock had she been buried under to be apparently clueless about this stuff?

"Don't go putting me on any pedestals," he muttered. "I'm here to help Deluca High. I'm not looking to be canonized."

"You shouldn't downplay this," she chided. "You've really gone to bat for us. For Pete. For Cerberus." She poked him in the chest. "It's a good thing you're doing."

Jake gave her a tight smile and drained his beer. She was looking at him like he was a god and he suddenly couldn't stand her praise. Ella had always been good – a good girl, a decent woman, a compassionate teacher – and he felt totally unworthy.

Standing abruptly, he said, "I think I better get back to the bar. Pete's looking snowed under again. I'll send over another round of drinks."

She let him out and Jake headed straight for the bar and the oblivion of hard work. Pulling beers and pouring shots – anything to distance himself from Ella's big trusting eyes. The aroma of hops filled his head as the floor grew tackier beneath his feet. People laughed, asked for autographs, women flirted, men shook his hand, a metallic beat played in the background. It was just what he needed to keep his mind off the black mood that had settled on his shoulders. The overwhelming desire to smash things itched under his skin, a feeling Jake from Trently knew too well and he struggled to push it back. It had been a long time since he'd used his fists and he was damned if he was going to regress on tonight of all nights.

Although Roger Hillman and his mates getting steadily trashed in front of him didn't help. Neither did the multiple TV screens plastered with Jake's arch nemesis turned sports caster – Tony Winchester. How he could even hold his head up in public, let alone score a TV gig, was beyond Jake.

He and Tony had started and ended their careers together and had spent the intervening years butting heads on and off the field. Tony Winchester was an asshole and having to look at him now on top of everything else was really grinding Jake's gears.

He glanced over to see Ella and Simon laughing at something Rosie had said and his gut twisted tighter. What had she said to him a few weeks ago in her office? He was *backward*. He was Trently and she'd come too far to go back.

Maybe she was right? A few weeks in her company, a couple of hours with good old *Rog* buzzing around and Tony fucking Winchester on the TV and he was spoiling for a fight.

Just like the bad old days.

* * *

An hour later, the group sitting at the booth were all feeling the hum from one too many cocktails.

"Jesus! This music is giving me a facial tic," Rosie complained. "I'm gonna put something decent on, then" – she walked her fingers up Simon's chest and smiled – "we should dance."

"Dance?"

Rosie rolled her eyes. "Yes, you know... moving your arms and legs to music."

"Decent music," Ella added.

"Not something I excel at," Simon admitted.

Rosie stared at him and shook her head. "What do I see in you again?"

"I... don't know exactly."

She grinned. "Well, lucky you excel at other things."

Simon smiled and Ella felt like the proverbial third wheel. Simon may not be Rosie's usual type but they *were* very good together. "I'll get the music," she announced.

Ella loaded the jukebox up with a selection of her favorites, effectively clearing the dance floor of all the bass junkies – which was pretty much everyone. Unperturbed, she and Rosie boogied until midnight, pulling out all the dance moves they'd perfected through their college years and TGIF drinking sessions at this very establishment in its previous incarnation.

Simon couldn't be coaxed out, watching them from the booth, laughing and shaking his head at their antics. Jake was watching them too. She should *feel* it. Ordinarily, that would have put her in a tailspin – Rosie was the mover – but her skin prickled with awareness and she was just lubed enough to not care.

When the oh-so-familiar opening chords of 'Sweet Home Alabama' oozed from the jukebox, the dance floor filled quickly.

Apparently even the *duff-duff* crowd had taste.

"This one always gets them up," Rosie said, undulating her hips and stomach.

"It's a classic," Ella agreed, doing a less successful version of Rosie's effortless shimmy.

"I'm getting Simon." Rosie strode to the booth, tugging on Simon's very reluctant hand.

Ella laughed as she dragged him onto the floor. For someone who claimed he couldn't dance, Simon got into the groove quite quickly. But then dancing with Rosie plastered to him didn't actually require a lot of movement.

"Thought you said you couldn't do this," Rosie shouted.

Simon pulled her hips in tighter. "This isn't dancing. This is fornication to music."

Rosie laughed. "I love how proper you make fornication sound."

"*Forn. A. Cation.*" Simon rolled the syllables off his tongue in a way that left Ella in no doubt that *fornication* was on his mind.

"See," Rosie said, "you *can* say an F word."

The song came to an end and the dance floor started to empty. Ella decided to give the love birds some alone time when a hard elbow jabbed her in the back. She swung around just as the man connected to the elbow stumbled and upended his frosty beer all down her front.

She gasped as cold, wet liquid soaked her bra and T-shirt. It was obviously loud enough to penetrate the love bubble as Rosie yelled, "Jesus, dude, watch where you're going."

"Oh shit, sorry, lady," he slurred. "Sorry."

"Simon," Rosie ordered as she continued to glare at the guy. "Go and see if Jake's got a towel or something."

The man reached out. "I'm really sorry," he repeated.

Ella dodged the hands. What did he think he was going to be able to do? *Rub her dry*?

"Hey, wait." The guy inspected her closely. "I know you."

Looking up from the state of her clothes, Ella focused on the beer spiller. Oh crap! *Roger freaking Hillman.*

"I don't think so," she said, shaking her head.

"No, no. I do." He grabbed her arm. "You're Ella Lucas. Little Ella Lucas. From Trently."

She tried to pull out of his grasp. "I think you've mistaken me for someone else."

Roger leered at her. "I don't think so." He ran the back of his forefinger down her arm. "Are you doing anything for the rest of the night?"

Ella's skin crawled as his hand encircled her wrist. Her stomach turned over. She'd seen that leer before. Occasionally she'd come face to face with one of Rachel's men and they'd get that look.

Like it wouldn't be long before she was on the menu.

She stared at Roger's hand on her arm, not really seeing it for the hundreds of memories that clawed at her gut. His touch was like the brush of a tarantula's legs against her skin and she could smell the rum on his breath but she couldn't move, a strange sense of paralysis rendering her incapable.

Rosie however, was not.

Keenly attuned to Ella's state of mind as always, she prodded Roger in the chest. "Hey pin-dick," she growled. "Take your hands off her."

Roger, very stupidly, laughed. That was when another voice joined the fray. "If you want to leave here with both your balls intact, *Rog*, I suggest you let her go."

Ella started as Jake's voice, right near her ear, sliced through her paralysis. She glanced at him briefly, noting that Pete and Simon were there too before Jake's grimness took up all the space. His green eyes were cold – reptilian almost.

She'd seen that face before. *Once.* At Trently High School, during recess, just before he'd taken a swing at some kid three years older than him who'd called Jake's father a stupid drunk.

Coming to her senses, Ella took advantage of Roger's distraction and wrenched her arm free, her heart rate kicking in to overdrive.

"Heyyyy, it's *The Prince*." Roger clapped Jake on the back, not reading the situation well at all. "Look who it is. It's little Ella Lucas. You know, *Rachel's* daughter. Come on, Jake, you remember Rachel, right?"

"Okay." Jake grabbed Roger by his lapels and hauled him closer until they were nose to nose. "Get out of my bar."

"Hey," Roger protested, his feet barely touching the ground. "It's okay. You want her, you can have her."

Ella felt as if she'd left her body as Roger's sickening implication sunk in. She could see Jake's fists tighten in Roger's shirt, the murderous look on Rosie's face. Could feel the steely band of Rosie's arm wrapped around her shoulders.

Yet, somehow, she wasn't *in* her body.

"Shut. Your. Face."

The unspoken threat in Jake's ground-out words had Pete leaping into action. "Help me," he barked at Simon before inserting himself between the two men.

Grabbing Roger by one arm, he indicated to Simon to grab the other. "Out!" he snapped.

"I'm fine, Pete," Jake growled.

"Sure, boss. But Ella's not." He indicated with his head. "Leave him to us and go take care of her."

"Don't *ever* show your face in here again," Jake spat before shoving Roger at Pete.

Still pulled tight to Rosie, Ella absently watched Pete and Simon hustle a loudly complaining Roger to the door. When they disappeared from view, she turned her attention to Jake who was looking at her like he wanted to burn the whole world down.

Instead, he said, "I've got some dry clothes in my office."

It was quiet and gentle and Ella nodded. "Thanks."

He turned to Rosie. "You guys go home, I'll take care of her."

It was a testament to just how outside her body Ella still was that she didn't protest Jake's *decree* or Rosie's easy acquiescence.

"Make sure you do," she said, her voice flinty. "Or you'll have to answer to me."

"Yes, ma'am."

10

Roger Hillman's words still dripped their venom into Ella's system as she sat on Jake's couch. She tried to recoil from them, from the ugliness of them, but they persisted.

"Put these on."

Ella looked up to find Jake holding something and it took a couple of moments to realize it was clothes. The air-con in the office blew on her wet T-shirt and she felt cold all over. Her nipples were pebbled, her brain function sluggish and she was rubbing at the raised goose flesh on her arms.

Relieving him of the items, she kicked off her shoes then stood, grabbing the hem of her shirt. Pulling it over her head, she absently registered the surprise on Jake's face before he turned his back and headed to his desk.

She supposed she shouldn't have done it but hell, the man wasn't exactly a stranger to bras. Hers included.

Given it was also wet, she whipped it off, pulling what she realized was a Founder's jersey over her head. His? Or just some old merch he had hanging around? Her skirt hit the floor next, and, with her underwear mostly dry, she stepped into a pair of baggy gray sweatpants.

"You can look," she said, smiling at Jake's propriety as she sat and huddled into the layers of the jersey.

Turning slowly, he plonked his ass against the edge of his desk and regarded her. "Roger Hillman is a giant asshat. Always was, always will be."

Ella nodded slowly, the pain of Roger's words a dull ache now. "I know. I just wasn't expecting it... it'd been such a great day."

"Yes." It was a bleak acknowledgment. "It was."

She stared at her fingernails, tuning into the muffled bass of the jukebox, the throb the perfect backbeat to her troubled thoughts. "Do you know how many years it's been since a guy spoke to me like that?" Ella locked her gaze on his. "*Looked* at me like that? Like I was a... commodity?"

Ella swore she could hear his teeth grinding as he said, "I'm so sorry."

The impotency she'd been feeling started to ebb as pure mortification took over. How many people had heard his ugly inferences? Had Simon? Had Pete? What about the people on the dance floor around her?

"Nineteen. Nineteen blissful years. And that" – Ella searched for an expletive worthy of Rosie and failed – "*moron* gets to throw the past in my face?" A crushing sense of unfairness pressed in on her and Ella hugged her knees.

"Forget about him," Jake growled.

Ella shook her head. If only she could. But if living in Trently had taught her one thing, it was that there was always another Roger Hillman. She'd just allowed time and distance to lull her into a false sense of security.

"How long, Jake?" she demanded, standing suddenly as anger replaced inertia. "How many years does it take? Until I get to be plain old Ella Lucas? Not Rachel's daughter?"

She glared at him. It wasn't his fault, she knew, but right now she wanted someone to vent at and he was it.

"I vowed when I left there I'd never look back. And here I am hundreds of miles away but everywhere I look lately there are reminders of Trently. Cam. Roger *goddamn* Hillman." She huffed out a breath, her eyes locking with his. "You."

"Yeah." He nodded. "I know."

His quiet acceptance took all the puff out of her sails. This *wasn't* his fault. And he did know. But she wondered if he truly understood where she was coming from?

Sighing, she sat again, pulling her knees up and placing her chin on top. "Roger Hillman and his cronies, they used to... ask me my... price."

Ella's voice cracked as all the old feelings of revulsion and fear swamped her. The gossips of Trently had called her haughty but so much of that had been a front to disguise her anxiety. She'd never quite been sure if one of the boys wouldn't try something on.

They may not have been men back then but they'd been experts at playing grown-up games.

To her horror, a tear leaked out of one eye and she brushed it away but not before Jake saw it. "Ella," he whispered before closing the distance between them.

Throwing himself down beside her, Jake pulled her into his arms as a strangled sob tore from her throat. Ella didn't want to be this person – *the weepy woman* – but another sob followed and another until her face was buried in his shirt and she was crying like she hadn't cried in a long time.

She'd wept two years ago as the orgasm he'd given her had tapped into the grief of her mother's death. But even then, she'd refused to give into soul-deep grief.

Not now. Now she was letting it *all* out. Crying for her lost childhood and Cam's. And Jake's chest was so big and warm and he smelled of deodorant and beer.

Or maybe that was her.

But she felt safe here with this man who knew all her secrets, so she cried until there were no more tears left to shed. Until there was nothing left inside. Until she was utterly exhausted.

And then she slept.

* * *

Jake drew the cue back and jabbed the white ball into the cluster of colored ones, picturing Roger Hillman's face on the front of it. The satisfying smack was like music to his ears and his gaze tracked the blur of color as balls flew around the table. He wasn't sure how long he'd been playing for, but it was his third game and he wasn't done with smashing snooker balls just yet.

Pete had stayed to help him clean up after closing, hovering like a mother hen, challenging him to a game. But Jake had ordered him home. His self-appointed role as Jake's guardian was amusing and Jake usually indulged him, but he was in no mood for Pete's wisecracking tonight.

He'd wanted to be alone in his anger.

Every time he thought about Ella – two bright stains of color in her chalk white cheeks – it tore at his gut and a silent roar of rage ripped through his chest. The urge to wipe Roger Hillman's face all over the bar resurfaced.

He wanted to pound on him, make him pay, make him *hurt*.

It had been such a great day until that son of a bitch had ruined it with his despicable inferences.

Jake inspected the table now the balls had settled into place and chose the longest shot, sending the white flying across the felt, smashing the yellow into the distant pocket.

The clink of balls as he set about annihilating the table was a good distraction from the echo of Ella's tears.

It was the second time she'd cried in his arms but it had been different this time. Two years ago, she hadn't allowed herself to wallow. She'd ruthlessly suppressed her grief and channeled it into their sex, *screwing* him through it.

This time she hadn't held back any of it and in every tear, he'd heard the echoes of his own lost childhood.

Jake stared at the last ball remaining, lining it up briefly before smacking it hard. It *thunked* heavily into the pocket and he wondered if Roger Hillman's face connecting with his fist would make the same sound.

Reaching under the table, he pulled the lever that released the balls and they thundered into the return slot. Plucking them out, he set up another game. He had no idea how long Ella would sleep but he had no intention of waking her up.

Ready to go again, he drew back his stick and set the game in motion, the chaotic careening of balls oddly satisfying.

"Is this a private game or can anyone play?"

Jake started, squinting into the gloom. He'd turned all the lights out except for the one directly above the pool table.

"You're awake."

"What's the time?" she asked as she moved into the stream of light spilling over the table.

There was a slight puffiness around her eyes that hinted at her crying jag and her hair was sleep tousled, but she looked better than she had.

Jake checked his watch. "Three-thirty."

They stared at each other for a moment, the silence stretching between them. Silence that seemed out of place in a bar where only an hour and a half earlier music had throbbed into every corner.

"Have you got any change for the jukebox?"

Wordlessly, Jake laid his stick on the wooden surround of the table and fished into the change pocket of his jeans. He pulled out some coins and deposited them into her outstretched palm. She smiled at him before ambling to the jukebox.

He picked up his stick, returning his attention to the table. Or trying to, anyway. Hard when he could see her out the corner of his eye, hunched over the jukebox, the jersey she wore – number eighty-seven, *his* number – slipping off her shoulder.

Her bare shoulder.

Forcing himself to focus on the shot, Jake jabbed the white toward the target.

It missed.

Harry Ryan, his first coach as a rookie, had always said that women ruined men's focus. He'd always been a wise old bastard.

The opening beats of Tracey Chapman's 'Fast Car' filtered out before Ella made her way back. Jake attempted another pocket ball, slamming the white hard but it missed again and he cursed under his breath.

"Bummer," she murmured, her hands sliding onto the edge of the table, her fingers caressing the wood grain.

Jake took a steadying breath then straightened. "Your turn." He reached for the nearby cue rack and grabbed one, offering it to her.

"Oh. No." Ella shook her head. "I'm hopeless. Rosie's the one that you need. Rosie can beat a bar room full of bikers."

Jake pushed the stick closer, hovering it just off the center of her chest. "I don't want to play with Rosie."

Her eyes widened a little at the innuendo but the haunting acoustics relaying a tale of small-town escape had set up a reckless kind of beat in his blood. And if he didn't do something with his hands, he was going to put them on her which was wildly inappropriate considering she'd cried herself to sleep not that long ago.

"Which ones am I supposed to hit?" she asked as she took the stick.

The action caused his jersey to slip off her shoulder and Jake's gaze dropped to the exposed flesh drawing attention to her braless state. Involuntarily, his gaze moved lower to where her erect nipples tented two spots.

"Don't worry about that," he dismissed, his voice husky as he dragged his gaze to her face. "Just go for the easiest."

"Alrighty then."

Choosing the closest ball – a green – she drew back the cue, botched the forward motion and missed the mark, grazing the side and barely budging the ball. "Wow." Jake blinked. "You really are hopeless."

Her stance was awful, her cue positioning terrible and her aim shocking. Ordinarily Jake would give someone this bad a few pointers, especially if they were an attractive woman. He'd be up there behind her, invading her space under the pretense of showing her how to hold the cue.

But he didn't need that kind of temptation tonight.

"You want me to point out the mathematical patterns on this table or work out the probabilities of each shot? I'm your girl. You want me to sink the ball? Not so much."

Jake chuckled. "That's okay. I'll just play really badly and let you win."

Setting the butt of the cue on the ground, she shook her head. "I know this may be a revelation to a jock like you, but I actually don't care about winning."

He snorted. That's what *she* thought.

"Yes, you do." Jake leaned over the table, setting up a shot that even Cerberus could make. "You just need the right incentive. Like a high school?" She'd fight to the death for Deluca and they both knew it. "Red into the center pocket."

Ella glanced at the indicated shot. A beat passed then she sighed, leaned over and smacked the white with her cue. The red bounced off the edge and ricocheted to the far side.

Jake winced. "Too hard." He strode to the other side of the table and positioned himself to line up another ball. "Sometimes you have to go softly." Gently Jake nudged the white to cozy up to a yellow that was sitting square with the pocket.

Lifting his eyes, he found her watching him intently and every cell in his body hummed with an electrical charge.

"Sometimes you need a slow hand," he murmured as her blue eyes locked on his. "A gentle touch."

For damn sure he wasn't talking about snooker now. But Tracey Chapman was crooning about city lights and being someone and heat flushed through his system and throbbed through his groin and it suddenly felt like every moment they'd ever had together had been leading them to this one.

Breaking eye contact, she righted her cue and Jake moved the hell away as Ella came around to take the shot. But if he thought distance would help with the heat situation, he was wrong. It only intensified as she leaned across the table in his too-big jersey and it slipped from her shoulder again, the neckline gaping a little.

There was no way in hell Jake could stop his gaze from drifting south to the swell of her breasts. To that creamy rise of flesh he remembered too well.

He drew in a shaky breath as he remembered how good her breasts had felt in his hands. Remembered how good she'd tasted.

His dick, predictable as ever, joined in the walk down memory lane and he knew there was no way it was going away while she was braless beneath his eighty-seven.

As if she could read his thoughts, Ella's eyes lifted from the ball and met his. There wasn't any doubt that she'd caught him looking down her top. She didn't object though, or call him out on it, she just took the shot.

Without looking at the ball. Or the table.

Just looking at him as she pushed the cue and Tracy Chapman promised things would get better.

She missed the yellow completely although it took her straightening before Jake registered it. And breathed again.

Clearing his throat, he said, "You should keep your eye on the ball when you're shooting."

Jake forced himself to peruse the table, to get the game back on track. The snooker game. It had been a tumultuous night. A tumultuous few weeks. It would be dumb to read too much into what was happening right now.

"Here, try this one."

He maneuvered the white into another good position and they played on, the jukebox pumping out easy tunes as they played the longest game of Jake's life. Between her hopeless aim and that damn jersey, he was fighting a losing battle with his temper and his libido. He talked her through the moves, giving her pointers as they went, demonstrating with his own stance, his own cue, but Ella was stubbornly uncoordinated.

Which should have made a difference to his dick, but it didn't. He preferred sporty women, ones who enjoyed this type of recreation and could hold their own. He especially loved the ones who could whip his ass. But his erection didn't seem to care how bad she was as long as she kept bending over, her tits flashing, her ass snuggled nicely into his old sweats.

The game finally came to an end when he potted the black with a resounding thud. It was 4 a.m. He was tired. And horny. He needed to get the hell away from her. Maybe he could dig out his little black book and ring one of a dozen women who would welcome a booty call even at this hour.

"Another?"

Jake opened his mouth to say no.

No way. No how. No siree. There was Alicia and Candice and Jennifer – three women he could name off the top of his head.

"A proper one. I think I'm getting the hang of it."

His jersey slipped off her shoulder again and his *honey, you have so not gotten this* was snatched away as the brain in his pants took over.

"Sure."

Jake cursed himself as he retrieved the balls and racked them up in the triangle.

Stupid. Stupid. Stupid.

"Can I break?" she asked as Roberta Flack started singing about a guy who sang a good song.

"Yup."

He stepped back a pace as she stood at the head of the table with him. Bending over, she balanced the tip of her cue between her second and third knuckles just as he'd taught her and he waited for her to take the damn shot and move away.

But she didn't. She straightened and turned until she was facing him. "Thank you," she said. "For before. For rescuing me from Roger. And being so... nice, in your office. I seem to make a habit of saving my meltdowns for you."

Jake felt like a complete asshole, thinking with his dick while she'd been working herself up to this. "Of course," he dismissed. "I'm just sorry you had to be exposed to his crap. I should have kicked his ass out the second I saw him."

"Oh yeah?" She smiled. "On what grounds?"

"Being a dickwad."

"You'd have to kick out half your clientele on that basis."

They both laughed then and she looked so carefree the urge to lean in and kiss her rode him hard. He didn't and the opportunity passed as she turned to line up the break shot.

Which she, naturally, screwed up.

Jake sighed as he hauled his gaze off her ass, so beautifully rounded and so very, *very* near. "Why don't we try that again?"

Using the triangle, he mustered the couple of balls that had managed to escape during the most pathetic break he'd ever witnessed. And then, because a part of him couldn't bear to watch her screw it up again – but mostly because he was weak – he leaned over her as she bent again to take the shot.

"Let me show you," he offered.

He half expected her to protest. To displace him. But she didn't, so he fitted his body snuggly against hers, his stomach and chest pressed along the length of her back, his crotch lining up with her ass like they were made to fit together even though he deliberately kept his distance down there.

"Like this."

Jake forced the tremulous tone from his voice, determined to stay business-like even though the silky caress of her hair and the aroma of warm hops wafting off her skin were digging seductive fingernails into his resistance.

"You don't have enough control of your stick," he murmured, feeling like a total hypocrite. At the moment he was damned sure she had better control of hers than he had of his.

"You have to slide it like this." Jake demonstrated the motion, gliding the cue between her knuckles, smooth and easy.

Back and forth. Back and forth. Back and forth.

Jake thought he heard something remarkably like a whimper reverberate in the back of her throat and his hand tightened on the cue. Her smell was intoxicating and it took all his willpower not to drop his head and bury his face in her neck.

"See what I mean?"

A second or two passed before she answered and even then, she only managed a breathy kind of, "Mmm."

"Let's do it together," Jake suggested, his voice husky.

She shifted against him slightly, bringing his crotch into full contact with her ass, causing his breath to practically strangulate in his throat.

His voice a veritable rumble now, he murmured, "Pull back. Then drive the tip of the cue into the center of the ball."

He punched the cue's tip into the white and it sailed down the table, hitting the cluster with a resounding smack, sending the balls flying around the table in a satisfying spider's web of color.

Which was their cue to move – but neither of them did.

Balls careened crazily around their joined hands, narrowly missing them but they didn't move. They were still standing plastered together as the balls eventually settled, the air heavy with anticipation.

She pushed back into him then, her butt cheeks grinding against the full force of his arousal, dragging a groan from the depths of his soul.

"*Ella.*"

11

Ella's nipples hardened to tight points at the thick, rough edge to Jake's voice. She was aware of him like never before. His lungs expanding, his pulse thumping against her back, the hard ridge beneath his zipper pressed into her ass.

She'd taken none of his lesson in since he'd pressed himself against her. Nor the wonderful randomness or the mathematical possibilities as the balls had bounced and collided, spiraling off each other like fireworks squirming into the night.

She was only aware of *him*. And the urge to rotate her hips like she was... *on heat*. An urge that apparently could not be denied as she involuntarily pressed into him, gasping as he slid hard against all her sensitive places.

"*Fuck*," he ground out, his hand shifting from the cue to her hip, gripping firmly.

Ella dragged in air thick as soup. *What was she doing?* This was all kinds of crazy. If they didn't stop this now it would be unstoppable.

Dredging up her last ounce of resistance, Ella straightened. He straightened with her, easing back a little as she turned. But he was still close enough to touch, his body pumping off heat and pheromones that were muddling her senses.

"I shouldn't." Ella shook her head as she drew in a husky breath. "We shouldn't." She looked into his hooded green eyes. "We're complicated. And we have to work together. I should get out of here."

He nodded. "You should."

But Ella didn't move because it didn't seem to matter how many times she told herself Jake was *backward* her body was screaming for his touch. For the magic she knew he had in his fingertips. For his mouth. For the rock of his hips.

She made one last appeal. "Please, just send me away."

"Shit, Ella," he muttered on a groan as he lifted a hand to cup her face. "I can't."

His head lowered then, his mouth capturing hers in a kiss that was out of control from the first touch. *All* she could do was hang on as it exploded around them, as his hands slid to her ass cheeks and lifted, setting her on the edge of the table before he stepped right between her legs.

She tore her mouth away, staring at him dazedly. His eyes were glazed and his chest was heaving air in and out like a bellows. He looked like she felt, so goddamn lust-drunk and confounded she was almost overwhelmed by the rawness of it all.

But then he swooped again and her pulse ratcheted up as his tongue tangoed with hers and somehow, she was falling back, and he was joining her, pushing balls out of the way as they went. Ella whimpered as his lips left hers but then they were at her neck and at that spot behind her ear, then licking along her collar bone.

He straightened and she almost mewed at the loss of him but his eyes were hazy with lust as he looked at her, the overhead lamp putting her squarely in the spotlight. His breath falling in rough pants, he placed a hand on her belly and the muscles beneath leaped at the touch. His hand moved then, pushing at the hem of the jersey.

Up, up, up.

Exposing her stomach then her belly button then her ribs and further still until her breasts were exposed, his gaze zeroing in on her nipples, hard as nickels.

"Fuck," he muttered, his eyes hot as they roved over every inch of her bare flesh. "I want to lick you all over."

Ella's stomach clenched at the naked desire in his gaze and part of her wanted to arch her back and yank him closer. But the other part wanted to lick him all over too and there were way too many clothes between them.

Her pulse tripping, she curled up, whisking the jersey off her head and throwing it on the ground. As far as she was concerned it was just one more thing in her way.

Sliding her arms around his neck, she kissed him full on the mouth as she grabbed his T-shirt from behind and pulled. Within seconds they were both topless, both breathing hard as they just looked at each other, their hungry gazes devouring the playgrounds before them.

And then they were on each other.

Ella pulled on Jake's shoulder, yanking him down and he climbed onto the table with her, dragging her into the middle as he went, pressing her into the felt, his lips plundering. His skin was warm and smooth beneath her hands, the muscles bunching enticingly. She'd forgotten how broad he was, how perfectly her hips cradled his.

His mouth moved lower, hot and wet, blazing trails, leaving devastation and pleasure in its wake. And when his whiskers grazed the aching tightness of her nipples, she writhed beneath the onslaught.

Ella needed him. *Now.*

Grabbing for the fly of his jeans, she tugged it open, her hand sliding into his underwear, wrapping her hand around his rigid cock. The groan that tore from his throat was so base, so *male*, Ella almost came from that alone.

She was vaguely aware of Kenny Rogers singing about being someone's knight in shining armor as her hands pushed at her sweats and underwear. Finally disentangling herself enough, she wrapped her legs around his waist and demanded, "Now."

His low chuckle buzzed against an impossibly taut nipple before he sucked into the heat of his mouth, dragging a moan from Ella's lips.

Oh *Lordy*. Good... So. Good.

But she needed more than that. Tugging his head from her breast, she yanked his face close to hers. "I need you in me."

"But—"

"I don't want the fancy stuff. Not now. All I need is this." She reached between them and grasped him again with rough hands, satisfied by his guttural grunt. "Inside me now."

Ella didn't care that she still had sweatpants and her underwear caught around one knee or that Jake had one shoe on and his jeans barely off his hips. She didn't even care about the carpet burns she sure as hell was going to have on her ass tomorrow or the distinct possibility that Jake was going to have to have the pool table professionally cleaned.

All she cared about was him putting a condom on and pounding all that hardness into her over and over. And she knew she shouldn't want it but it had been too long between drinks for them and she *needed* it.

In a way that wasn't just sexual.

"Mmm," he murmured, a smile on his lips. "I love it when you use your bossy teacher voice, Ms. Lucas, ma'am."

As if to prove it, he was suited up in twenty seconds flat. Considering her ankles were locked around his waist and her tongue had gone to town on his neck, it was an impressive feat.

But then he was pushing inside her on a low deep groan and everything outside the pool of light ceased to exist. There was just their breathing and the combined knock of their heartbeats and the entwined heady musk of their arousal. The deep, hard thrust of him and her *yes, yes, yes* every time she clenched around him and the way every stroke hit that spot he was so good at finding.

The spot only Jake seemed to know how to find. No hand-drawn map, no GPS coordinates just – *bam!* Every damn time.

"God... *Ella.* You feel so good," he panted as he gripped her bent knee, pushing it back further, lifting her foot off the table and thrusting again.

Ella cried out as the different angle went deeper and pulled down hard in all the right places, heat suddenly coalescing then bubbling and finally rippling out in ever increasing waves. She shut her eyes, trying to hold it back, wanting him to keep doing just *that*, just *there* forever.

But she could feel the tremble of his biceps beneath her hands and knew he was as close as she was. So she let it go, falling into an abyss of such intense pleasure she didn't think it was possible to survive it.

Until Jake joined her and they came out the other end, together.

* * *

Jake woke the next morning to a hand sliding up his chest. He cracked his eyes open as Ella draped a leg over his thigh and snuggled her head into his shoulder. Her hair brushed his chin and he shut his eyes again. He'd only been asleep for a few hours and the post-coital buzz had set firmly in his marrow, leadening his bones and eyelids.

A smile touched his lips as his mind drifted back to their brisk walk from the bar to her place as the first blush of dawn streaked the sky. They'd slipped into the darkened house like teenagers late home for curfew and hit her mattress, Ella's hand over his mouth, smothering his laughter, finally kissing him to shut him up. And then passion reigniting, racing to shed their clothes and do it all over again.

And again.

Ella Lucas was insatiable. To prove his point her hand drifted south and his smile grew wider. *Very* insatiable.

"You asleep?" she murmured, her hand traversing the flat of his stomach.

He grinned. "Not anymore." Neither was his dick.

She trailed her finger across the soft vulnerable strip where his belly met groin and he moaned appreciatively, eager for her to stay and play a little longer.

"Mmmm," Jake sighed.

Even the brief, loud knock on the door wasn't enough to kill his morning glory despite Ella withdrawing her hand like a child who'd been caught with her hand in the cookie jar.

His cookie jar.

"Ella, are you awake?" Rosie whispered loudly on the other side of the door. "I've been worried about you."

Jake chuckled and Ella dug him in the ribs. "I'm fine."

"Jake? Is that you?"

"Morning, Miss Rosie."

"When I said take care of her I didn't mean seduce her."

Jake could hear the smile in her voice all the way through the door. "What makes you think *I* seduced *her*?"

Rosie snorted. "Almost twenty years of friendship. Ella thinks too much."

He laughed, remembering how she'd asked him to send her away. "That she does."

"Hey, smart asses, I'm right here," Ella grouched.

"I'm making bacon and eggs," Rosie said. "You must both be famished?"

Jake was starving. But now Mr. Woody was involved, food was low down on his list of priorities. "No."

"I do some mean mushrooms."

"No."

"And grilled tomatoes to die for."

Jake laughed. "Go away, Rosie. Ella needs some more TLC."

"No. I'm good," she said, her stomach rumbling audibly.

"Really?" he asked, sliding a hand up to cup a breast.

It was gratifying to see her swallow. "Well..."

Jake brushed a thumb over a nipple that seemed more responsive to his suggestion than Rosie's. "Really?" he murmured again, lower this time.

"Maybe I am having a relapse."

Jake smiled. "Another time, Miss Rosie."

"Okay, okay. But you know you're passing up one of the best experiences of your life."

Jake smiled into Ella's eyes. "No, I'm not," he murmured as he rolled on top of her and she spread her legs to accommodate him.

"Rosie really does make the best breakfast in all fifty states," she said, twining her arms around his neck. "I know lumberjacks who've wept at her breakfast table."

"I'm craving something a little different for breakfast," he said, waggling his eyebrows before disappearing beneath the sheets.

* * *

Twenty minutes later, having thoroughly succeeded in wiping Ella's brain of not only food but even more basic things like speech and the ability to name simple objects, Jake rolled onto his back, dragging in ragged breaths. The fact Ella lay beside him in a similar state of breathlessness made him feel like king of the fucking world.

The mid-morning sun pushed bright fingers around the drawn blinds, allowing him a proper look around her space. Ella's room was surprisingly... girly. A lot of purple. A lot of bookshelves crammed with books. A print of

Van Gogh's *Starry Night* hung on the wall opposite the bed. Above it was a picture rail boasting a collection of nick-nacks.

"Your room's not what I imagined."

Her eyebrows lifted. "*You* imagined my room?"

"Well." He grinned. "Only insofar as you being naked on the bed."

She laughed. "So... what *did* you imagine then?"

"I don't know." He lifted his head. "Not so... purple."

"Does it offend your masculinity?"

"Absolutely not. But seriously, don't you think a big-screen television would look great on that wall?" He pointed to where *Starry Night* had pride of place.

She gave a faux horrified gasp. "That's a Van Gogh, Jake."

"You could hang it in your office. Or, better still, have it as a screen saver."

She tutted. "Philistine."

Jake grinned as he inspected some gauzy purple fabric thrown over a tall free-standing lamp in one corner. Suddenly, he was hit by a fragment of a memory. "Actually... Deidre Hillman had a purple room. More than this though. And frilly too." He shuddered. "The whole catastrophe."

"Oh, *really*?" Ella pursed her lips.

"Hey," Jake protested. "Just because Roger was an asshat, didn't mean his sister was. Deidre was actually *very* accommodating."

"Let me guess. She flashed her breasts?"

Jake smiled at the fond memory. "How do *you* know?"

"She did it for *everyone*, Jake." She rolled her eyes. "It was her specialty." She glanced at him after a beat. "Did you and she...?"

Jake grinned as she worried her bottom lip with her teeth and couldn't quite meet his eye. "Jealous?"

She shrugged unconvincingly. "Curious."

"No."

Rolling up onto her side, she inspected his face. Her hair fell in a sexy kind of dishevelment around her head. "So, who was it? Your first? Who got to deflower Trently's bad-boy jock?"

"Ella." Jake feigned a stern look. "A gentleman never divulges that sort of information."

"Okay, fine." She pursed her lips. "How old were you then?"

"Fourteen."

"*Fourteen*? Jesus, Cameron's fifteen and he's flat out stringing a sentence together most days let alone something witty enough to convince a girl to do the wild thing with him."

Jake shrugged. "I was an early starter. Plus, if it helps, I was really bad at it."

Ella laughed. "Don't tell me the great Jake Prince finished a little early?"

"You could say that." He grinned at the memory, at his mortification. "But she was more experienced and very patient. Plus... I'm a fast learner."

"And I bet your teachers always said you had difficulty concentrating."

Jake chuckled as he also rolled up onto his side and nuzzled the swell of her breast, his hand sliding to her warm, naked thigh. "What about you?" he asked, his lips trekking higher to where her neck met her shoulder. "How old were you?"

Her blissed-out sigh curved Jake's lips into a smile as he buzzed them against her flesh.

"I was clearly decrepit at the grand old age of twenty."

His chuckle was interrupted by a loud banging on the door. "Jake. It's Pete."

Pausing his assault on Ella's neck, Jake pressed his forehead to her sternum. "It's like Grand Central Station here, isn't it?" Glancing at the door he yelled, "Go away."

"Rosie says last chance for bacon."

Jake fell back against the bed on a groan as Ella muffled a laugh. "We said no, already."

"She says it's like an orgasm for the mouth."

Ella laughed again as Jake shook his head. "Does the kid not realize that I'm trying to score a real one here?" he murmured. "Pete," he said, louder this time, "I hired you, I can fire you. Go away."

"Jeez, okay, I'm going, I'm going."

Jake collapsed back against the mattress and Ella pressed her body into his side, snuggling her head into the crook of his shoulder. His arm came up around her, his fingers stroking up and down her arm, her contented sigh echoing one of his own.

Lying with women after sex had never been Jake's thing. It didn't usually take them long to get to the hard sell, the *when can I see you again* speech which usually had a lot more to do with his celebrity than anything else.

When he'd been younger the *hey baby, sure I'll call* lies had been easy. The older he got, the more gnawing his arm off in the middle of the night appealed. But being here with Ella, escape was the furthest thing from his mind.

A flash of color amidst the nick-nacks sitting on the shelf above the Van Gogh caught Jake's eye. A stray beam of sunlight had pierced a path through swirling dust particles and struck two red glass objects, throwing a deep ruby glow on the wall behind.

"Hey." He knew what that was. "Are they the vases your mom had in her room on the window ledge opposite her bed?"

12

_____

Ella had been drifting away to the deep rhythm of Jake's heartbeat when his comment ripped her by the roots of her hair back to consciousness. For a few seconds everything stopped as his words sank in.

How in the hell did he know that?

Ice-cold dread spread frigid tentacles through her veins. Her heart beat like bullets, hitting her chest from the inside. She pushed herself away from him, dragging the sheet with her, anchoring it firmly under her armpits.

Ella looked at the vases and for the first time in her life they revolted her. They'd been the only thing – aside from Cam – she'd taken from the house after she'd packed it up and left it for the lawyer to sell.

The only link to her mother. *Not* Rachel – her *mother*.

The woman she'd loved and known before the ugly truth of who she was had infected her memories like a cancer.

A rising urge to hurl the vases against the wall and watch them smash into a pile of ruby shards shook Ella to the core.

"Ella?"

She must have looked strange because he was looking at her warily, a frown crinkling his brow. "Yes, Jake." Her voice trembled which Ella hated but her feelings were too big right now to act cool. "They are."

Seemingly reassured by her answer, he nodded, glancing at them again. "I thought so. I always thought it was pretty cool how they refracted that weird red light around her room."

Oh God. Oh God. Oh God.

The vain flicker of hope that maybe he'd just heard about the vases through grubby boys' talk was brutally snuffed out.

Ella leaped out of bed, her mind scattering as she searched for something to put on. Jake's coyness earlier about the experienced woman who had taken his virginity formed a bilious slick in her gut.

Oh God... she should have guessed who it was then.

Roger Hillman's words from last night – *come on, Jake, you remember Rachel, right?* – caused a pain in her chest so severe she thought she was having a heart attack. Ella rubbed at it, trying to ease it as she threw Jake's jersey over her head before turning to face him.

Adrenaline flooded her system as her fight-or-flight response took hold. "I think it's time you left." She crossed her arms around her middle to stop her hands from shaking.

How could he?

How could he have touched her, *made love* to her, when he'd been with Rachel first?

The frown from before returned, the furrows deep enough now to plant seeds. He levered himself upright. "Okay... what the hell just happened?"

"Oh, Jake." Ella fought against the urge to crumple as she was swamped by a tide of despair. "Don't be so bloody obtuse. The vases, Jake. The vases."

She saw the moment he got it, the moment it dawned on him.

"Oh, hang on." He ripped back the sheets and scrabbled for his own clothes. "This is insane."

Ella, her chest a cold block of ice, watched him step commando-style into his jeans and she prayed his dick would get stuck in the vicious teeth of his fly. Maybe then he'd know a bit of the pain that was tearing into her flesh.

Unfortunately, he pulled it up without incident.

"You think I *fucked* Rachel?" he hissed as he yanked his shirt down and shoved his hands on his hips.

Even hearing him say the words was like an icepick to her heart. Her brain busily conjured images that made her want to retch. She needed a shower. A scrubbing brush.

She needed hospital-grade disinfectant.

"Damn right I do, Jake."

He raked a hand through his hair. "I *didn't*."

Right. As if she'd believe anything he said right now. "Sure you didn't."

He stalked toward her. "You *seriously* think that of me? After everything these last weeks? This is bullshit, Ella."

A noise came from the back of her throat she didn't recognize. Hell, it defied description. It was guttural and ugly, a cross between a roar and a mortally wounded whimper, ripping at her vocal cords.

"You have to have been *in her room*," she said, her voice thick with emotion, "to know about the sunlight on the vases."

And men only went into Rachel's room for one reason.

The vases were one of the happier memories from Ella's childhood. From when she was really little and used to snuggle in her mom's bed every morning, watching and waiting for the sun to get high enough to strike the vases. The mystical garnet hue usually lasted a couple of hours and often she and Rachel would lay there until the last of it had disappeared.

The sense of magic and wonder created in those moments had always stayed with Ella. And the fact that her mom had apparently done the same thing with *her mother* had imbued the spectacle with family tradition.

Now that was all gone.

Ella gave Jake's chest an angry shove which only managed to rock him back on his heels a little. "What do you think?" she asked, tears pricking her eyes as she shoved again, harder this time but still making no dent to the solid wall of his chest. "Was I as good as her?"

He reared back as if she'd struck him across the face and for a moment he was speechless. Then he opened his mouth as if he was going to say something.

But what?

Was he going to try and justify how he'd gotten into the pants of not one but two Lucas women? Ella sure as shit didn't want to hear that and she was relieved when his jaw clicked shut.

"You know what, Ella? If you *really* believe that of me, I don't think there's much else to say." He raked her with a contemptuous gaze before he turned away to gather the rest of his belongings.

Ella watched him with a strange sense of dislocation, hugging herself hard to stop the shakes, sniffling loudly as she blinked back the tears. How could she want him gone but be bereft at the thought of him leaving?

A whimper rose in her throat and she swallowed it down, biting her lip to stop herself from blurting out that it didn't matter what happened over twenty years ago.

Because it really shouldn't. *But it did*.

Most of the guys Ella had gone to school with had paid Rachel for sex. It had practically been a Trently rite of passage – why should Jake have been any different? He'd been a testosterone-driven, screw-anyone-who-said-yes teenager. And the entire town knew that Rachel was Trently's favorite yes-woman.

Just because she'd felt some feeble connection with him back then didn't mean he had. Just because the kiss he'd given her that night at home-coming had meant something to her, didn't mean it had meant anything to him.

Maybe that's what was making her so mad?

Could the lips that had touched hers so gently, so tentatively at homecoming, really have touched Rachel's first? Had she tutored him in how women liked to be kissed? Where they liked to be touched? All their secret places? Did she have her mother to thank for Jake's prowess as a lover?

Ella shuddered just thinking about it.

She must have looked a fright when he faced her again because the hard mask of his face softened and he took a step toward her. "*Ella*."

The thought of him touching her right now was too much to bear and Ella took a step back. "Just leave the money on the table on your way out, Jake."

His eyes widened for a second then the mask was back. He was gone five seconds later, the door slamming with such finality on his way out.

* * *

Jake watched the Demons do drills on Wednesday afternoon. He'd been working them hard all week, having brought them down from the high of their win with brutal honesty on Monday morning. He'd hammered into them that the comp would only get harder and he and Pete had made the team watch the video from the game several times, pointing out each player's weaknesses and strengths and replaying their errors ad nauseam.

Then they'd spent all week running endless drills targeting specific areas.

The fact that he'd been pissed since storming out of Ella's house on Sunday had certainly kept the fire burning in his gut and he'd replayed that conversation over and over. Replayed that moment she'd looked at him and everything had gone from warm and loose to cold and tight.

She'd *seriously* thought he'd slept with her mother.

The solution had been an easy fix, of course. Just sit her down and make her see. Explain how he knew about the vases. Because he *had* wanted to – despite her horrible accusations. He could see how she could have leaped to that conclusion and he'd wanted to comfort her with the truth.

She'd looked so disheveled and almost fragile, standing there in his jersey, hugging herself so tight. But her words hadn't been fragile. They'd *bludgeoned*. Particularly her parting shot and anger and pride had kept his mouth firmly shut.

Sure, Jake had been subjected to people's insults his entire career. He'd expected it on the field. He'd expected it from the press and the paparazzi and the social media trolls. He hadn't expected it from *her*.

Not after that incredible night.

In one sentence she'd sullied everything that had happened between them and he'd been so damn *furious* with her, getting the hell out had been his only option. And, five days later, the bitter lump of injustice lodged high and hard in his throat was showing no signs of dissolving.

So... they'd fucked like they were made for each other. Sex he could get – with uncomplicated women. Women who wanted to say they'd screwed the famed Founders' tight end and didn't give a shit about the one-horse town he'd grown up in nor who he'd bedded – or *had not* – while he lived there.

When he'd calmed down enough, he'd go set her straight. But that wasn't today. The way he was feeling right now, it wouldn't be tomorrow either. And besides, he was the coach and she was the principal. It was a line they should never have crossed anyway. Professional boundaries and all that crap.

Oh, and he was *backward*, right?

Why did he even care what a woman who considered him a backward step thought?

He tracked Cameron around the field for a bit as he worked on his passing. The boy had loads of stamina, but he was a ball hogger, relying on his bulk to bust through the opposition's front line instead of using his brains and his team members.

He watched some of the other guys working with Pete on their tackling. They needed some training machines. Deluca High had no equipment and no budget to buy any. The Demons' training sessions seemed archaic compared to the high-tech sessions during his professional career.

It put them at a disadvantage and, God knew, they were already handicapped enough.

"Pass the goddamned ball, Cameron," he shouted from the sidelines.

He made a mental note to start getting some basic stuff. What the hell else was he going to do with all his money? The teams they were up against had equipment, top-class equipment. Not that he really thought they'd make it to the playoffs. But if they won enough games they might be invited to play Chiswick Academy and *they* sure as shit had every bit of whizz bang training tech on the market.

If Ella wanted him to save her school, then he needed the right tools.

"Jake!"

Jake turned to find Miranda bounding along the sideline with all her usual indefatigable vigor. Honestly, if he hadn't seen her feet as she'd emerged into the world fifteen years ago, he'd swear she'd been born with springs instead.

She enveloped him in her trademark enthusiastic hug as Trish brought up the rear. "Miranda. Stop it. You know you're not supposed to hug Jake at school."

Jake grinned at Trish, an older version of her daughter, her step still springy despite the march of time. He kissed her on the cheek and they chatted briefly about the debut game before Miranda spat out what it was that had her shifting from foot to foot like a Cocker Spaniel on speed.

"I want to form a cheer squad."

Jake glanced sharply at Trish. The years fell away between them and he could see her in her little bitty skirt, her ponytail bouncing as she did the splits in mid-air, the team logo emblazoned across chest. "You okay with this?"

"Course she is," Miranda jumped in. "Mom even said she'd coach us."

Trish shrugged. "I've tried to talk her out of it."

Jake looked at Miranda again, not comfortable with the idea of her flaunting her ass and legs and shaking her chest in front of a bunch of horny teenage boys. As a professional, he understood cheerleaders were part of the showbiz of the game.

The *razzmatazz*.

But cheerleading wasn't all pom-poms and routines. He and Trish knew that better than anyone.

He'd hate to see history repeating itself. Hate to see Miranda crushed like her mother had been. But he didn't have the heart to tell her no.

He'd *never* been able to say no to her.

Then a sudden thought had him smiling – *Ella* could do his dirty work for him. "Okay. But you gotta get Ella's permission first."

Miranda squealed and grabbed him around the neck. "Oh thank you, Jake. Thank you, thank you."

Jake chuckled as he untangled himself. "Yeah, well, don't count your chickens."

"Could you come with me, Jake? Ms. Lucas has been a real grouch all week and she likes you."

Liked him? *Liked to castrate him, maybe.* "Grouchy, huh?"

"Cameron thinks she might be, you know..." Miranda lowered her voice. "Going through the change."

Trish rolled her eyes and Jake threw back his head as a huge belly laugh escaped. How old did they think Ella was, exactly? "Best not mention that to her."

"So you'll help me? Tomorrow before training?"

It was on the tip of Jake's tongue to tell her no. He doubted whether his presence would do much for her cause.

But wasn't that what he wanted?

"Okay. Sure."

"Yes." Miranda squealed again. "You're the best, Jake." And she ran back to a group of girls who huddled together and they all started squealing together.

"Oh God," he said to Trish. "I've created a monster."

* * *

Ella, already well and truly shitty with the world, was tearing up another letter that had arrived in an ominous yellow envelope when the knock came.

"Come in."

She smiled as Miranda opened the door and entered. Jake followed her in and the smile died. She hadn't spoken with him since Sunday and had, frankly, been dreading the prospect.

She'd lived that dreadful sinking moment when she'd realized Jake had been in Rachel's room over and over and it didn't matter how hot he looked right now in his tight, gray T-shirt, screwing her mother was unforgiveable.

Maybe it wasn't fair of her to hold Jake to a higher standard than other guys from Trently – but she did.

Miranda shifted nervously in front of her and Ella dragged her mind off the mess with Jake. The young woman gave her a shy smile and Ella wondered where peppy Miranda had gone.

"Can I help you with something, Miranda?" She didn't bother to acknowledge Jake, which was petty but, too bad.

"I asked Jake yesterday if we could form a cheer squad and he said you had to give your permission first. So... that's why I'm here."

Ella frowned. Her gaze cut to Jake. What the hell was he playing at? He knew how she felt about cheerleaders. "I see." Ella steepled her fingers, buying some time.

"My mom said she'd coach us," Miranda added into the growing silence. "We can practice in the afternoons on the field while the guys are practicing."

"Your... mother?"

Miranda nodded her head enthusiastically. "She was a professional cheerleader. That's where she met Jake."

Ah. So *that* was their origin story. The thought that he and Trish had been lovers reared its ugly head again, adding to her grievance with him. Were there any women on this planet – and their mothers – who hadn't ended up between his sheets?

Studying Miranda for a moment, Ella chose her words carefully. She'd always applauded initiative but this was a hot-button subject for her.

"I have to be honest with you, Miranda. I'm really not in favor of this."

"Oh but, Miss—"

Ella held up her hand. "Have you heard of Emmeline Pankhurst?"

"Of course." Miranda looked affronted. "She was a British suffragette. Although I prefer Ida B Wilmott or Lucrecia Mott."

"Excellent." Ella nodded, pleased to see there were still young women interested in that part of history. "So let me ask you, how do you think any of them would feel to see young women prancing around in itty-bitty costumes providing *entertainment* for males at sporting events?"

"If you don't mind me being frank, Miss Lucas, I think that's a rather outdated opinion."

In her peripheral vision, Ella saw Jake hide a smile with a jaw rub. Miranda paused as if she was expecting to be chastised but Ella just waved her on. She definitely wanted to hear what an articulate young woman who knew her suffragettes had to say.

"Cheerleaders are classed as professional athletes these days and are now even eligible for the Olympics. And surely women's suffrage was born out of the idea that women can be and do whatever they want?"

Ella blinked at Miranda's cogent argument. "And what about the message cheerleading sends to younger, less informed girls? That women are just there to prop up male egos while they chase a ball around a field."

"No." Miranda shook her head. "I don't think it's about that and we shouldn't make it about that. This is about what we can do to support Deluca High."

Ella opened her mouth to speak but Miranda didn't break for comment. She plowed right on.

"Look at the Cats last weekend. Their cheer squad was *ahh*-mazing. And right away they had a mental advantage over us because they had all the bells and whistles and we didn't. With every chant, they were saying our team's better than yours because we have all the luxuries, like a cheer squad. This isn't about girls pandering to boys. It's about school spirit. About us all pulling together and doing our bit to save the school."

Ella fell silent at the impassioned plea. She caught Jake's eye. He shook his head and mouthed, "*No.*"

Wait... *Jake* didn't want it either? She'd have thought the tight-end jock would be all for it. But he shook his head once more, bugging his eyes as he mouthed, "*No,*" again.

Okay, well... *that* was curious. She opened her mouth to say something but Jake got in first.

"I think Miss Lucas has made herself clear, Miranda," he said. "I don't think we should take up any more of her time."

"But..." Miranda protested as Jake grabbed her elbow.

Ella narrowed her eyes. "Wait right there!"

What the hell was his problem? Whatever it was, she was sufficiently angry with him that she was happy to sacrifice some principles just to *yank his chain* in any way she could. "I think Miranda's made some very salient points."

"Ella."

She arched an eyebrow at his clearly irritated voice. "We don't want to come across as the poor cousins, do we?"

"What about *Emmeline*?" he asked through gritted teeth.

"I'm sure Emmeline would have approved of Miranda's daring to stand up for something she believes in."

Several seconds of mutual eye... whatever the opposite of *eye fucking* was – eye hating? – elapsed before Ella dragged her gaze from Jake to smile at Miranda. "I'll call and talk to your mother this afternoon."

Miranda quirked an eyebrow. "Is that a yes?"

Ella gave a brief nod. "That's a yes."

"Oh my God. Oh my God!" Miranda turned to an immobile Jake and hugged him. She turned back to Ella and beamed. "Thank you. Thank you so much."

Ella smiled but held up her hand to curb Miranda's enthusiasm. "There are conditions."

"Name them."

"I don't want to walk around the school grounds and feel like I'm on the set of *Mean Girls*. No beauty pageants, no popularity contests – all comers regardless of size, sex and nationality are welcome to be in if they want."

Miranda nodded eagerly. "Diversity. Check."

"The uniforms are to be *modest*. No tiny skirts, no bare skin."

Miranda nodded again. "Functional. Check."

"Chants are about school spirit, okay? No ego-stroking."

"Deluca chants only. Check."

Ella laughed. Miranda was brimming with enthusiasm which was infectious. "Alright, then. Keep me up to date."

"I will," she promised. "I will." Then she bounded out of the office.

Which left Jake and Ella scowling at each other across her desk. "All you had to do was say no."

"This felt better," she snapped.

More eye hating followed as Jake glowered at her. For a moment she thought he was going to say something but then he turned on his heel and stalked for the door. He made it halfway before he stopped, clenched his fists, turned and strode back.

"Listen up," he growled as he planted his hands on her desk. "I'm only going to say this once. *I. Did. Not. Sleep. With. Rachel.*" Pushing off the desk, he shoved a hand through his hair. "My father was one of her clients. Sometimes he was too drunk to get home and Rachel would ring the bar and I would go and pick him up. That's how I knew about the damn vases."

Ella stared at him, his fervent denial and explanation seeping into the cracks of her famous reserve that had been papered over one too many times. He looked part pissed off, part exasperated, and tired as hell.

But, she believed him.

The weight Ella had been carrying on her chest suddenly lifted but it didn't make her feel any better. Because now she felt like a fool and a *shrew* going off half-cocked like that. Kicking him out of their still-warm bed.

And saying some pretty terrible stuff in the process.

"Why didn't you *say* something?" she demanded.

"I *did*," he retorted.

As he prowled to the window, Ella wanted to refute his statement but it was the truth. He *had* denied it and she'd pushed it aside because her brain had gone into frantic damage control, protecting her from images and scenarios she hadn't wanted to contemplate.

"Not hard enough," she said to his back. *Why hadn't he tried harder?* "Why didn't you tell me it was your father?"

"Because..." Jake stared out the window, his back to her. "Maybe I'm as ashamed by my father and the things he did as you are your mother? Maybe I didn't want to admit to the woman I'd spent the night with that my loser dad used to pay her mom for sex, especially after Roger fucking Hillman's insults. And maybe" – he turned then, his eyes bleak as they settled on her – "after all our history, I thought you knew me better than that?"

The barb struck her in the center of the chest. He was right. She should have. They had a complicated relationship that had sprung from a shared history neither had ever really talked about but she *did* know him.

The way only another misfit from Trently could.

Ella inspected her hands, embarrassed and ashamed by her hasty condemnation. *Stupid, stupid, stupid.* "I'm sorry." She lifted her gaze to his. "I'm really sorry."

He shook his head, sighing as he leaned his ass against the windowsill. "It doesn't matter. It was probably for the best, right? We're trying to achieve something here and if this... incident has taught us anything it's that complicating the situation with" – he pointed back and forth between the two of them – "a *thing* between us, probably isn't very smart."

Swallowing hard, Ella nodded. He was right. He was absolutely right. The last few days had been full of angst and stupid amounts of avoidance. They needed all their drive and energy to pull this thing off.

Not petty distractions.

"We should keep this strictly professional," he continued. "You're the principal. I'm the coach. Respect the line between us, concentrate on the team, the kids."

His words rang true. The last thing the Demons needed was any spillover between *Mom* and *Dad* fighting.

"Okay." Ella stood, determined to be as matter of fact as Jake. It was the only sensible way forward and she'd always aced sensible. "I agree." She stuck out her hand. "Shake on it?"

Regarding her for a brief moment that made her insides swoop, he pushed off the windowsill, crossed to the other side of her desk and slid his hand into hers.

"Principal Lucas," he murmured, his gaze hot on hers.

"Coach," she said, his touch far cooler than his gaze but burning a swathe of heat up her arm anyway.

She gave two very firm, very business-like pumps to quell the sudden urge to tear his clothes off and do him on her desk.

Because, despite everything – the competition, the school and their newly minted professional boundaries – she really, *really* wanted to do him on her desk.

13

Ella couldn't believe what a difference two months had made. The weather had turned along with the leaves, and jeans and sweaters had appeared as the evenings started to draw in. But that was nothing compared to the changes that had happened within the grounds of her beloved school.

Sitting in the crowd nervously awaiting the referee's whistle for the kick-off, in her very own Demons jersey, she had to pinch herself.

The Deluca football field had undergone a complete facelift. The grass was now tended to lovingly by three volunteer grandparents of Deluca students who had been gardeners before they'd retired. New undercover bleachers sat on opposite sides of the field. The goalposts had been replaced and the score board had been repaired and repainted, towering pride of place over the proceedings.

All this was in large thanks to Jake's generosity but also the hard work and fundraising efforts of the newly established PTA who had hit the ground running.

Two years ago when she'd had the principal's job thrust upon her, Ella had tried to form a PTA, tried to engage parents. But nobody had been interested.

How things had changed.

With a team that had put some wins on the board as well as grit, determi-

nation, vision and the fairy dust of a star ex-football player, things were definitely looking up for Deluca.

She glanced at Jake who was already prowling up and down the sideline
like a caged beast. In his regulation aviators and baseball cap, he was all hard
muscle and sleek lines, something his dark Henley showed to perfection.

It was hard to believe, now their relationship had morphed into one of
painstaking professionalism, that he'd ever pushed her onto a pool table and
pounded into her until she'd had carpet burn on her ass. And while there'd
been many a night she'd laid awake burning with those memories, it had
been for the best, drawing a definitive line through their past, both distant
and recent.

Channeling their energy into saving the school.

And tonight, everything was riding on the outcome of this game. The
Demons were battling it out with the Sabers for a spot in the playoffs. Which
was a remarkable feat considering they'd only made it to this point by the
skin of their teeth.

A short, decisive trill pierced the electric hum and the crowd roared as the
Sabers kicked the ball.

"I'm going to throw up," Ella said to Rosie.

"You say that every time," Rosie murmured, her gaze firmly glued to the
action.

"Yeah, but this time I think I mean it."

"They're going to be fine, babe." Rosie squeezed Ella's hand. "They're
going to kick some Saber ass."

"Come on the Demons!" someone yelled from behind.

Ella turned, viewing the crowded seats – another miraculous change. The
Deluca supporters, a sea of black and red complete with their signature red
horn headbands, had turned out in force. As the season had progressed and
the Demons had won a few games, the bleachers had gradually filled with
Deluca families – both home and away – until it had become *the* thing to do
on a Friday night.

A lump rose in her chest as she gazed upon what seemed like the entire
school community attending this, their final home game. Ella had hoped that
they'd win enough games to save their school from closure, maybe show her
students that hard work and determination could pay off.

But she'd never expected this.

She certainly hadn't expected the way the entire male student population had undergone a magical transformation. Every one of them had traded their awful, shaggy hairstyles for sleek number twos. It had been a gradual change to begin with, subtle, not something she'd noticed. But slowly, as the Demons had done the school proud, more and more boys had joined the ranks.

And, sitting here tonight, it was a sight to behold. She could see eyes again, faces.

Another surprising outcome had been the gradual decline in her truancy rate, not to mention the spring in everyone's step, from the teachers to the students. Her staff were energized and kids who used to mope around with the weight of the world on their shoulders were walking tall, smiling at her, greeting her with enthusiasm.

The sense of pride and accomplishment Ella felt glowed like a furnace deep inside, warming her soul on this cool evening. Deluca had finally found its mojo and she was starting to really believe that it all might just work out okay.

But perhaps the biggest change of all had occurred in her. For a start, she never would have believed that she'd be voluntarily spending this much time on or near a football field – not in a million years. In fact, a couple of months ago, she'd have rather had root canal and, while she did still think football was stupidly macho, she couldn't deny its positive effects.

The crowd in the stand opposite started to roar and Ella tuned into the game. The Saber running back was rushing the ball along the ground, storming toward the end zone. Cameron and several Demons were hot on his heels and Ella's heart crept into her mouth.

Go Cam. Go Cam. Go Cam.

As she watched her brother gaining, Ella realized that even her relationship with Cam had come a long way this past couple of months. He was the happiest, the most settled she'd seen him since she'd dragged him out of Trently.

He attended school, he trained hard, he'd become polite and respectful. And way more talkative. She knew that them becoming *friends* was a ways off, but for the first time in two and a half years, Ella actually felt it was a possibility. He and Miranda had become quite close, too, and it was encouraging to see that he had the capacity to form human relationships.

He'd always been so distant – it was a relief to see him engaging finally.

Cameron dragged down the speeding Saber and everyone in the hometown bleachers rose to their feet, cheering.

"Good tackle, Cam," Jake called.

Cameron untangled himself from the wildly kicking Saber and stood, turning to Jake with a huge grin on his face and Ella's heart lurched in her chest. Cam adored Jake and she knew her brother's changes had as much to do with the coach – wanting to please him and make him proud – as they did football.

From the sidelines, the Deluca cheer squad did their thing, plump red-and-black pom-poms fluttering through the air as the squad shook them high above their heads.

> *Deluca, Deluca, we're the best,*
> *Better, way better, than all the rest.*
> *You wanna, you wanna, put us to the test?*
> *You're gonna be sad, you're gonna be sorry,*
> *Cos we're gonna win, don't you worry.*

Ella had to admit, despite her initial misgivings, the squad was a credit to Miranda and Trish. A melting pot of genders and sizes and ethnicities, they had become an integral part of the Demons' games in their distinctive red cotton leotards with mandarin necklines, black cargo-style pants and the signature red devil-horn headbands.

Better still was how the entire school, rallied by Miranda, had united to produce them. The senior textiles students had made the uniforms, the art students had enthusiastically taken on the project of the leotard design from the logo – a pitchforked devil – right through to the screen printing, and the PTA had funded them.

And the squad looked amazing. Not hot pants, cutesy-pie like the Sabers but fit and strong and, with red-and-black stripes slashed on each cheek, warrior-like.

Miranda had even roped Cerberus into the team spirit, making the Jack

Russell a doggy coat with "Deluca Demons" handstitched across it. And, so he wouldn't feel out of place, she'd modified a headband to give him his own pair of red horns.

Jake had taken one look at Cerberus that first time and rolled his eyes. But, like a true stray, Cerberus loved the attention and when he wasn't sitting by Simon's feet, he pranced up and down the sidelines, barking encouragement at his team.

A roar came from the Sabers' stand and Ella didn't have to see to know the opposition had just scored their first try.

"Oh no," she wailed and clutched Rosie's hand.

"Don't worry," Simon said. "Plenty of time left."

Simon had become a permanent fixture both at the games and in Rosie's life and Ella loved how their relationship went from strength to strength. No guy had ever lasted this long the entire time she'd known her bestie.

"I know," Ella said, but still her insides felt like they'd been scrunched in a tight ball and she watched until half time through the cracks of her fingers when she could bear to watch at all.

At the half-time siren, the Demons were trailing and Ella went to the restrooms and threw up. When she ventured back, Pete, Jake and the team were huddled together and she made a beeline for them.

After assuring Jake she wouldn't say break a leg again, it had become a tradition for her to talk to the team at the start of the game. But she wanted them to know that no matter what happened in the second half, she was proud of them.

Jake frowned as she approached. "Miss Lucas?"

"Can I have a quick word, Coach?"

He nodded warily but stood aside in the unfailingly polite way he'd adopted ever since they'd shaken hands two months ago.

"Don't be discouraged, guys." She gave them all a big smile, letting it linger on Cameron. "And I want you all to remember, I'm so happy that we even got this far. You've done me and Deluca proud."

The whistle blew as she finished up and the starting team ran back onto the field. Ella stood beside Jake, watching the team get into position, her gut twisting. Miranda led the squad in a cheer and the Deluca crowds yelled, "Go Demons," and "Demons rule."

"You okay?" Jake asked, his eyes on the field.

"Fine."

"You look like you're going to throw up."

She peeked at him but he was watching the field, his dark shades giving nothing away, the shadow from the brim of his cap throwing his face into hard-to-read lines.

"Already accomplished." She slid her hand to her stomach then, as the silence built between them, she said, "They're playing well, right?"

"Yes," he assured. "Something you'd probably know if you didn't have your hands over your face."

Ella gave a self-deprecating laugh. "I can't bear to look."

"I know the feeling."

This was the most personal conversation they'd had, just the two of them and it gave her courage to say the next thing.

"Look, Coach." It had felt weird calling him that at first but it slipped easily off the tongue now. "I just wanted to say that I know we made you do this and I know coaching a high school football team wasn't how you planned to spend your retirement. So, it's okay if we don't make the playoffs."

Especially if it meant they still got the Chiswick Academy gig. They'd come further than anyone had given them credit for, which *might* just be enough.

Apparently though, that wasn't acceptable to Jake.

Very slowly he turned his head to look at her, removing his glasses. Ella almost took a step back at the fierce glitter in his eyes.

"Listen to me *very* carefully, Ms. Lucas." His voice was almost menacingly calm. "Nobody makes me do anything I don't want to do. And you better believe we're going to win this *and* make the playoffs. After that, the competition is a whole different level and I don't know what happens. But tonight is in the bag."

Ella was captivated by the blaze of conviction in his green gaze. She really wanted to believe him. Wanted to believe they could win.

"Jake..." She bugged her eyes at him and whispered, "They're ahead by twelve points."

"*Ella*," he cautioned and damn if the barely contained growl in his low voice didn't go straight to her ovaries. "Have some faith."

And with that, he replaced his glasses and turned his attention to the field.

Clearly dismissed, Ella returned to her seat. Trish had joined Rosie and Simon and Ella smiled at her absently, still thinking about that raspy rumble. It had been a long time since they'd had such an intense one-on-one and she'd forgotten how much of an impact he had close up.

Thankfully Deluca's quarterback chose that moment to go long and thoughts of Jake and their *relationship* were completely obliterated as the crowd surged to their feet.

She spent the rest of the game on the edge of her seat, hiding behind her fingers as it progressed. With two minutes to go, Deluca was trailing by four points. The crowd behind her were stomping their feet on the wooden floor of the bleachers and her heart thundered along in time.

Twenty seconds out, Deluca's giant wide receiver, Dwayne Morgan, caught the ball from the quarterback and ran into the end zone to score a touchdown and win the Demons the game.

And the Deluca supporters went *wild*.

"Oh my God, *we did it*," Ella yelled at Rosie, her heart hammering so hard she thought it might just burst out of her chest. "*We did it!*"

Rosie, who was crying and laughing all at once yelled back, "Yaaas, babe! We fucking did it!"

A potent swell of relief almost took her knees out from under her, but Trish and Rosie grabbed her into a three-way hug, holding her upright as they jumped up and down excitedly.

Jake and Pete ran onto the field and tears streamed down Ella's face as the team – *her* team – huddled together in a big group hug. Then the boys picked up Jake and Pete and carried them off the field into the swarming Deluca supporters.

The cheer squad joined the fray and Ella, Rosie and Simon got swept up in the crowd, everyone reveling in the high of sweet, sweet victory.

Cameron found her and lifted her off the ground in a huge bear hug. "We did it," he yelled over the noise, grinning down at her. "We did it!"

Ella almost fell over from the shock at such a show of affection and was glad he was still hanging on to her.

"You did it," she said, beaming up at her brother, struggling to remember a time her heart had been so damn full. "*You* did it."

* * *

Half an hour later Jake found himself standing in a circle with Cameron, Miranda, Rosie, Simon, Pete and Ella. The crowds had largely dispersed, the night had cooled rapidly and the dew was on the grass but none of them, it seemed, were willing to call it a night.

"Time to celebrate," Rosie announced. "I've got a curry in the slow cooker and you're all invited."

The only one of them to look enthused was Cerberus, who had grown fat on the curry treats that appeared regularly under the table from anyone who dared to attempt it. He gave an ecstatic little shudder and whined appreciatively at her.

"Ah, count me out," Jake said.

He glanced at Ella who was *glowing*. He hadn't been back to their house since Ella had kicked him out and, in the effort to keep it professional – and avoid temptation – he should probably stay the hell away.

"Oh no. No, no, no." Rosie shook her head vehemently. "It's not a celebration without the coach."

"She's right," said Pete.

"Yeah," said Cameron. "Please, Coach."

"Please, Jake," Miranda said, her arm around Cameron.

Jake took in the eager faces, knowing that part of their motivation was how much less curry they'd all have to consume with one more at the table. And then there was Ella whose hair was loose and mouth was curved into a permanent grin and she was still *glowing*.

"Please, Jake," she murmured.

There were those words again. *Please, Jake.* And it was Jake, not Coach and she was staring right at him which was like a hot fist straight into his groin. Between her and Miranda – two women who'd had his nuts in a vise forever – he knew he was sunk.

He gave a grudging nod. "Looks like I'm outgunned."

"Yaas!" Rosie whooped. "I've sourced this great new spice that adds a little extra zing. You're going to love it."

Jake blinked. If Rosie's curry had any more zing it'd need to be classified as a poison.

"We'll go ahead and get the rice cooked," she said with a little jiggle as she dragged Simon away.

"I'll stop off and buy yogurt," Pete offered.

"Buy extra," Jake ordered, resigning himself to death by curry.

* * *

Even though it was a brisk night, they still ate on the back porch. Thanks to Rosie's curry it wasn't remotely possible for any of them to feel the cold. The heat was like a thermonuclear reaction in the stomach, likely to keep them warm to the end of their days.

Was her secret spice plutonium?

Simon took a large gulp of his water and passed around the yogurt bowl for second helpings. "Delicious." He smiled at Rosie.

Miranda and Cameron had excused themselves earlier, taking their meals into the living room to watch Netflix. Cerberus had followed them in and Jake had no doubt most of the curry would, by now, have found a canine host.

Daisy and Iris were, as usual, tucking in heartily as the conversation turned to football. "I still can't believe we made the playoffs," Ella said.

"Believe it." Pete grinned.

"Just," Jake clarified. They'd exceeded expectations but the playoffs were a real step up and he didn't want to give anyone false hope.

Pete, who was clearly in an optimistic mood tonight, shook his head. "Doesn't matter. We wipe the slate clean now and start all over again."

"And we go in as underdogs," Rosie pointed out.

"Which can work in our favor," Simon added.

"Yep." Pete nodded. "And even if we're knocked out of the playoffs, we're the most improved team in the competition so we should have done enough to secure the game with Chiswick and that sucker gets a lot of attention."

Ella looked across the table at Iris. "What do the cards say?"

The older woman didn't hesitate, she put down her fork, moved her bowl aside, shuffled the worn, ever-present pack and laid out a spread.

"They're still favorable," she murmured, staring a bit longer before she grimaced. "But it's going to get worse before it gets better."

"What does that mean?" Jake asked.

Irish shrugged as she collected the cards. "Time will tell." Then she picked up her fork and started eating again like predictions of doom were nothing much to worry about. Certainly not enough to put her off her curry.

But it sure as hell shot an itch up Jake's spine.

* * *

Half an hour later, Jake stood to leave. He didn't want to, he was enjoying himself too much. Laughter flowed and the company was great. Daisy had dialed up Ella Fitzgerald on Spotify and with her crooning 'It's a Lovely Day Today' the atmosphere was decidedly mellow. Three beers had finally doused the fire in his mouth and his buzz fit the mood quite nicely.

But the other Ella hadn't stopped *glowing* (non-curry related) and it was driving him nuts. Her hair was loose and her Demons jersey fit snug across her breasts and he was having a hard time remembering why they were keeping it *professional*.

Not even the niggle of Iris's warning was enough to blunt his desire to burrow his fingers in her hair and put his mouth on hers. Telling himself he was backward didn't help either.

Libido had no pride.

To much protest, he made his goodbyes, nodding at Ella as he departed and he *almost* made it out unscathed before she said, "Wait up. I'll see you out."

Jake gave an internal groan as he followed her through the house, her round ass swaying in front of him. The same ass he'd gripped as he'd sat her on the pool table.

The same ass he dreamed about night after night.

Dragging his thoughts back, he called goodbye to Cameron and Miranda before he stepped outside after Ella, barely noticing the naked branches of the trees planted sparsely along the sidewalk or the fact the nearest streetlight had blown, drawing the night in around them.

She stopped at the gate, not opening it. He stopped too as a weird vibe descended. She seemed like she wanted to say something and part of Jake urged him to leave but the message wasn't getting through to his legs.

The faint strains of 'A Fine Romance' floated out to them which couldn't have been a more perfect song for the state of their relationship.

He cleared his throat. "Ella Fitzgerald, huh?"

She nodded. "They play it for me. They know Rachel named me after her, that she was a huge fan."

It was on the tip of Jake's tongue to tell her he knew. How many times had he been to Rachel's while Ms. Fitzgerald sang the blues? But given what had happened last time he'd mentioned being at the house, he didn't feel so inspired.

"You didn't have to walk me out."

"I know. I just wanted to say..." Her fingers slid to the top rail of the gate and absently caressed the metal. "Thank you. I didn't get a chance to say it after the game."

"There was a bit of a crush."

"*That*, is an understatement." She gave a half-smile. "Well, anyway... thank you. You don't know how much this means to me."

"Oh, I think I do."

He'd seen the improvements around the school these past couple of months. The way the kids carried themselves – and not just the team. The entire student body was walking a little taller, a little prouder and he was very aware that this had become about more than keeping the school open for Ella.

It had become about restoring their dignity and purpose.

Maybe that's why Iris's tarot caveat about things getting worse before they got better, was still playing on his mind. Ella cared a little *too* much.

"How much stock do you put in Iris's tarot readings?" he asked, his warm breath fogging into the air. Not that he was feeling the cold. Between the aftereffects of the curry and Ella's nearness he was *burning up*.

"I've been privy to her accuracy on more than one occasion to *not* put stock in it. I know as a math nerd I'm supposed to be all logical but, as someone who draws the eight of swords on a freakishly regular basis, I've learned that there are some things you just can't quantify."

"Are you worried about the worse before better thing?"

"Well." Her face might have been in shadow but he saw the small smile curving her mouth and hell if it didn't curl right around his heart. "I prefer to concentrate on the whole *cards being favorable* bit." She shrugged. "Why borrow trouble?"

Jake chuckled at her deliberate avoidance as the song ended and the music morphed into 'Cheek to Cheek' and for a crazy moment it felt like they might be *in heaven* smiling at each other despite everything between and ahead of them.

The impulse to pull her into his arms rode him hard and he was offering his hand before he could check it. "Care to dance, Ms. Lucas?"

Because that kept it professional, right?

Jake held his breath as she looked at his hand for a beat, then at him. "Coach," she murmured and slid her hand into his.

He expected her to maintain a formal waltz position, but she didn't. She stepped in close, sliding her arm around his waist and pressing her cheek to his chest which stoked the fire a little more. For a moment, he contemplated putting some distance between them, but he was weak where she was concerned and he relaxed, fitting his chin snuggly on top of her head as they swayed from side to side.

Suddenly he was fifteen again at the homecoming dance, his heart thudding, his palms sweaty. Was she feeling it, too?

The song ended and she stilled in his arms, a beat or two passing before she eased away, her face upturned. Their gazes locked and she was smiling wistfully like maybe she *had* felt it.

And it was just so easy for him to drop his head in that moment and press his mouth to hers as he had back then. Not moving, not deepening, just holding in this one perfect moment on a brisk Inverboro night, far away from Kansas yet wrapped in the tendrils of their past.

Jake wasn't sure who stepped back first but suddenly there was space and clouds of dragon's breath between them.

He didn't know whether to apologize for crossing the line or to just leave it be as it was, existing without comment. He decided on the latter.

"Goodnight, Ms. Lucas," he murmured, unlatching the gate.

"Night, Coach."

14

Ella thought of little else all weekend and was still smiling at the memory of the kiss on Monday morning. She literally had a head full of far more X-rated images associated with Jake but, she couldn't help it. That press of lips, so reminiscent of that other press of lips in Trently, so long ago, had her happy sighing like a goofball.

She should have known it wouldn't last long.

It took about three minutes sitting at her desk to burst her bubble in the form of another yellow envelope from Donald freaking Wiseman.

Dear Ms. Lucas – *blah blah*. We note your numbers have dropped by a further six – *blah blah*. You need to present to the board in two weeks – *blah blah*. Show cause as to why Deluca shouldn't be closed at the end of the year.

Blah, blah, blah. Blah.

Ella's heart sank in her chest. No praise for her vastly improved truancy figures. No mention that the reason her numbers had dropped was that two of her families had parents who were in the armed forces and had moved to another post.

They *couldn't* do this. She *wouldn't* let them. Not when Deluca had come so far. Not when Iris's prediction of a favorable outcome hung like a shiny bauble in her mind's eye.

Before she could fully think it through, Ella lifted the phone. "Bernie, can you find me a number for the *Deluca Daily* please."

She'd promised Jake no press but this was just a free suburban paper. Popular with locals but not big enough to make a splash on a wider scale. It was time to tap the fledgling support the Demons had birthed within the school and get the wider community involved.

It was time to go public.

There'd be no need to mention Jake at all. It would be about the school and their battle with bureaucracy. And it wasn't like his presence hadn't been noticed despite the low riding ball cap and aviators.

As a schoolteacher, Ella had never been on social media but Bernie, whose screen time alone must surely have put him on dozens of watch lists by now, had shown her several posts featuring Jake. From Facebook to Instagram and TikTok he'd garnered quite a bit of attention but mostly from students or their families. None of the posts seemed to have gone viral, but people *were* talking about him.

He was *on* the radar. Whether he liked it or not.

* * *

As soon as the *Daily* was delivered to the school on Wednesday morning, Bernie brought it through. "I think you're gonna love this."

He smiled, holding it up to reveal the front-page headline. *The Little School That Could* said the bold black type and then under it in smaller print but still readable from across the room: *Education Dept Threatens To Shut Down Local School*.

"Front page?" Ella practically leaped off the chair. "Oh my God! Much better than I hoped for."

Ella took the paper from Bernie and he departed. Her hand trembled a little as she cleared a space in front of her and laid it flat. The team's official photograph – the one minus Jake and Pete – which she had emailed to Suzy Barton, the young reporter, took pride of place in the center of the article.

Devouring the piece, *which spilled over to page three*, Ella couldn't have been happier. Suzy, who'd apparently spent a lot of time covering fluff pieces, had been most eager to really dig into something juicer.

And it was a very comprehensive article.

Everything she'd discussed with Suzy was there. The Education Department's threats to close the struggling school and the desperate measures Deluca High was employing to stay open. She'd also summarized the Demons' successes on the field concluding with Friday's win which had put them in the playoffs.

Somehow, Suzy had managed to ferret out that Jake "*The Prince*" Prince was the coach but it was only one sentence among many from the hard-hitting story which raved about the school spirit and how the cheer squad, tutored by Trish Jones, herself once a professional cheerleader, had become a whole school project. There were also mentions of Cam and Miranda, to demonstrate how Deluca High was one big family and praise for Ella herself, for leading the charge and standing up to The Man.

The piece ended with a diatribe on heartless bureaucrats who were ripping the soul out of a severely depressed socio-economic area to pinch a few pennies. Phrases such as *denying kids access to free education* and *discrimination* leaped off the page.

It was exactly what Ella hoped it would be – a stirring piece of journalism to inspire even the most apathetic in the community to rally to the cause. It may not be Watergate but Ella hoped it'd have Donald Wiseman on the run.

Or silenced, at least.

She leaned back in her chair, reveling in the buzz of a job well done, until a loud knock on her door startled her out of the glow. Before she could open her mouth to say *come in*, the door was flung open and Jake strode in to her office.

He was wearing his standard jeans, jersey and ball cap. "What," he asked, holding up the paper, his mouth a grim slash in his face, "the hell is this?"

Ella blinked and the buzz disappeared like a genie in a puff of smoke. She'd hoped it might last longer. And that this wouldn't be their first interaction after their cheek-to-cheek moment on Friday night. Their kiss.

"I can explain."

But he clearly wasn't in the mood for explanations as he slammed his copy of the paper down. "Didn't I say no press?"

Ella stood. "Yes, I know you did but—"

His loud snort cut her off. "Damn it, Ella." He ran a hand over the top of his head. "I think I was fairly specific."

"I got another letter from the department. They're demanding I show cause as to why they shouldn't close the school at the end of the year. I just thought this might drum up some broader local support."

"I don't care what you thought," he roared.

Ella blinked at the outburst, so far removed from the man who had kissed her so lightly not that long ago.

"Look, Jake, I know you didn't want any media attention drawn to you, that you wanted to stay anonymous and I didn't mention a word about you. Suzy obviously found that out by herself. But it's hardly anything. I don't think there's any need to overreact."

"Overreact?" He gaped at her. "You don't have a fucking clue, do you?"

"Jake..." Ella frowned. "It's the *Deluca Daily*. Not the *Washington Post*."

He gave another snort and stalked over to the window, slapping his palm hard and high against the frame as he muttered, "I knew this was going to be trouble. Right from the beginning. I just knew it."

He sounded so much like Iris, Ella would have laughed had he not been so angry.

"There's no such thing as local, Ella," he said after a beat or two, his back to her. "Every national paper, every TV and radio station will see this story. They pay people to comb independent newspapers looking for juicy tidbits like this. It'll go viral before you know it."

"I've already seen social media posts about your coaching the team, Jake. You didn't really think it would stay a secret, did you? With every person in the world attached to their phones?"

"No. But I had hoped to keep out of the goddamn newspapers."

"Your name's barely mentioned," she reiterated. "There's like, two sentences in the entire article."

Jake turned back, took two steps toward her desk, flipped the paper over and stabbed his finger at a headline that read, *The Prodigal Prince*.

"Wrong."

Ella looked down to find a large picture of Jake beneath the headline. He was in the foreground in his Demons jersey, standing arms crossed on the sidelines. Sure, he was wearing his dark glasses and baseball cap, but it was clearly him. In the background were Trish and Ella, their blank gazes glued to the action. And beside them, Rosie and Simon.

"Okay." That she hadn't expected. "That's more than a couple of sentences."

"Ya think?" He glared at her. "Where were you hiding him?"

"Hiding who?"

"The photographer."

Ella frowned. "I wasn't hiding *anyone*. The reporter who interviewed was going to send someone to take some shots of you and the team at practice on Monday but then she called to say that, coincidentally, their sports photographer had snapped some pics at the game on Friday night and they'd use them."

Jake scrubbed his hands over his face then dropped them to his sides, his blue eyes bleak. "You have no idea what you've done."

There was a bleakness to his tone as well which triggered Iris's words from Friday night again. *It's going to get worse before it gets better.* "Look... Jake—"

Her phone rang and Ella was grateful for the reprieve from Jake's accusatory stare and the eerie kind of shiver skating chills up and down her arms. "Yes, Bernie?"

Their gazes stayed locked as Bernie prattled away in her ear, Jake's expression not helping with the chills. "Some radio station wants to talk to me," Ella said as she replaced the receiver.

He shut his eyes briefly, nodding his head. "And so it begins." A resigned expression came over his face. "Okay." He nodded, then almost as if to himself, he said, "I quit."

Ella's pulse spiked. "*What*?"

"I told you I'd walk if the press became involved."

"But..." Ella searched around for something to say that would fix this – ASAP. "I'm sorry if there's going to be more attention in your life for the next little while but... isn't this a little extreme?"

He looked at her, his eyes blazing with conviction. "It's the only way I can think of to make the story about Deluca."

"*Jake.*" Ella couldn't believe what she was hearing. "You can't do this to the team."

"They have Pete," he dismissed. "They'll be fine."

What? Oh hell, *no*. Ella walked around the desk and stood directly in front of him. "It's not *Pete* they're doing this for. It's *you*."

The desire to curl her hands in his shirt and shake him – to make him *see* – was almost overwhelming.

But she didn't.

"They look up to you. You can't walk out on them now. Not with the play-offs in two weeks. You'll *devastate* them."

"Well…" He shook his head, his eyes shuttered. "Maybe you should have thought about that before you went to the press."

He turned away, heading for the door and leaving Ella dumbfounded. Okay, she'd brought this on herself but the driving need to make him *understand*, forced her legs into action.

"Jake, please." She put her hand on his shoulder just before he got to the door and he reluctantly turned to face her. "I really am sorry I went behind your back with this. But you can't just walk away. You made these kids believe in you. Kids who didn't believe in *anything*. Don't walk out on them when the going gets tough like so many adults in their lives have done."

He shrugged off her hand. "Go and do your radio, Ella. Milk the publicity for all you can. Just leave me out of it, okay?"

The indifference in his eyes was more devastating than his anger, clawing at her gut as he walked out, and she stared blankly at the back of the door as it closed. Her heart drummed wildly, thudding loudly through her head.

What had just happened? What had she done?

* * *

By the time the final bell of the day had rung, Ella was all talked out. Between conversations with Deluca businesses and community figures, two local radio slots and a chat with a journalist from a bigger Inverboro paper, it had been a lot. As requested, she'd avoided Jake's name, but it did seem to be the one thing they were the most interested in.

So she'd downplayed it as much as possible, trying to recork the bottle, mentioning only when repeatedly pressed that Jake's involvement was purely serendipitous. That it had evolved out of a chance meeting with an old school friend and wasn't some orchestrated career move.

She hoped like hell, as she made her way to the field, that would satisfy both the media's appetite and make some kind of amends to Jake. But he wasn't on the field when she arrived.

There was only Pete.

Jake hadn't been serious, had he? Surely, he wouldn't *really* pull out on them? He was mad, she got that. But he wouldn't do something so damaging, would he?

"Hey." Pete nodded.

She forced a smile. "Jake running late?"

Pete returned her smile with a sympathetic one of his own. "He's not coming, Ella."

There was tenderness in Pete's tone and she knew he was trying to let her down gently but it didn't help. "He'll be here tomorrow," she said as the knot of nerves in her belly tangled tighter. "After he's had a chance to calm down."

"I think Chernobyl's nuclear reactor has a greater chance of cooling down before Jake does."

"He can't just walk out on the team, Pete. Can you talk to him?" she implored. "Please?"

"If I thought it would make a difference, I would. But he won't listen to me. I don't know if you've noticed but he can be stubborn AF when he wants to be."

Ella nodded. Yeah, she'd noticed. "Okay." She sighed, accepting defeat – for today anyway. "Just do me a favor? Tell the team he's not well and he'll see them tomorrow."

"What happens when he doesn't show?"

"He will," she said, her confidence wafer thin.

* * *

Thursday was as ridiculous as Wednesday. More ridiculous. The phones ran hot. Everyone wanted a piece of her. She avoided all media but embraced all comers from the community as the conversations she'd had yesterday started to bear fruit.

There was a petition circulating and a letter-writing campaign – to the mayor, the governor and the district Board of Education – being organized.

And the cherry on top came in the form of Donald Wiseman ringing to express his displeasure at the negative press she was generating for the department.

Ella relished it all, grateful for something to occupy her mind, to keep it off that afternoon's practice session.

Would Jake be there?

He hadn't returned any of the umpteen messages she'd left on his cell since yesterday afternoon and she'd barely slept for fretting about it.

Was it possible to develop an ulcer overnight?

A last-minute phone call kept her from being early to the field and she arrived with the team stragglers to find Jake another no-show.

"Coach still sick, Pete?" Cameron asked.

Pete glanced at Ella and she gave him a slight nod. "Yep. You know these old blokes. Can't keep up. He asked me to work you guys extra hard though."

The team grumbled but hit the field for their warm-ups in good spirits. "Thanks, Pete," Ella said.

"They're going to have to know sooner or later."

Ella chewed on her bottom lip. "I know. I know. Did he tell you he wasn't coming?"

"Couldn't get hold of him. He hasn't been in to work either."

"At least we've got another two weeks before the game," she murmured.

Last week the thought of waiting three weeks for the playoffs to start had been pure torture. Today Ella was prepared to get on her knees and praise the football gods.

Her life had officially gone to hell.

"What's his problem, Pete?" she asked as she watched the team go about their drills. "Why's he so damn media shy? His face was on practically every tabloid and magazine in the known universe during his career. He picked a really bad time to go all reclusive on me."

Pete looked at her like she'd been dropped on her head. "You should ask Jake."

"Yeah." Ella nodded. "I will."

But not before she'd google-fu'd the crap out of it first.

* * *

When Ella arrived home an hour later, her head and heart were heavy with the information she'd gleaned about Jake with just a few easy clicks. She was cranky that she hadn't done even a cursory internet stalk of him before now. She might not be on any social media, but she knew how to fire up a search engine.

She understood why the furor surrounding his sacking from the Founders had escaped her notice. Apart from the fact that no one in their household followed football, it'd all happened around the same time Rachel had died and she'd gone to Trently to deal with all that. Which was obviously why he'd been there too, not anything to do with an old groin injury that he'd clearly recovered from *just fine*.

And then Cam had entered their lives and had consumed everyone's time and attention.

Still, she should have been more curious a few months ago when they'd roped him in to coaching the team. Wasn't that what everyone did these days with people coming into their lives?

But it wasn't like he was new entity. And really, their reconnection had felt a little too *woo woo* to look at too closely. Like this unspoken... *bond* that had been forged in Trently had always been leading them to this point in time.

Him and her in Inverboro, saving her school.

Yeah, the less she thought about *that* and all its potential ramifications, the better.

She found the three Forsythe women sitting at the table on the back porch drinking. Daisy took one look at Ella's face and poured a decent slug of bourbon from the half-empty bottle near the overflowing ashtray.

The sisters had stopped smoking in the house when Rosie and Ella had arrived and had never smoked in front of them but had resisted all attempts over the years to get them to quit.

"You look like you could do with this," Daisy said, passing it over.

Ella gave a wobbly smile as she accepted the glass and had never been more grateful to be part of the Forsythe family. They may not be her blood but they'd opened their door and their hearts to her unconditionally, and Ella had felt loved and accepted from the second she and Rosie had walked through the front gate.

"Are you okay?" Rosie asked, her brow furrowed in concern.

God... where did she even start? "No." Ella took her seat at the table and downed half the glass. "Jake's quit and it's all my fault."

Daisy glanced at Iris then topped up everyone's drinks as Rosie reached out and squeezed Ella's hand. "Jake wasn't impressed with the media coverage?"

Ella gave a half-laugh, half-snort. "That's putting it mildly." Rosie had spent the previous night at Simon's and Ella hadn't wanted to bother her bestie with the unfolding drama. "I couldn't figure out why someone who's had his picture out there more often than the Kardashians would be so rabidly media shy. Then I googled him."

"Oh." Rose grimaced. "Not good?"

Ella gave her friend a grim look. "There was this sexual assault scandal a couple of years back."

Rosie gasped. "Jake raped someone?"

"No." Ella shook her head quickly. "God, no!" She shuddered at the thought. "Apparently it was some guy called Tony Winchester?"

"Okay. So... who's he?" Rosie asked.

"An ex-teammate of Jake's. They did their rookie year here with the Sentries. A few years back, Tony was accused of rape. He protested his innocence and his club at the time backed him but then Jake made a statement in support of the woman claiming he knew Tony had almost raped someone else eighteen years prior when they were both playing for the Sentries."

"Wow." Rosie whistled. "Gutsy."

"Yeah." Ella nodded. "But because he refused to name the first woman, he was discredited amidst all the controversy. Then he was sidelined, then he was sacked."

"What happened to the Winchester guy?" Daisy asked.

"Nothing. He *retired* and is now some hot-shot sports caster."

Rosie blew out a breath. "That's... a lot."

"Did Simon not know?" Ella asked. Apart from Cameron, he was the biggest football fan she knew.

"I suppose so." She shrugged. "If it was as big a scandal as you say, he probably assumed we already knew?"

Yeah, probably. Who'd have thought a subscription to ESPN would be more valuable than three university degrees?

"So, I'm guessing that Jake has bowed out because he's worried media attention will rekindle the scandal?"

"Yup."

Ella stared morosely into her drink as Rosie drummed her fingers on the table. She wished she could travel back two days and *not* have made that call to Suzy. Glancing at Daisy and Iris she asked, "What am I going to do? How do I fix this?"

The two older women had lived and seen much in their lives. And between Daisy's pragmatism and Iris's psychic ability they always seemed to know just what to do or say.

Daisy regarded her over the rim of her whiskey glass. "Go and talk to him."

"I'm pretty sure he doesn't want to talk to me. And even if he did, I doubt I'll be able to change his mind."

"So don't try," she said. "This must have stirred up a lot of crap from his past. Talk to him about what he's feeling."

Ella almost laughed at the suggestion. Jake had never struck her as a guy who talked about his feelings.

"He likes you," Iris added. "He likes you very much." She grabbed her cards and laid them out in a quick spread. Nodding briefly, she announced, "The cards are favorable."

Ella sighed. Far be it from her to question the cards.

15

To say Ella was intimated by where Jake lived was an understatement as she knocked tentatively on his apartment door an hour later. She'd called Pete, expecting him to refuse to divulge his boss's address but he'd given it to her with his blessing and wished her luck as he disconnected.

She'd always assumed he lived somewhere nice but this was *prime* real estate. The luxury apartment block towered high over Greenmount Park Beach overlooking Lake Michigan and, up here on the forty-second floor, she was guessing he'd have a pretty spectacular view of said lake.

Ella knew in that vague kind of way she knew *anything* about football, that players earned a lot of money during their careers but she'd never thought about Jake's bank account.

Nor had she thought to google it when she was checking him out earlier. She supposed because he'd never flaunted it?

Two years ago he'd been pulling beers behind The Rusty Nail in Trently. Two months ago he'd been pulling beers behind the bar at The Touchdown. Which he owned. *And* worked at. He wore jeans and T-shirts and seemed perfectly at home eating lethal home-made curry on the back porch of a southside bungalow.

He made sure an ugly stray had found a home and was volunteering his coaching services to save a school in one of the city's most economically depressed suburbs. Yes, he drove a BMW but she was pretty sure from this apartment and its fancy AF lobby, he could have been driving a Lamborghini.

There was no reply to her knock so she repeated it, a little firmer this time. Pete had said he was home with no plans to go out anywhere which meant he was ignoring it. Or possibly her if he'd checked through the peep hole she could see in the center of the door.

"I know you're in there, Jake," she called, giving another knock. "Answer the damn door."

Still nothing.

She thumped on the door. "I'm not going away and I'm only going to get louder."

Of course, there was probably super fancy security to go with this super fancy building so if he called them, she'd be screwed.

"Jake! Stop being such a damn coward and talk to me."

She pounded on the door this time, almost falling into his apartment as the door opened abruptly and Jake stood before her in a pair of jeans and nothing else.

Bare chest, bare feet, a Corona in hand.

He looked scruffy and disheveled and like he'd hadn't slept in days. But he still looked better than any cleanly shaven, well rested guy she'd ever laid eyes on.

"I don't want to talk to you," he said belligerently, his gaze boring in to hers as he took a slug of his beer.

Ella swallowed hard, hoping Daisy was right. "Or maybe you do and you just don't know it?"

He regarded her for a moment. "I have company."

Company? Did he mean...?

She'd been trying not to ogle his shirtless chest but now its very presence made sense. His inference was like a rusty spoon scooping into the center of her brain.

"You're... having *sex*?"

Ella blanked for a moment as the thought of him doing to another woman the things he had done to her, scooped out more of her gray matter. She had no claim to him – she knew that. They'd had sex twice. Well, two *sessions* of sex, anyway. Yet in this moment, how quickly he'd moved on was deeply wounding.

"Everything is falling apart," she hissed, the emotional whammy turning to an icy kind of rage. "And you're... *tumbling* around between your sheets with a woman?"

"Jake? Who's there?"

Ella tensed as a distant female voice reached them. Horrified, she glanced over his shoulder, every cell in her body preparing to flee. *God.* She did not want to come face to face with some bar hook-up who had perky *everything*.

As if he was taking some kind of sick pleasure from her obvious consternation, he didn't take his eyes off her as he called, "Wrong number," over his shoulder.

Suddenly though, Trish appeared from behind.

"*Ella*! Did Pete send you to talk some sense into him too?" Giving Jake a playful shove, she ordered, "Go put a shirt on," as she grabbed Ella's hand and ushered her inside.

On autopilot, Ella followed Trish through Jake's open-plan apartment minimally decorated in what would be best described as *industrial chic*. Gunmetal gray rugs littered the cavernous floor space while ceilings with exposed ducting and sleek chrome fixtures, soared overhead. A staircase with wire railings and black metal treads lead to a mezzanine level.

They entered a massive black marble and stainless-steel kitchen. "You look like you could use a drink," she said.

It was the second time today she'd heard that and it had been right both times.

Trish opened the fridge door and pulled out a bottle of white wine, placing it on the marble top of the central island. Next, she opened a cupboard, produced a glass that twinkled in the chrome down lights and poured a generous slug. The other woman clearly knew her way around Jake's apartment which shot an itch up Ella's spine.

Maybe Jake *had* been in bed with a woman? With Trish?

Confronted with her domestic familiarity, the questions Ella had always harbored about Trish and Jake's relationship resurfaced.

"C'mon." She handed Ella the glass. "We're out front."

Ella followed again, passing a theater room where she glimpsed black leather recliners and a TV screen that would have been right at home at an Imax. Ahead though, the unimpeded view dazzled as Trish led her into a sunken area that ran the length of the apartment, large windows showcasing the vastness of Lake Michigan.

"*Wow.*" There were no other words.

Trish laughed. "Yeah, that's what I said when he bought it at the beginning of the year."

It was almost too much to take in as Ella wandered over to stand in front of the display, her head moving from side to side like a carnival clown just to absorb the scale of it. There was more leather and chrome scattered throughout the space but it was the greenery at one end that eventually caught her eye.

Crossing to it, Ella admired the way the wall had been turned into a vertical garden with all kinds of potted herbs splashing green against the austere graphite paint. Beneath them, sitting on the slate flooring, were several terracotta pots sporting a range of plants from a fiscus to a red chili to a dwarf lime tree groaning with dark green fruit.

Smart investment for someone who drank so much Corona.

It appeared to be the only corner of Jake's apartment that hadn't been decorated by the United Steelworkers Union.

"You like my handiwork?" Trish asked. "Miranda and I keep buying him plants. And of course tending them, otherwise they'd be dead." She grimaced as she looked back into the sparse apartment. "If it wasn't for the view I'd feel like I was in a factory."

Ella drew in a deep breath as Trish's words painted a cozy picture of the three of them in this apartment and it occurred to her for the first time that maybe Miranda was Jake's daughter. Miranda never mentioned a father but she knew he and Trish went way back and it wouldn't be the first time paternity was kept secret from a child.

"Yes," she murmured, distracted by this latest conundrum. "It's very... masculine."

Trish laughed. "That's one word for it. I prefer too much money, not enough give-a-shit."

Ella laughed despite her racing thoughts. Damn it, she really wanted to dislike the ex-cheerleader but Trish Jones, who had been nothing but super lovely *and* supportive of the school and the Demons, was impossible to dislike.

"Is Jake Miranda's father?"

She hadn't planned on blurting it out. Hell, she hadn't planned on *asking* the question at all. It just slipped out. And, given Trish's shocked expression, it should have stayed unasked.

"Oh God, I'm *so* sorry." Ella's cheeks burned. "That was terribly rude and none of my business."

Trish finally spluttered out a laugh. "Good grief, no. Jake and I aren't... we don't have that kind of relationship. We're friends. *Good* friends. But there's never been anything *romantic*. Miranda's father was someone I was with briefly who ran a mile when he found out I was pregnant."

While embarrassed to be so wrong, Ella couldn't deny the relief was overwhelming. "I'm sorry," she repeated. "It's just you seem so... I thought—"

Trish laughed again. "Don't worry about it," she assured, giving Ella's arm a squeeze.

Which was the moment Jake, now in a black button-down shirt, decided to make an appearance. "Alright," he announced, stepping into the sunken area, beer in hand. "Let's get this over with."

Plonking himself down in one of the leather chairs situated around a low smoky-glass-topped table, he glanced from one to the other. "So is this going to be good cop, bad cop?"

Trish, obviously already moved on from Ella's gaffe, quirked an eyebrow at her. "You wanna be good cop?"

Ella shook her head. "Nope."

"Looks like it's just bad cop, bad cop," she said as she took the seat beside him, gesturing for Ella to take the one on the other side.

Sighing, he took a quick hit of his beer. "Why don't I just save you both the trouble. Nothing either of you say will change my mind about coaching the team."

"Jake," Trish chided. "Miranda's going to be very disappointed in you."

"Well, Miranda's going to have to get used to being disappointed. It's a big, bad world out there."

Trish frowned. "You think *I* don't know that?"

"Oh come on, Trish." He shook his head. "You know why it has to be this way."

Ella watched their back and forth, understanding that their couched language was for her benefit but impatient with it. Daisy had encouraged her to talk to Jake about the past so she'd rather cut to the chase.

"I know what happened all those years ago," she announced. "About the sexual assault. I've been googling. And I'm really sorry I stirred it all up again for you."

* * *

Jake closed his eyes and expelled a breath as his past rushed out, swirling around him in all its vivid, sullied glory. Somehow the fact that Ella's loathing of football had kept her ignorant to his sordid decline had been refreshing. Almost twenty years later the shame still clung and a part of him hadn't wanted her privy to all the murky details.

It had meant something that she didn't know and he wasn't sure if he could bear to see the judgment in her eyes. Because she was wrong – she didn't know what happened.

Very few people did.

"I wish I could walk it back. I really do. But the team shouldn't be punished for a mistake I made." She turned pleading eyes on him. "Don't you want to finish the job you started?"

Jake drained his beer and set the bottle on the table. Walking away from the team had been harder than he'd imagined. The boys were raw but they had that magical combination – balls *and* heart. And they were playing for much higher stakes than the other teams in the competition.

Hell, if he didn't recognize himself in those kids. A misfit from a small town against what had felt like the entire world.

"This isn't about me," he said, his gaze flicking from Ella to Trish and back again.

He was in serious trouble with them both here, ganging up on him. Trish and their history. Ella and all their *stuff* – modern and ancient. There wasn't enough Corona in all of Mexico to help him navigate this situation.

"When this all blew up two years ago, there was a lot of pressure on me to name the mystery woman, which was not then, nor is it now, an option. She's been through enough without the media beaming her nightmare into every living room across the country."

Jake watched as realization dawned over her face. "So you're protecting her?"

"Yes."

She didn't say anything for a beat or two just nodded, her ponytail bobbing as she obviously absorbed the information.

"Pete will manage," Jake added.

"Yes." Ella's brows beetled. "Of course."

Trish plonked her glass down so hard on the glass top the wine sloshed precariously close to the rim. It was a wonder the fancy AF stem hadn't snapped in two.

"No. *Not* of course." She glared at him. "This is utterly ridiculous, Jake. It's time."

Jake shook his head despite Trish's fierce face. "*No.*"

"*Yes.* If John Wilmott figures it out, then so be it."

Ella looked from one to the other. "Who is John Wilmott?"

"A journalist," Jake muttered. "He does features on issues in sports. He's very persistent and he almost connected the dots. He just doesn't realize it."

"If it happens, it happens," Trish dismissed. "Miranda's older now and I'm not the same scared little mouse I was back then. And maybe it's time I got to tell my side of the story and hang the confidentiality agreement." She turned to Ella. "Jake is protecting me. *I'm* the one who Tony tried to rape."

Ella's eyes widened at the admission and she was momentarily speechless before recovering. "Oh, Trish... I'm so, *so* sorry. That's awful, just... terrible." Then her eyes widened again. "Oh God." She put her glass down on the table with a light tap, sitting forward in the chair. "You were in the background of that picture. I'm so sorry." Glancing at Jake, she said, "Will this John Wilmott guy see it?"

"Yep." There was no doubt in his mind.

Ella shook her head, shooting an apologetic look at Trish. "I'm so, *so* sorry. I made a complete mess of everything."

"No," Trish denied. "You haven't."

But Ella was not going to be so easily assuaged of her guilt, turning her gaze to him. "After everything you went through to protect Trish—"

Jake cut her off with a harsh laugh. "Don't put me on a pedestal, Ella. Eighteen years ago, Tony Winchester tried to rape Trish while I stood by and did nothing."

His words fell into the space between them like boulders into a shallow pond. Ella's lips parted, shocked by his admission.

"No." Trish shook her head vehemently. "That's not what happened," she said to Ella before looking at him again. "By the time you heard me screaming, I'd already gotten away. You need to stop blaming yourself. I'm the aggrieved person here. Not you. Let it go. I have."

Jake picked up his empty bottle and absently rolled it between his palms, staring at the lime wedge. "If I'd been sober I might have realized what was going on."

"He was my boyfriend, Jake. How could you have known?"

He shook his head. "I should have pushed past those goons at the door sooner."

"You pushed past at the right moment. If you hadn't busted through the door when you did he'd have caught up with me and I'm not sure I could have fought him off a second time."

Trish switched her attention to Ella. "Jake was amazing. My dress was all torn and he wrapped me up in his jacket. He punched Tony in the face. He took me home."

"Not to the police station?"

Jake could feel Ella staring at him but couldn't bear the thought of what he might see in her eyes.

Anger? Distaste? Reproach?

There wasn't any look she could give him that hadn't stared back at him from the mirror for the longest time. Even after all these years the memories of that night still scratched deep into the murky swamp of his guilt, pulling at the crust, lifting the ugly scab a little, making it bleed all over again.

"I refused," Trish said. "I didn't want to. Not right then. I was a hysterical mess. I was crying... shaking so hard. I just wanted to get away, go back to my house where I felt safe. Jake called around the next day to take me to the precinct but... who was going to believe me, Ella?"

Trish's question was beseeching, one woman to another, and it didn't surprise Jake when Ella gave a resigned, "Yeah."

"Tony and I were in a relationship. I went into the room with him more than willingly. Fooled around quite happily. I'd had a couple of drinks." Trish ticked the points off her fingers. "I knew how these things went down. *Still* go down. It's never the guy who ends up looking bad."

Another resigned, "Yeah," from Ella was such a searing indictment on the way things were Jake's jaw clenched.

"I guess I was in shock," Trish continued. "We'd only been going out for a month but I think I fell for Tony the first time I laid eyes on him. He was so big and strong. He had this curly blond hair – I swear he looked like an angel. I couldn't believe he was capable of that. I knew he was impatient with my decision to wait before taking our relationship to the next level, but I never thought he'd try and force me."

"I'm so sorry that happened to you," Ella said, reaching across the table to give Trish's arm a squeeze.

Trish gave a half-smile. "Thanks."

"What happened after that?" Ella asked, looking between them. "Were there *no* repercussions for Tony?"

Shaking his head, Jake took over the story. "When Trish refused to go to the police, I went to the club. Told them *everything*. Demanded they get the police in to investigate. Demanded Tony be dropped from the team."

Jake found it hard to believe he'd been that naive.

"I take it they didn't quite see it your way?" Ella said.

"No, they didn't." Jake's lips flattened. "They played hardball which resulted in Trish being offered cash to go away."

"Which I took. I couldn't face a protracted legal thing, all that media attention and" – she shook her head – "messiness. So I signed their NDA, took the money and walked away."

"And I requested a trade."

"I see," Ella said although she was clearly clueless to how uncommon it was for rookies to be traded.

"Doesn't it stick in your craw to know that Tony Winchester got away with it?" she asked Trish.

She nodded. "That's why I couldn't stand by two years ago and watch him walk over another woman. If I'd spoken up when he'd assaulted me, maybe it wouldn't have happened to her but... there was the confidentiality agreement."

"Ah," she said and Jake saw the moment it all fell into place for Ella as she turned to him. "So you spoke up."

"He did," Trish confirmed. "The media were going on like Tony was this bastion of respectability. A happily married man, a great father, a stalwart of the community. *Blah, blah, blah.* I didn't want to sit by and watch them crucify her without them knowing he had history."

"But you couldn't because of the NDA."

"Right." Trish nodded. "So Jake waded in all guns blazing. He went to the police and the media and told everyone what had happened all those years before at the Sentries. Which created a huge frenzy especially when he refused to identify me. The NFL closed ranks and after a shit ton of bad press, the Founders gave him an ultimatum. He could *retire* to great fanfare; after all, he was playing past the age a lot of players decide to hang up their cleats. Or he'd be let go."

Old bitterness boiled to the surface and Jake was unable to sit still while all this old ground was being so casually turned over. He rose, heading for the windows, staring out at Lake Michigan and the dying rays of sunshine.

"Jake refused to retire, forcing them to sack him, forcing them to have to publicly defend their decision to get rid of one of the best tight ends the game has ever known. Someone who *despite his age*, was still playing brilliant football."

"That was very honorable."

Jake could feel the heat of Ella's gaze between his shoulder blades. He opened his mouth to deny the charge because he didn't think he should be lauded for just doing the right thing but Trish got in before him.

"It was magnificent," Trish enthused. "I know you had a lot going on during that time with your mom and Cam but... you would have been so proud of him, Ella."

"Sounds like it," came her soft response.

"But it's time for me to step up now."

Jake whipped around. "No way."

"Jake." Trish shook her head.

Much to his surprise, Ella backed him. "I agree with Jake." Her gaze briefly flicked to his, her ponytail swishing. "There's no need. I understand why Jake quit and I have no desire to draw attention to what happened to you. You've been through enough. Pete's good with the boys and they're really motivated."

In the face of Trish's steely determination, Jake could have kissed Ella for siding with him. But he could hear more bravado than conviction in her statement.

"Nonsense." Trish stood this time, her brow beetled as she stared him down. "There are some things bigger and more important than me and this is one of them. I've brought Miranda up to believe in fighting for what's right, sticking up for the underdog. And that's *us*. Deluca. It's time to fight and I'm not going to be the one responsible for Deluca not putting its best foot forward which" – she bugged her eyes at him – "is you."

Jake sighed. It was all very idealistic but Trish and Miranda were more important than any team. Even *Ella's* and he was, *God help him*, falling hopelessly in love with her.

"What will happen, will happen, Jake, but you can't walk out on those boys. Not now. You've got them this far – you need to take them the rest of the way. And I won't let you use me as an excuse to hide away and lick your wounds anymore. You fading into obscurity means those assholes have won. Especially when this is *exactly* what you should be doing with your life."

Trish had been very vocal this past year about him wasting his talent and pushing him to coach. It was the first time she'd essentially called him a *coward*, however.

Was it true? Had he been hiding away, licking his wounds?

"I have to go." Trish picked up her wine glass and downed it in three swallows. Turning to Ella she said, "Convince him for me," then she left.

Ella stared after Trish for several beats. The other woman may be diminutive, but she'd been as tall and straight and fierce as a freaking Amazonian right now. She glanced at Jake, her head spinning from this afternoon's revelations, to find him inspecting her with brooding eyes.

"Well, I don't know about you," he said, "but I need another drink." He picked up her half-finished wine glass from the table. "I'll top you up."

Ella followed him into the kitchen and stood quietly while he busied himself. Passing her the refilled glass, he popped the top on a Corona, pushed a wedge of lime into the throat and took a swig. Cocking a hip to rest against the granite bench top a couple of feet from her position, his gaze finally met hers.

"Bet that was more than you were expecting, huh?"

The bitter edge to his voice pricked like a Brillo pad on her skin. Did he think she was going to judge him about what had happened all those years ago? Because it was clear he was still beating himself up over it.

"Do you hate me?" he asked, his gaze anguished.

Ella sucked in a breath at the surprising question. "Of course not."

Hate him?

Nothing could be further from the truth. She'd heard too much good stuff about him just now. Hell, she suspected she *loved* him. Not that she was about to blurt *that* out. Their situation was complicated enough without half-baked declarations in emotionally intense settings.

"I think you found yourself in a situation a long time ago that made you feel angry and powerless. I think it still does."

He threw his bottle cap into the bin on the other side of the kitchen with the precision of a trained athlete. "Damn right about that."

"That's fair enough. But..." Ella hesitated as she took a tiny step closer. She was new to all this information and it was hardly her business, so she had to tread carefully. "If Trish is determined to relegate it to her past, perhaps you should too? Maybe it's time to stop hating yourself, Jake?"

He nodded but she could see the whiteness of his knuckles as his hand tightened around his beer and Ella wanted to reach out, remove his hand, press his palm to her racing heart. Drag him back from the past, ground him in the here and now.

"Do you think it's true what she said? About you hiding away?"

He shrugged. "Yeah, maybe."

Ella watched the bob of his whiskery throat as he took a drink. The bottle *tink'ed* as he set it down again on the marble top, seeming very loud in the silence between them. The last time they'd been alone like this – six days ago – they'd danced and kissed and even though it was stupidly inappropriate to be thinking about that now, it was *all* she could think about.

Every cell in her body hummed with the memory. And the way his gaze lingered on her mouth, she wondered if he was thinking the same.

"So... knowing all that you do now you still want me to coach the team?" he asked, finally breaking the silence in a low rumble that sent warm air currents spilling over her skin.

She nodded because she didn't quite trust her voice for a beat. "They need you, Jake." In more ways than one.

A team of impressionable young men could do worse than Jake as a role model.

"And what about you?" His gaze dropped to her mouth again and she swayed a little. "What do you need?"

The air in Ella's lungs felt as heavy as wet sand at his blatant invitation. She needed only one thing in this moment but if she cracked that seal for a third time, she was worried she'd never be able to slake her thirst and her needs had to come second for a little while longer.

There was a school to save.

Giving a husky little half-laugh, she waved dismissively and said, "That doesn't matter right now."

And she actually believed it for a split second. Until Jake snagged her hip and dragged her flush to him, all his heat and hardness pressing into her and she barely stopped herself from whimpering.

"*Ella.*" His rough whisper drew her nipples to tight, aching points. "It's okay to want things for yourself. To be selfish every now and then."

Raising his hand, he gently tucked a strand of hair that had worked loose from her ponytail behind her ear, firing off a swathe of goosebumps down the side of her neck. She shut her eyes at the gentle touch, feeling it *everywhere.*

"Damn it," he muttered and groaned a groan so low and rumbly it was practically subterranean. Her eyes fluttered open to find him staring at her mouth like he was starving for it and she was suddenly ravenous, too. "I wish I didn't want to kiss you so much."

Ella wished she didn't want to kiss him either but suddenly that's exactly what they were doing, his lips hot on hers, her breasts squashed against his chest, her arms snaking around his neck. Passion exploded full roar between them as the kisses deepened and they pressed closer, the long, hard thickness of him grinding into the apex of her thighs setting her instantly aflame, making her *dizzy* with need.

Too damn dizzy. He filled her up too much. Made it hard to breathe. Hard to think.

She broke off, dragging in much-needed air, her heart pounding like a massive sub-woofer at a rock concert. His mouth was wet, his pupils so dilated there was only the thinnest rim of green iris as he closed in again.

"Wait."

Her pulse thrummed as she held herself back from him. As much as was possible anyway with their thighs pressed so intimately and his aroma – beer, lime and pheromones – drowning her good sense. But she was determined to finish business before she got to pleasure.

"Ella?"

His voice was a ragged pant and it was gratifying to see him looking just as sucker punched as her.

"I take it this is a yes? You'll coach the team."

"Yes." He huffed out a pained laugh then reached for the hem of her blouse and yanked it over her head in one swift movement. "Paradise," he muttered, staring at her pink bra before sliding his hands to cup her breasts, kneading them, lowering his mouth to the swell of her cleavage.

Ella dragged herself back from melting into a puddle on the floor. "Wait," she said again, pulling his head up.

"What?" he demanded, his breathing hard.

"We're supposed to be keeping this professional."

He snorted. "*Fuck* professional."

Then he reached for the twinkling diamante clasp in the depths of her cleavage, flicking it with an expert twist of his hand. Ella looked down as her breasts sprang free.

"Is there some place you go to study that?"

"University of life." He traced the ridge of her collar bone with his index finger. "Got myself a PhD."

The finger headed south over the swell of a breast to the rapidly hardening nipple which shot a bolt of pure, unadulterated need right between her legs.

Oh God.

"Jake," she whispered, grasping his shoulder as the whole room tilted. She had to keep her head here. Be the responsible one. "I'm serious about the professional thing."

"Fine," he muttered as he bent his head and his lips followed the path of his fingers. "Tomorrow."

And, as his mouth closed over one taut, achy, flushed tip, Ella figured she could be professional tomorrow, too.

* * *

The dogs greeted them enthusiastically as she and Jake walked up the front path the next afternoon. Cerberus almost wriggled out of his skin, he was shimmying so much, and Ella watched as Jake gave the dog – *his* dog – some extra love. It had been a tumultuous twenty-four hours but suddenly things felt like they were back on track.

They'd just come from practice where Jake was given a hero's welcome by the team before getting straight down to the business of putting the Demons through their paces. Considering the man had barely slept a wink last night – *lucky her* – he was firing on all pistons.

Which was just as well with the playoffs two weeks away.

Cam, who'd already disappeared inside the house chatting to Miranda on the phone, was happier than she'd ever seen him, and after the revelations and catharsis of yesterday and the night in Jake's arms, so was Ella.

For two long days everything had felt helplessly derailed and now suddenly, it wasn't. Ella was feeling quietly confident that this *testing* they'd been put through was the *worse* Iris had referred to and things would be easier moving forward.

They found Daisy, Iris, Rosie and Simon in their usual places at the table on the back porch. At five-thirty in the afternoon, the light was fading and the cooler night air was creeping in but it took more than that to drive the aunts from their beloved porch.

"Jake!" Rosie, sporting a black *Drac Sucks* T-shirt, leaped up from her chair and gave him a big hug. "It's so good to see you back."

Simon greeted him with a smile when Rosie eventually unhanded him. "Hey," he said with one of those manly chin-tilt movements that Simon, despite his Hugo Boss suit, actually pulled off quite credibly.

Daisy, less enthusiastic, eyeballed him for a long moment. She flicked a glance between him and Ella and back again. "You sticking?" she asked in her gruff, two-pack a day voice. "Cos we're getting older by the moment and we don't need to waste our precious time on someone who ain't going to stick."

Clearly unperturbed by Daisy's straight-talking, he grinned. "I'm sticking."

And damn if that didn't make Ella swoon just a little.

Daisy stared for a moment longer before giving a nod of approval. "Good."

Jake switched his attention to Iris. "Hello, Iris. What are the cards saying lately?"

Iris glanced worriedly at the tarot deck she was gripping. "There's more to come," she said.

Ella blinked. More? They were in the middle of a media feeding frenzy. How much *worse* could it get?

But then Jake slid his arm around her shoulder and squeezed and said, "We'll get through it," and she forgot all about Iris's tarot predictions as her heart skipped several beats.

Apart from some very explicit dirty talk last night, they hadn't spoken at all, much less about what was next for them. Maybe because they both knew that their priority was the team.

But it did seem like Jake wasn't going anywhere.

For God's sake, the man could have chosen to go home to his quiet, expensive Lake Michigan *bachelor pad* condo after practice but he'd chosen to come here, to this suburban bungalow and this zany found family she loved so much.

In a million years she never would have pictured herself with someone from Trently. Someone who was privy to her past in all its messy disappointment.

And certainly never Jake.

But suddenly the thought didn't scare her as much. A shared background made things easier in lots of ways. She didn't have to explain or justify anything to Jake. Because he understood her, like she understood him – in ways other couples might take a really long time to figure out.

Ella's pulse fluttered madly at the thought and she barely stopped herself from breaking out into a happy dance. She certainly couldn't concentrate much on the conversations that followed as they all sat at the table talking about Deluca High and football. Although that was mostly due to Jake's blatantly sexual gaze seducing her from across the table. His eyes roving over her face and hair. Lingering on her mouth. Dropping to her cleavage.

All she could think about was excusing them and picking up where they'd left off at dawn and she wondered how long was polite enough to make conversation before they could get away.

In the end she was saved by Cam who called out to her. Ella leaped up gratefully. "Coming," she said, sliding Jake a side-eye which she hoped like hell he could interpret.

His answering look left her in no doubt that he'd picked up exactly what she'd put down and he'd follow her in *ASAP*.

She dealt with Cam's math homework query quickly and was heading to her bedroom when she heard a car door slam out on the street then the latch lift on the gate. In an instant, the dogs barked from the porch, almost bowling her over in their haste to the front door and Ella heard Jake say, "I'll check and see who that is," and she smiled to herself.

Attaboy...

Letting the dogs out the door, she vaguely heard Jake talking to Cam as she followed the barking rabble at a more sedate pace. Stepping out onto the front porch, she found the pack all barking at two men who had retreated behind the safety of the fence and were regarding the animals warily.

Ella rushed down the steps, calling the dogs back as she assured the visitors, "They're all bark, no bite," and then yelled at Genghis, "*Heel.*"

All the dogs retreated to where Ella stood on the bottom step, positioning themselves in front of her like a canine shield, protecting their human. Except for Cerberus, clearly conflicted between loyalty and his need for love and attention. Especially if the newcomers had some kind of food.

They didn't have food. But one of them had a camera. A big ass one. And it took Ella a beat or two with all the dogs and the barking to compute he was taking a picture of her. Multiple pictures if the rapid-fire clicking was any indication.

She blinked. "Umm, can I help you people?"

"Just wanted to ask some questions about the team, Ella," said the guy without the camera. "You must be pleased with how the Demons are going. This is the kind of publicity your beleaguered school needs, right?"

"I'm sorry." She frowned. "Who are you? Which outlet are you from?"

"The *Herald*," he confirmed.

Ella's mind blew a little to think the city's flagship newspaper was interested in their story and what kind of exposure that could give them. But, exposure, she was coming to learn, could be a double-edged sword. "Very pleased," she said, non-committally and turned to go.

"You've done well," he continued. "Deluca didn't even have a football team a few months ago and here you are at the playoffs. Kudos to you."

Ella shrugged, cautious of the flattery. None of it had been her idea and she certainly didn't want to jinx anything by getting too cocky and running her mouth. "I'm just a math nerd who's trying to keep her school open for the kids, that's it."

"Quite a coup to score the services of Jake Prince. How'd that come about?"

She stiffened at the mention of Jake, the air suddenly feeling ten degrees cooler. And then, as if by just naming him, Jake was by her side. "Don't answer that," he said, as he slipped his arm around her waist.

It was a total alpha move but Ella was here for it.

The guy asking the questions smiled as the cameraman went all trigger happy again. "Jake."

"John."

The response was terse and Jake's lips flattened into a hard line in Ella's peripheral vision.

John?

Was this the John Wilmott that Trish had mentioned yesterday? She guessed it was given the tension as the two men stared each other down. Had this been the Wild West, their hands would be hovering over their pistols.

"What do you think, Jake?" John Wilmott leaned his elbows on the gate, earning a low growl from Genghis. The journalist stood, eyeing the dog warily as he continued. "Is she just a math nerd? You and Ella go back a long way, don't you?"

"No comment."

"I don't suppose while I'm here you'd care to name the mystery woman from all those years ago?"

"No comment," Jake repeated, his voice utterly glacial.

"What about you, Ella? You and Jake are obviously..." His gaze drifted to Jake's possessive hold. "Close. Any pillow talk you care to share?"

A bubble of irritation at the impudent question popped behind Ella's eyeballs at the same time Jake's hands tightened on her waist. "We're done here," he announced as he urged her back up the stairs.

Ella followed without argument, the clicking of the shutter sounding ominously like bullets as they stepped inside the house.

* * *

It took two days for the bullets to hit, but at seven minutes past ten on Sunday morning they found their mark squarely between Ella's shoulder blades. Everyone, except Cam who was still asleep, was out on the porch, eating pancakes that Jake had fixed. Practice was scheduled for the afternoon but for now, nobody had to be anywhere.

The morning was crisp and cold and clear, the sky a dazzling blue, sunshine bouncing off neighborhood roofs and railings and glistening in the water droplets pearling at the ends of bare branches. The dogs were lazing off to one side all fully reclined near the back stairs in a sunny patch, their bellies full of table treats.

The coffee was hot – bourbon laced for Iris and Daisy – and the company was wonderful. Jake had spent the last two nights at the house which had been intense and intimate but also cozily domestic and Ella couldn't wipe the smile off her face.

She should have known things were going too well.

"Uh-oh," Simon announced, sitting forward in his chair, frowning at his phone.

"What?" Jake asked.

"*Herald* site," Simon said, glancing at Jake. "Page five. Not good."

Everyone at the table picked up their devices except for Iris who leaned close to her sister to look at the iPad screen.

Ella's fingers shook as she navigated to the *Herald* and clicked on the link that took her to today's edition. Her heart thumped as she scrolled to page five to find it dominated by a picture of her and Jake standing on the front porch, the dogs in the foreground. Above, the headline screamed:

THE PRINCE AND THE PAUPER

And just beneath that in slightly smaller print:

Former NFL jock slumming it in the suburbs.

Daisy grabbed the bourbon and poured an extra slug into hers and Iris's mugs as a wave of nausea roiled through Ella's gut. Her gaze dropped to the byline.

John Wilmott.

Part of Ella didn't want to read the rest. But part of her couldn't *not* read it either.

In a run-down house in the run-down southside suburb of Deluca, ex-Founders tight-end royalty, Jake Prince, whose net worth exceeds 100 million hides out in plain sight.

Ella blinked. Jake was worth one hundred *million* dollars? *Sweet, Jesus.* But that wasn't what the article was about. Not by a long shot...

Two years after his career ended in great ignominy, Prince has quietly remerged as the unlikely coach to a high school football team that didn't exist prior to this season. After turning down several lucrative coaching contracts, how did this come to be?

The answer to that possibly lies with the principal of Deluca High School, Ella Lucas, who hails from the same small Kansas town as The Prince. Ms. Lucas, it seems, is exceptionally persuasive, a talent she no doubt inherited from her mom who eked out an existence in Trently as the local hooker.

All the color leeched from Ella's face. "Oh. My. God. *Oh my God.*" She rubbed a hand across her forehead. "Oh my God."

Jake, always less wordy, just said, "*Fuck.*"

There it was, right there. The *worse* Iris's cards had been predicting. On the cusp of getting the one thing she'd desperately wanted, she was about to lose probably the most important thing she'd gained since leaving Trently.

Her anonymity.

The article went on about her mother's sordid history, including quotes from people in Trently, and repeated the old rumor that Ella had run away with her high school principal. It questioned her moral integrity, challenged the appropriateness of her being a role model for school children *and* her ability to raise her fifteen-year-old brother.

But Wilmott hadn't stopped there. He'd done a little more digging and found out that Iris and Daisy, the two *circus freaks* – his words – that had taken Ella in after her scandalous exit from Trently, had never lodged a tax return. Suddenly they were tax evaders in the order of Al *freaking* Capone.

Glancing up from her death grip on her phone, Ella said, "You two seriously haven't ever lodged a tax return?"

The sisters traded a look. "Never could wrap my head around those damn forms," Daisy said, pouring another slug of bourbon.

Ella returned her gaze to the screen where John had moved on to their beloved dogs. Apparently, he and his photographer had been *menaced* by a pack of mangy, unruly, *unregistered* dogs. She flicked her gaze to the picture again that had caught Cerberus mid-wriggle, obviously ecstatic at the attention.

He ended with a lot of inference about the state of public education in Wisconsin intertwining it with a freaking *treatise* on the moral choices made by people who were in charge of impressionable students. Ella wanted to cut John Wilmott's heart out of his chest and stomp on it.

Throwing her phone on the table, she buried her face in her hands. "I feel sick."

"Fucking. Bastard," Rosie muttered as she tossed her phone next to Ella's.

"Can he say that stuff?" Ella asked, lifting her head.

Simon nodded. "Unfortunately. Most of the facts are essentially true. And he's been really careful to wrap the more outrageous things in phrases like 'it's rumored' and 'sources say'."

"Yep," Jake concurred, his hand sliding onto her shoulder, his thumb absently stroking her collar bone.

Ella's head pulsed like it was about to explode. Prior to today, the only people outside of Trently who knew her story were the people sitting at the table. Now everyone in Inverboro, *anyone* with a *Herald* subscription, knew her shame.

When Simon had alerted them to the article, Ella had been prepared to pick up the pieces for Jake. She'd had no idea that the media machine she'd so eagerly embraced last week to push her agenda would turn around and kick her in the teeth.

She'd brought this on herself.

"You okay?" Jake asked, his voice low and soothing.

"Not really." She cradled her face in her hands. "But I've got no one but myself to blame."

"No." He shook his head as his hand moved to her nape and massaged. "This stuff is inexcusable."

"I don't understand." Ella frowned. "Most of this is just salacious gossip wrapped up in some loose public interest excuse. What does he hope to gain from this?"

Rosie shrugged. "Notoriety?"

"Circulation," Simon said.

Jake shook his head. "He's hoping to flush me out. Yank my chain enough that I'll give him what he wants in exchange for him backing off."

Ella laughed. There was a slight note of the manic about it, but she couldn't help herself. "He doesn't know you very well."

But she did. She knew Jake Prince was his own master and didn't dance to anyone else's tune.

"What are you going to do?" Daisy demanded, looking directly at Jake.

"Nothing. For now. I'm not going to feed this monster any more morsels. None of you should." He stood, the chair scraping back loudly, his mouth a grim slash in his face. "I have playoffs and hopefully the game against Chiswick to concentrate on and I will not let that asshole distract me. But after we're done, I'm not going to rest until John Wilmott is writing the fluffi-est-cat-in-show stories for some cowboy operation in fucking Siberia."

17

The impact of the article was as terrible as Ella imagined.

People on everything from TikTok to Jake Prince fan sites to talk-back radio were talking about her morals – *her* morals – and her suitability as a principal. Arguments broke out in comments sections of social media posts which only aided in amplifying the furor.

Television cameras were waiting for her – and anyone else who fancied their face on the six o'clock news – at school on Monday morning and the phone ran hot with interview requests.

But by the time she got to her office, several messages from concerned parents had built up as well as a more ominous one from head office indicating they would call back. By midday, five families had announced their intentions to pull their kids out of Deluca and the phone calls from the media kept coming.

And then the phone call she'd been expecting – dreading – the most came. "Ms. Lucas, this is unacceptable," Donald Wiseman said. "It's not good for any school to be dragged into this kind of disrepute."

"Mr. Wiseman, I can explain."

"I've had media and angry parents on my phone all morning."

"Join the club."

"By my reckoning, if the number of people who say they will pull their kids out of your school *actually* do, then your numbers will no longer be viable."

Ella's grip tightened on the pencil she was flicking in her hand. Was that gloating she heard in his voice? She'd worked so hard to keep Deluca open and the change in the school and the students over the last few months had been truly miraculous.

She didn't know whether to cry or slam the phone against the wall.

"I'm sure after this has blown over in a few days, parents will see it's all been a media beat up and things will calm."

"So, it's not true what they're saying? About your mother, about the affair with your high school principal?"

Ella gritted her teeth. "What I'm saying is that it's nobody's business, and once some other juicy news item has come along it'll all be forgotten."

"And if it isn't?" His pompous inquiry set her teeth on edge. "It might be just as easy to affect an immediate closure. Stop dragging it out."

Ella, usually calm and professional, felt that all snap at his preposterous statement. The rage that had been building since yesterday morning coalesced with the rage from all those goddamn years in Trently. She stabbed the pencil into the fake leather inset of her desk, snapping it in half.

Her hand shook as she rose to her feet, gripping the phone hard, wishing it was Donald Wiseman's testicles instead.

"Go ahead," she hissed. "Try it. This will be old news soon enough and no one is going to give a flying *fuck* who my mother slept with or how many times I supposedly porked the principal."

Donald's mortified spluttering about her *language* fed the roiling pit of rage as Ella plowed on.

"You think *this* is a media storm? This is nothing, *nothing*, compared to what you'll have on your hands if you try to shut me down now. You might like to remember, Donald, that I have a very popular NFL player and his rather large platform up my sleeve and nothing left to lose. And you better believe that makes me a completely loose cannon."

Ella slammed the phone down. And for a moment felt so alive, so invigorated, she could fleetingly understand why people took drugs.

Then her legs gave way and she flopped into an unceremonious heap in her chair.

* * *

On Wednesday, things were still manic and Ella felt like she'd been on the rack for months. Iris's prediction had been eerily accurate – everything was a mess.

Her urban family had been exposed to ridicule, the negative publicity had taken a toll on the students and teachers alike and the Demons were finding it distracting. None of it was conducive to putting them in the zone for their first playoff game the following Friday.

Her phone rang not long after the bell had gone for the first period and Ella picked it up with some trepidation in case a journalist had managed to get through to her private line.

It was Gwen, Cameron's biology teacher. "Cameron's not here."

Ella frowned. "Oh." Cameron hadn't missed a day's school since Jake had picked him for the Demons. None of them had.

"I thought you might like to know."

Ella thanked Gwen and hung up. *Where the hell was he?* He'd been quiet the last few days but then they'd all been a little preoccupied.

She called his cell phone and it went to voicemail. She left a terse get-your-ass-to-school message, then she texted the same for good measure. In fact, over the course of the day, she called and texted Cam dozens of times.

But she wasn't overly worried. She was annoyed for sure, but she knew where he'd be come three o'clock.

Except he didn't show to practice either. "Cam not joining us?" Pete asked.

Ella frowned. "Apparently not."

"Everything okay?"

She gave a half-laugh, half-snort that sounded like an asthmatic horse. "What do you think?"

Pete nodded. "Some of the guys said Cameron's been taking some shit the last few days from the other kids. About Rachel."

Ella bit her lip as tears sprang to her eyes. Goddamn it – the woman had lived hundreds of miles away and was *dead* for crying out loud but still managed to cause Ella and Cam grief.

"Thanks, Pete."

Heading back to her office, she called Jake, who was en route to the school and hadn't seen Cam. She called Trish – not there. Thinking outside the box, she called a couple of the boys he used to hang with before football had set him on the straight and narrow, but they hadn't seen him either.

Clutching at straws, Ella went to the arcade he'd frequented during his truant phase but there was no sign of him. She went home – not there either.

By now it was late afternoon and Ella was imagining him dead on a road somewhere or kidnapped by a serial killer. He'd never done this before. He may have been sullen, rude and hard to get along with, but she'd always known where he was – even when he'd been cutting class.

And they'd been making such progress.

It was almost dark and getting chillier by the second when the front gate squeaked. Ella flew to the front door as Cam stepped inside the house. She was so relieved to see him she didn't know whether she wanted to hug him or spank him.

His casual, "Hey," morphed her relief to anger.

"Don't *hey* me," she snapped. "Where the hell have you been? I've been worried sick all afternoon."

"Around," he muttered, that mulish look she knew so well on his face.

"Around?" Ella winced at the shrillness of her voice as she tried to keep herself in check, aware that Daisy and Iris – no Rosie thankfully – were out on the back porch. But seriously, *around*? "Are you kidding me right now?"

Cameron went to push past her. "I don't want to talk."

Ella stood her ground. Two years ago, the expression he was sporting would have had her backing down, not wanting to push him too much. But she was a lot surer of their relationship now.

"I don't give a good goddamn what you want. Where the hell have you been all day?"

"Places."

"Who were you with?"

"No one."

Ella curled her fingers in her palms in case her temper got the better of her and she wrapped them around his neck. "Have you forgotten your promise to Jake when he put you in the team? What about your practice session today? What about your teammates?"

Yeah, she was pushing him but the adrenaline that had been pumping through her system needed a release somewhere.

"Jeez, Cam, I thought you'd moved past thinking of nobody but yourself? What about the Demons, about Deluca?"

Cam rounded on her then, his face red, his eyes bulging. "What about them?" he roared.

Ella startled at his sudden vehemence. His anger pulsed toward her on a hot cloud. But there was a crack in his voice and tears shining in his eyes.

"They don't give a shit about me," he yelled. "Jesus, Ella, why'd you have to go and open your mouth to that reporter? For the first time in my life, I was living someplace where no one knew all my dirty secrets." He thrust his face right up in hers. "And now the entire school does. *Fuck, t*he whole country knows that my mother was a *whore*."

Ella gasped as he spat the word with such contempt it blew her hair back. She was pretty sure not only Daisy and Iris had heard it but the entire neighborhood had as well.

"Don't say that."

Cameron blinked as tears spilled down his face. "For fuck's sake, Ella, I'm not some kid you have to protect from the truth." His breathing was choppy as he struggled with his emotions. "I knew who she was two years ago. I knew who she was from very early on. You can go on saying things like, *oh Rachel liked to entertain* or *Rachel had a lot of men friends,* to protect me for as long as you like, but I'm not an idiot."

He was right, she *had* done that – made excuses for their mother. Tried to pretend she wasn't who she'd been. Ella had tried to protect him from the truth, just like she had tried to protect herself for so many years.

"And now the whole world knows. How could you?" he demanded. "*How could you?*"

Cameron whirled around and stormed out of the house as she called, "Cam," after him. "Cam, *wait!*"

But the gate opened then slammed closed, the metallic scrape like a rusty nail down a pane of glass.

He was right. *How could she?* It didn't matter that she had no idea the sequence of events it would unleash. That talking to one local paper would lead John Wilmott to Trently and their sordid past.

Daisy appeared in the back doorway, her gaze locking with Ella's. "He'll cool down," she said.

Ella nodded through a blur of tears. Daisy had always been the tough-love aunt, Iris the softie, but there was empathy in her gaze and she appreciated that it was coming from Daisy.

"Yeah." She nodded and sniffled. "I'll just..." She held up her cell. "Call Jake."

"Okay."

Daisy departed and Ella let the tears flow as she scrolled to his number. But she was shaking all over and crying so hard she could barely see the screen and she had to pull herself together to make the call, to be composed enough to speak.

He answered on the third ring. "Did you find him?"

The fact he asked about Cam first had Ella crumbling. "Yes but... we... we y... y... yelled and... and C... Cam was so... so mad... and he was cr... cr... crying... and—"

She choked up then, emotion completely overwhelming her, a huge lump in her throat rendering her incapable of coherent speech. Her nose was running like a tap, so were her eyes. Her ribs were tight around her lungs, biting into them, making it impossible to grab enough air.

"Ella?" Even through a telephone line, Jake's voice was thick with alarm and when she didn't answer – *couldn't* answer – his alarm intensified. "*Ella? Where are you?*"

"At h-home," she wailed.

"I'll be there in ten."

He made it in eight, screeching to a halt in front. Ella, who was sobbing into her hands looked up in time to see Jake practically hurdle over the gate to get to her. He took the steps in two strides, throwing himself down beside her and pulling her into his arms.

"I've m-messed everything up." She'd reached the hiccoughy stage of her crying jag.

"Hey, hey," he said. "It's okay. I'm here."

"No... Please. Go find Cam." Ella shrugged out of his arms. "He's so angry... I don't know what he'll do."

"Cam can wait," he dismissed, his voice firm. "He'll be fine for a few minutes. Tell me what happened."

Ella opened her mouth to tell him but her face crumpled again and nothing came out but a sob.

"Shhh," he crooned, stroking her hair, pulling her into his lap like he had that night in his office and they sat for a few minutes while Ella's tears subsided.

"What happened?" he murmured when she'd grown silent and all that could be heard was the drone of distant car engines.

Ella raised her head from the comforting curve of his neck, took a deep breath and the whole messy argument tumbled out.

"Damn it, how can Rachel still be causing this much trouble so many years down the track? I thought we were both putting it behind us, but it just won't let us be. Why can't Trently just *let us be*? It's always there, between us. She's always there."

He rubbed his cheek against her hair. "Maybe she's always there because you've never let go of the anger? Maybe Trently keeps sucking you back because you keep trying to erase it from your memory banks instead of coming to terms with it?" He dropped a gentle kiss on her head. "You never even grieved her passing, Ella. Maybe it's time to just let it all go?"

Ella's heartbeat filled her head. She knew he was right, even as the rejection came to her lips. "No."

"Yes," he whispered, looking directly into her eyes. "Instead of railing against your origins, maybe you need to embrace them? Whether you like it or not, whether *I* like it or not, Trently's part of us. Rachel's part of you. *And Cam*. Just like my drunk, gambling father's part of me. Like them or loathe them, they made us who we are today." He brushed his thumb across her mouth. "Stronger. And better."

"What about you?" Ella searched his face, looking for an out. He was asking too much. "Have you let go of your anger?"

He nodded. "Over Trently? Sure. Mostly anyway. I had to, years ago. It was interfering with my game too much."

Somewhere, amid the storm of her emotions, the irony that the *jock* was more emotionally evolved was not lost on Ella.

"Have you ever thought that maybe Rachel was just doing the best she could with what she had?" He paused. "I think by and large, people just do the best they can. Even my father. They're not all strong like you, Ella."

Ella gave a little laugh, her voice wobbly. "I'm strong?" Frankly, in that moment, she felt like she was going to break into a thousand pieces. She'd cried three times in the last two years and Jake had been there for each meltdown.

He grinned, easing away from her again. "You're one of the strongest women I know." He stroked her cheek. "It's okay to have loved her, Ella."

Ella felt a lump in her throat. "I did love her."

"Of course you did," he murmured. "She was your mother. It's okay to miss her and to grieve for her. It's also okay to admit you didn't like her. You don't have to make excuses or atone for her sins, no one's asking you to do that. She was a grown woman and her actions were her own. But you do have to find a way to make peace with them, with her. Or you're never going to be able to move forward. Neither will Cameron."

Ella's eyes filled with tears. Maybe he was right. She'd spent the last nineteen years in a knot of conflicted feelings about Rachel. She'd always thought admitting she loved her mom was tantamount to approving of her. But maybe she could love Rachel *and* not like her all at the same time and that was okay.

"She used to dance with me. When I was little. She'd put on 'Blue Moon' and she'd pick me up and waltz me around the room."

"She used to feed me," he said with a smile. "When I came to pick Dad up. I think she knew with my aunt gone there wasn't a lot of routine. She'd say, *Jake, you must be starving. I've made some choc-chip muffins for Ella, help yourself.* Then she'd whip up this shake with honey and ice-cream and she'd sprinkle the top with cinnamon and she'd sit and chat with me while I ate." He rubbed his forehead against her hair. "She asked me about school. About football. She talked about you. A lot. She was proud of your achievements, Ella."

A single tear trekked down Ella's face as she remembered the garnet glow in her mother's room, the choc-chip muffins that had been such a staple of her childhood. When she'd cried in his office that night after the Roger Hillman debacle, she'd been crying for herself, for the sucky hand that life had dealt her. But now she was crying for her mother, mourning the person Rachel was beneath the label Trently had given her.

The real person that no one, including her as she'd grown older, had bothered to see.

Ella dashed the newly falling tears away. She'd cried enough for one day and this wasn't finding Cam. Wriggling off Jake's lap, she sat beside him again, her head on his shoulder.

"Better?" he asked.

She nodded as a rush of the love that had been growing inside her for this man pressed against her vocal cords, wanting out. If she'd had to pick anyone in the world to fall in love with, it wouldn't have been Jake, but she'd done it anyway.

Or maybe she'd always been in love with him – even back in Trently – and this moment had always been inevitable?

Whatever.

It could no longer be denied. And, weirdly, she wasn't afraid to say it because it felt overwhelmingly *right*.

Even amidst the shambles of her life.

"I love you," she said into the cold, crisp night as she stared at the house across the road.

"I love you, too."

The words settled around her like the missing pieces of a jigsaw puzzle, making her whole. She sucked in a breath and glanced at him to find him looking at her. There were no choirs of angels or thunderbolts from heaven that she'd always thought would mark such a moment.

Just Jake. Looking at her. Smiling at her.

Loving her.

Maybe that's why she hadn't been afraid. Maybe she'd known somewhere that he felt the same. Maybe, like her, he'd *always* felt the same?

Ella's lips curved into an answering smile. "You do, huh?"

"I do."

"So this isn't just a sex thing?"

Jake chuckled. "Nope. This is the *real* thing and I'm not going anywhere. I'm afraid you're stuck with me."

Ella's heart practically glowed in her chest. It was hard to believe not that long ago she'd wanted him as far away from her as possible and now, she couldn't imagine her life without him in it.

"Thank you, Jake," she whispered, sliding her arms around his neck and hugging him close, absorbing his strength, his solidness, his *goodness*.

She wasn't sure how long they sat there, just holding each other, their hearts beating as one, but eventually he roused, dropping a kiss on her forehead. "I better go find Cam."

"Oh God, yes, please."

Ella nibbled at her bottom lip as her anxiety returned. This moment on the stoop with Jake had been a calm interlude in the chaos and she'd needed it more than she'd realized. But it was back to reality now.

"I don't know where he'll be."

"I think I do." Dropping a lingering kiss on her mouth, he said, "Sit tight."

* * *

Jake pulled up at the Deluca football field ten minutes later. It had been a momentous night. Getting that frantic phone call from Ella after practice had been like a pickaxe to his heart. Her distress had caused a physical ache in his chest and the state of her when he'd arrived had ramped up the ache to a vicious stabbing pain and he'd realized he wanted to be the one to fix the situation.

That he *always* wanted to be the guy who fixed things for her.

Of course, she didn't *need* him to ride in and rescue her but that didn't stop him wanting to be that guy.

Her guy. Her *first* call. Fixing her shit would be his love language from now.

Love language.

Hearing her say *I love you* had been like opening a door he'd shut a long time ago. Or maybe it hadn't ever been truly open to start with. But it had been wrenched wide tonight and the feelings he'd already been experiencing for her in all their depth and glory, had flooded in.

Ella Lucas loved him. And he loved her right back.

Smiling to himself, he unbuckled and got out of his car, his step lighter than it had been in years despite the conversation ahead. Glancing at the bleachers he could see a lone human shape sitting on the top row. The face was obscured by shadows and a hoodie but he didn't need to be psychic to know it was Cameron.

Jake had always gone to the field when he'd been troubled or needed to think, too.

Jumping the fence with ease, he crossed to the bleachers, striding up them then navigating to where Cameron was sitting. It was evident from the waft of rum that greeted him that the kid was drinking.

"Cam."

Cameron took a swig out of the bottle, not bothering to acknowledge Jake's appearance. "My sister sent you, didn't she?"

Jake sat. "She's worried about you."

"Well it's a bit late for that now."

The bitterness in the teenager's voice hung heavy in the air and Jake remembered they weren't that different, he and Cam.

"Getting drunk?"

Cameron shrugged. "You gonna snitch?"

"Is it helping?"

Cameron held the bottle up to the ambient light, inspecting the line of amber fluid sloshing against the glass. "Give it another ten minutes."

"So, what? You're just going to drink till you pass out? Is that your way of getting back at her?"

"Got a problem with that?"

Jake held onto his temper, forcing an air of nonchalance. "Well, it's not particularly smart."

"Oh, right," Cameron sneered. "You telling me that you've never drowned your sorrows before?"

"Nope. I'm telling you as someone who's drowned his sorrows a little too often, that it's a dumbass thing to do."

Cameron glared at him. "I'm the laughing stock of the school. I thought I'd gotten away from all that crap when she took me away from Trently. She should have just left me there."

Jake nodded and stayed silent for a few minutes letting the angry teenager drink and stew for a little longer.

"You know what I learned a long time ago, Cam?" he asked eventually.

"You can't control what people say about you. You can only control how you react to it. Now, you can get mad, you can get drunk, or you do what I do."

"What's that?" Cameron eyed him with suspicion.

Jake held his hand out for the bottle. "You get even."

Cameron regarded his open hand for a moment and Jake could see both the conflict and the sheen of tears in his eyes. After a beat or two his jaw clamped tight and he said, "Okay." Taking one last swallow, he handed the bottle to Jake. "I want even."

Jake grinned. "Good choice." He tipped the bottle upside down until the last drop of amber fluid had drained away to the grass below. "Now let's go win this game."

18

A few days later, Ella was standing in front of a glass door simply labeled *Lawyer*, conscious that Trently was, as always, watching her. She couldn't believe she was back. She almost turned around and told Jake to forget it. But he squeezed her shoulder and the urge to flee subsided.

He was right. She needed to find some peace.

Taking a deep, fortifying breath, she pushed the door open, the blinds swinging slightly from side to side with the movement. The door shut behind them and she was aware of the rattling as their momentum settled.

Ella blinked as her pupils adjusted to the low light inside Sol Levy's wood-paneled office. There was no pretentiousness in here – no highfalutin' secretary, no gilt-framed art, no leather Chesterfield. Just Sol in his three-piece suit sitting at his big old mahogany desk with real leather inlay, framed by a bank of mahogany bookshelves crammed with leather-bound texts.

"Ella, how lovely to see you, my dear."

Jake's warmth behind her was welcome as the elderly lawyer peered at her over the top of his bifocals and half stood, acknowledging Jake with a nod. "Please, sit, both of you."

He indicated the chairs opposite and they sat. "Thank you for seeing me, Mr. Levy," Ella said.

Sol smiled at her. "I'm pleased you decided to come." He reached down, opened a drawer and extracted a thick, cream-colored envelope. "I believe you're after this."

Ella took the envelope she'd refused two years earlier. She'd instructed Sol to shred it and was exceptionally grateful he hadn't.

"Your mother came to me about a year before she died," Sol said, giving Ella the background she hadn't wanted to hear at the time. "She'd had a premonition she wasn't going to be around for much longer."

Ella looked up from the envelope, surprised at the information. Of course, the good folk of Trently had had a few premonitions of their own, none of which involved the rather pedestrian heart attack that had killed Rachel at fifty-three. They'd been expecting a much stickier end.

Lord knew there were any number of scorned women who hadn't shed a tear when the town tramp had collapsed in her front yard and not been able to be revived.

Sol steepled his fingers and pursed his lips. "There are things in there she desperately wanted you to know."

Ella nodded, slipping it into her handbag. "Thank you."

"Your mother was a good woman, Ella," he said gently. "She always had the time of day for me and that can't be said for everybody, even if I am the only lawyer in town."

The affection in the older man's voice was palpable and Ella was reminded that despite the way the town had painted her, Rachel had always possessed an innate kindness. It had been an easy fact to forget growing up in a community that hadn't cared about the finer points of Rachel's character.

But Jake obviously hadn't forgotten nor had Sol Levy.

"She liked you a lot," Ella murmured.

She stood then and Jake and Sol followed. But she didn't know what to do next. She wanted to leave but wanted to hear more about her mother even as she shied away from the emotional baggage of it all. So she just stood there feeling awkward AF until Jake placed his palm on the small of her back.

"I think we'll be on our way now," he said to Sol.

The lawyer nodded. "Of course. Nice seeing you both."

* * *

Ella stood in front of the non-descript tombstone, her warm breath misting into the cold air. There was just a name and two dates. No lament. No words to usher Rachel's spirit into the afterlife.

No flowers either.

All around them, neatly kept graves boasted vases of freshly cut blooms. Only weeds grew where Rachel lay.

Trently would probably think that was fitting. In fact, Ella wouldn't have put it past the town to deliberately infect her mother's final resting place with such ugliness.

Rachel, who'd always had an eye for beauty, would have hated it.

Ella fell to her knees and started yanking at the scrawny weeds, her movements agitated as she clamped down hard on the rising block of emotion threatening to blind and choke her. The ground was cold, her hands colder as she plucked at the ground.

"Hey," Jake murmured, kneeling beside her, one hand on her back. He placed his other hand over hers, stilling the frantic movements. "Let me do this. Why don't you read the letter?"

Ella rested back on her haunches and looked at him. "She'd hate them."

"I know." And he took over where she'd left off.

Ella watched him for a moment or two before she slowly opened her bag and located the cream envelope. She turned it over a few times before summoning the courage to open it.

The paper was beautiful – expensive and delicately perfumed – so very, very Rachel. But the shock of seeing her mother's flowery handwriting again rocked Ella and she was gripped with a sudden sense of foreboding.

"You're never going to know unless you read it." He stopped what he was doing and looked at her with calm green eyes. "I'm right here." Then he returned to the job, throwing another weed in the pile near his right knee.

With a heavy heart, Ella settled cross-legged on the grass in a patch of sunlight and started to read.

My Darling Ella,

I guess if you're reading this then the prayers of every spoken-for woman in Trently have been answered. They've had their rosary beads and voodoo dolls out for a lot of years and it's nice to know, for them at least, that persistence pays dividends.

Don't be mad at them, darling. Or at me, for that matter. You're a long time dead so life shouldn't be wasted on things that you can't change.

I know you don't understand why I do what I do. It was so much easier, darling, when you were little and would look at me with those huge blue eyes of yours and say, "You look so pretty, Mommy," and not care about the whys.

But then of course, you grew up and I couldn't protect you from the truth. Nor Cam. Please know that if I could have, I would have. But gossip is rife in small towns and it was only ever going to be a matter of time.

I'm truly sorry, if I could do something else, be something else, I would. But the truth is, I'm good at what I do.

And I love it.

You've always made me so proud, darling, but I'm not like you. I didn't have much schooling nor the brains or patience to work for someone else. I never really had any ambition other than falling in love and being loved and being surrounded by beautiful things.

It's why you always gave me so much joy and why Cam continues to do so – you two are the most beautiful things I've ever done.

I've been lucky that men have loved me and allowed me to live in beauty. People in Trently can call it whatever they like – I know the truth.

I give love, darling – and what is more important than love?

Even the young boys, so cocky and full of bravado, leave this place knowing that. They arrive wanting only one thing but leave knowing how to love a woman – truly love her. How to touch her. How to read her. How to appreciate her.

I know that I've made you ashamed, but please, darling, don't be ashamed on my behalf. I'm okay with what I do.

What I am.

Trently, I guess, will be breathing a sigh of relief knowing that I can now be relegated to the annals of history – the dark years when Rachel Lucas preyed on their men. For that I am sorry. I've always held my head up in this town and the thought that I will be judged harshly doesn't sit easily. But, as I said earlier, time shouldn't be wasted on things you can't change.

It is my fervent wish that history will treat me kindly but even I'm not fool enough to believe that. I shall have to settle for being notorious – for that is better than slipping from this life without anyone ever having known you existed.

I'm sorry, my darling, that I'm not the Brady Bunch mother you and Cam yearned for and deserved. But I hope you know that I love you and that I'm happy you have the life now that you always wanted.

I know you will take good care of Cameron. He has perhaps suffered even more than you for what I am. I rejoice, knowing that you'll finally be together.

Be happy, my darling. Remember, life is short. Your loving mother, Rachel xxx

Ella wasn't sure how long she stared at the letter after she finished. She was sad.

So very sad.

Jake finished weeding and plonked himself down next to Ella. "You okay?"

Ella handed him the letter and he read it without comment. When he finished, he folded it up and tugged her close, kissing her head. "Pragmatic to the end."

She nodded and they sat in the patch of sunlight for a while longer.

"Back to Inverboro?" Jake asked eventually.

With a sudden blinding certainty, Ella shook her head. "Back to Levy's."

* * *

"Ella?" Sol rose to his feet, surprise at seeing her again so soon written across his face. "Is everything alright, dear?"

"It will be," she said firmly. "I'd like to set up a Rachel Lucas University Scholarship for disadvantaged students at the high school."

Ella couldn't change the past but she could see to it that her mother wouldn't slip from this life without anyone knowing she'd existed. Trently may want to forget Rachel Lucas – but they could all go to hell. She wasn't rich but she could factor a couple of thousand dollars every year into her budget.

Sol smiled. "Good for you, Ella. Good for you."

* * *

Deluca lost their first playoff game and were knocked out of the competition. After all the excitement of making the playoffs, it was a blow and the team was bitterly disappointed but Ella wasn't. Her small, down-and-out, hard-luck school had made it all the way to the playoffs in their first year.

And, earlier that day, had scored themselves a ridiculously fancy written invitation to play Chiswick College the following Saturday.

They'd done it. They'd really done it.

The entire school community had notched up the first step in saving the school from the Education Department axe and, in the process, united as she'd never imagined possible. It was as if Deluca had gone into a chrysalis all broken and defeated and emerged a thing of beauty, cohesive and unified.

Sure, the last couple of weeks had been exhausting. Between the continued media interest, the intense training schedule and her sexy night times with Jake, there hadn't been a lot of sleep going on. But Ella wouldn't have traded them for anything even if the furor had been unwelcome and uncomfortable. Because she wasn't the same person she'd been before her most private information had been bandied around as *entertainment.*

And that, as it turned out, had been a good thing.

Jake had been right – her anger had been holding her back and taking steps toward letting it go had been incredibly cathartic. Her trip to Trently had helped as had enrolling Cam and her into counseling. There was still a long road ahead but at last Ella felt as if she and Cam were on the right track.

More good news came in on Monday with an official from the NFL calling to talk about funding some practice clinics at Deluca. Several months ago, Ella would rather have burned the school to the ground, but today she felt a little trill of excitement at the possibilities.

And, sweetest of all, Donald Wiseman rang to – rather stiffly – inform her that with a host of new enrollments the district review panel no longer had Deluca on its closure list. It seemed that despite some families not wanting their children at the school, even more families did. The story of the *little school that could* had become a beacon of hope in an area that often ran a little short on that particular commodity and people wanted to be part of it.

Best of all, Donald had let her know that, with their expanded numbers, Deluca High would also qualify for two more teachers and a deputy principal.

So there was a lot to celebrate that night as they all gathered around Daisy and Iris's dining table – the inside one given the freezing rain outside. The household of five had grown to seven with Jake and Simon being at the house more often than they weren't. Add multiple four-legged residents and Miranda and Pete into the mix and it was a raucous affair.

Dinner – curry, of course – was accompanied by the low hum of Ella Fitzgerald and the louder hum of everyone laughing and talking, enjoying each other's company. Watching Jake talking tarot with Iris, Ella realized that all the warmth and love at this table tonight was because of Rosie's aunts.

They had opened up their perfectly happy, chain smoking, spinster existence twenty years ago to two small-town runaways without complaint.

A lump swelled in Ella's throat. She'd been truly blessed.

"What?" Daisy asked, squinting suspicious eyes at Ella.

Ella laughed at the crotchety inquiry. "Nothing."

"Nothing my ass," she chortled. "What was that look about?"

Ella sighed. "I was just thinking how marvelous you and Iris are. You took us in, became our family." She shrugged. "You gave us this amazing life."

"Nonsense," Daisy dismissed. "Our lives hadn't begun until you girls came along."

Iris nodded. "You *are* our life."

Ella's vision misted over and Jake's hand squeezed her thigh under the table. "To urban families," Rosie said, her eyes also bright as she picked up her red wine.

Everyone toasted then Cam and Miranda stood. "Can we go and watch some TV?" he asked.

"Sure," Ella agreed. "Door open though, please."

"And not too late," Jake warned. "Early to bed for the next week. Miranda, I'm taking you home in an hour."

"Yes, Coach," they chorused, rolling their eyes in the way of teenagers the world over.

The adults watched them go. "They're good together," Iris murmured.

Nobody disagreed.

As dinner continued, reminiscing about the season took center place. "I'd just like to say at this juncture," Simon said with a grin, "this whole thing was my idea."

"So it was," Ella agreed. She had no idea where they'd be now if it hadn't been for Simon.

Rosie slung her arm around his shoulders. "He's brilliant, isn't he?"

"Definitely," Ella agreed. "And for that I give you permission to do unspeakable things to my best friend."

"Don't take this the wrong way, Ella, but I'm going to do unspeakable things to this woman whether you permit it or not."

Ella lifted an eyebrow at Rosie. "I see your penchant for dominance is rubbing off?"

"What can I say?" Rosie sighed. "The man's a quick study."

The conversation soon turned to the game with Chiswick the following Saturday. The exclusive private school hosted the event at their state-of-the-art football field and they'd won this particular exhibition game for sixteen years straight.

And, as Jake had stated a few months ago, a public school had never beaten Chiswick in this arena.

"I managed to get hold of some footage of Chiswick's last game." Pete dropped the morsel into the conversation and everyone turned to stare at him.

"Have you seen it?" Jake asked.

He nodded. "The first ten minutes. They're *really* good."

"And?" Daisy demanded. "Did you bring it with you?"

Pete winked at her. "Of course."

"Well don't just sit there," she bellowed. "Show us the damn thing."

They adjourned to the living room, Pete casting the footage from his phone to the television. The vision was muffled and amateur but there were good close-ups of the action and Jake kept muttering, "This is gold," as he watched the play.

"Well done, Pete," he said at half-time as the person videoing obviously decided crowd shots and scenery would suffice until the game started again.

They used the break in play to analyze the game. "There's some great stuff on there," Simon said.

"Yep." Jake nodded. "Pete and I will go over it in more detail tomorrow morning and with the team in the afternoon."

"They look amazing," Rosie commented.

"They do," Jake agreed. "Chiswick are champions, no doubt. But the Demons have come from nowhere, with very little and made the playoffs which is not nothing. And we have something that they don't. We have something to prove."

Ella couldn't dispute that but watching the game had put a real itch up her spine. Chiswick scared the bejesus out of her.

She turned to Jake. She loved him. He'd turned her entire life upside down and somehow in the process managed to turn it right around. But she wanted him to know that it was okay to be beaten by a superior team. That winning this one didn't matter.

That they'd *already* proved themselves.

"Jake, this game... it doesn't matter. Not anymore. Deluca's not under threat of closing and the team have exceeded all expectations. But these guys" – she tipped her head at the television – "they're in a league of their own."

A frown furrowed his forehead. "I got into this whole thing for the Chiswick game. It's the *end* game. You need me to win it and that's what I'm going to do."

Ella blinked. He'd essentially been *badgered* into coaching.

"I'm just saying that... no one's going to think less of you, *or* the Demons, if they lose this game."

"*I'll* think less of me."

Okay, he *really* wanted this. The guy who'd been happy drinking Coronas and flirting with women at his bar. Was this some kind of redemption for him, too? Maybe he needed the Demons to restore his reputation as much as they'd needed him to restore Deluca's?

The thought set off a warm glow around her heart but still... expectation management seemed prudent.

"Look... I get it. I do," she said. "But Chiswick is an exclusive boys' educational facility. They obviously have the best equipment and coaches money can buy."

"*You* have the best coach money can buy," he said.

She raised an eyebrow. "You're free, Jake."

"What can I say?" He blasted her with his steely green gaze. "The school principal drives a hard bargain."

Oh *Lordy*. Her body took that in an *entirely* different way than it was intended considering how affronted he looked.

Ella cleared her throat. "What I'm *trying* to say, is the boys have done their best and I don't want them to get their hopes up too high. It's alright to admit defeat, you know. There can even be honor in it."

A shout on the video drew everyone's attention to the television as the Chiswick College boys ran back onto the field. The person behind the camera said, "What do you think, Coach?" and swung around for a close-up of a man wearing a shirt that said Coach.

The shot was blurry and came slowly into focus.

"We've got this one in the bag," the Chiswick coach said. "The opposition are a pack of limp dick, pansy-assed cry-babies that play like a bunch of girls. They might as well have their cheerleaders play the game for them. At least we'd have a bit of tits and ass action to look at."

Everyone stared in horror at the screen. "Yeah," Pete said sheepishly over the continuing tirade of abuse. "Thought I'd leave that bit to last. Tony Winchester's son plays for Chiswick. He's just scored the head coaching gig there."

Ella stared at the face on the screen as it continued to mouth horrible obscenities about the opposition like they were brainless zombies and their cheerleaders like they were there for his sexual pleasure. A wave of disgust swept through her, heating her skin and flushing her face. She already detested the man for what he'd done to Trish but this tirade was turning her vision red.

"Forget what I just said." She turned to Jake. "I want you to win. Not just win but I want you to *crush* that smarmy asshole into the dust. And then when he's down, I want you to *stomp* on his neck so he can *never* utter another vile word."

Grinning, Jake performed a mock salute. "Yes, ma'am."

"Good," she muttered and reached across to the table for the remote, flicking a button to switch it off.

Tony Winchester wasn't welcome in their house.

19

Ella sat in the plush locker rooms at Chiswick College on a cold clear Saturday morning listening to Jake and Pete give their pre-game talk to the Demons. She could see the impossibly green, manicured field through the slats of the blind covering the window. As if a team of trained leprechauns had individually trimmed each blade of grass.

Occasional shouts from the large crowd filtered in as the astringent aroma of Deep Heating assaulted her senses. There was a kaleidoscope of butterflies in her stomach. Butterflies that had swallowed elephants.

She wanted to *win*. Not for her or for Jake or for Deluca, but for Trish. She wanted to see Tony Winchester go down.

"Ella?"

Jake and Pete were looking at her expectantly and Ella guessed it was her turn to speak. She enjoyed the tradition of her principal pep talk more and more each time and so, she thought, did the team. Or at least, it was a ritual they'd dare not buck in case any deviation from routine brought bad luck.

And they called women flighty!

She looked at each of the boys in turn. She could tell they were a little awed by their surroundings. Chiswick College was a physically impressive campus – landscaped gardens, space-age classrooms, intimidating sandstone buildings reeking of wealth.

And they were looking to her to tell them it didn't matter. That how you played the game and the size of your heart trumped money and tradition.

But today she was reluctant.

Today she wanted to say things she never thought she'd ever think, let alone contemplate giving voice to. She wanted to say kill them, smash them, play dirty if you have to, gouge their eyes, punch them in the kidneys, spear their rich little heads into the ground if needs be – just win.

At any cost.

It went against everything she believed in but it was right there on the tip of her tongue, waging a battle against her political correctness to be heard.

"Ella?" Jake prompted.

She glanced at him. He was nodding at her to get on with it and she stood automatically, her gaze falling on Cameron. He was sitting so tall. So confident. And when he smiled at her she knew she'd come too far with him to take him backward.

Her legs trembled a little as she cleared her throat. "I'm not going to say much," she said. "You guys have already done me and Deluca and Jake and Pete so proud. You've come a long way and earned yourselves a fearsome reputation. I know you want to win today. Well, guess what? I want you to win today, too."

The Demons glanced at her with confused looks. They weren't used to their principal being so outcome focused. But, as her words slowly dawned on them, they started to grin and, one by one, they started to clap and stomp their boots until the locker room was filled with an almighty clatter.

"So go on now," she called out above the din, holding up her hand and waiting for the racket to die down. "Let's get out there and show them how we do it on the southside."

The team sprang to their feet, cheering and clapping and Ella laughed, caught up in the heady mix of exuberance and testosterone.

"Way to go, Ms. Lucas," Jake murmured as the boys filed out of the room.

Ella favored him with a steady stare. "Annihilate him."

"I love it when you talk dirty," he whispered, flicking a towel at her butt as he followed the team out.

Ella stayed until she was the only one left in the room, taking a moment to center herself, thinking about all that had got them to this point and the game ahead. She supposed others might have prayed but she didn't think it was appropriate to ask for divine assistance in something as frivolous – compared to real life horrors – as a football game.

Or Tony Winchester's demise, for that matter.

Instead, she wished for things to be *right*, then stepped out into the cool darkness of the tunnel that led from the locker rooms to the field.

"Ella?"

"Cam?" She frowned. "Everything okay?"

"Yes." The scrape of his boot against the concrete floor echoed around the tunnel as he shuffled his feet.

"Shouldn't you be on the field?"

"I just want to... I'd like to talk to you for a moment."

Ella peered over his shoulder, satisfied to see the game hadn't yet started. "Okay."

Taking a deep breath, he looked at his sister. "I'm sorry for being such a jerk."

Ella blinked, completely taken aback by his apology, the only one she'd ever heard come from his mouth. "About our argument a few weeks ago?"

"No. Well, yes... that too. But I mean, just generally. I know I haven't been very easy to get along with. It's just... growing up in Trently was hard, you know?"

"Yeah." She knew.

"And I dreamed for years my big sister would come and rescue me and when you didn't it was easier to... hate you."

Tears needled Ella's eyes. "Oh, Cam! I would have, if I'd known, I would have."

She took a step toward him but he took a step back and held out his hand to pause her movement. "I know that now. I do. And I *didn't* hate you, not really. Miranda reckons I'm lucky to have such a cool big sister. And so do I."

His voice cracked a little and Ella's tears threatened to spill. A lump in her throat grew bigger, stretching to painful proportions. Maybe the counseling she'd insisted upon was making bigger inroads than she thought?

"I love you, Cam," she whispered. "We may not have been brother and sister for long but we're part of each other and I love you."

Cameron's gaze dropped to his boots. "Same," he mumbled.

"Cam!"

Ella jumped as Jake's exasperated command ricocheted around the cavernous tunnel. "What are you doing? It's twenty seconds to kick-off."

Cameron looked at Jake then at her. "Go," she said, giving him a quick, fierce hug. "Go!"

He ran toward the light, his cleats clacking on the cement. Jake slapped him on the back as he passed and ran beside him, accompanying him to the field. Ella followed at a more sedate pace, her mind turning over the things Cam had said and their import. He'd been taking baby steps these past weeks but this was one giant leap.

For the first time she *knew* they were going to be alright.

The sound of boot hitting ball rang like a shot around the field as Ella emerged into the full light of day. The packed stadium erupted into a hearty cheer, the large contingent of Deluca supporters standing out in their red demon-horn headbands. They looked amazing and she slid hers in place as she hurried to the sideline bench.

Ella noticed a large contingent of press roped off on the opposite side of the field. John Wilmott was right in the middle, a smug look on his face. This game usually got plenty of press attention but it had been significantly elevated since Wilmott's scandalous exposé on her life.

The story wasn't about two high school teams anymore. As far as the national media was concerned it was about two old rivals squaring off against each other.

As though the pressure on the Demons wasn't bad enough.

Ignoring the media, Ella plonked herself between Rosie and Trish and grabbed their hands. Simon was on the other side of Rosie and they were all sporting a set of devil-horn headbands. Pete was standing off to one side watching the play while Jake prowled along the sideline, a bedeviled Cerberus at his heels.

"What's happening?"

"Nothing yet," Rosie said.

It didn't take long for that to change. And it wasn't a change for the better.

Chiswick wiped the field with the Demons in the first half with their superior ball skills, as though it was their God-given right to win. Ella, as per her usual position, spent half the time with her hands over her eyes, begging Rosie and Trish to tell her what was happening.

Tony Winchester spent the first half on the opposite side of the field, yelling at his team despite their exemplary play. A slight fumble, a misstep, and he was hurling insults that made even Rosie blush.

It was a shame really, because Ella had to admit that, objectively, he was still an impressive-looking man. He hadn't gone to seed as a lot of ex-jocks did. Tony Winchester still had *it* and it was easy to see why Trish had fallen for him. But as far as she was concerned, his black heart and cruel tongue made him uglier than a hat full of assholes.

After a particularly awful tongue-lashing, Trish curled her fingers around Ella's so hard she winced. "He's such a tyrant." She shuddered. "Where the hell was my head?"

Ella shrugged. "Time has a way of eroding facades."

"And he's just butt-ugly under his," Rosie added.

Trish laughed. "Yes, he is, isn't he?"

"He's a fucking mad man," Rosie said. "Aren't there rules against this kind of behavior in kids' sports?"

Not that any of Chiswick's team looked like kids.

* * *

At half time, Chiswick led by sixteen points, with Deluca only managing to get six on the board from one touchdown. Jake followed his team back into the locker room. Ella, Simon, Rosie and Trish joined them, as did Cerberus, who found Cam immediately and collapsed on the floor at his feet.

Jake eyed the dejected players, struggling to find the right words to inspire and empower. He glanced at Ella, who gave him an encouraging nod. He opened his mouth, hoping to God the words that came out were the ones the Demons needed to hear. But before he said a single thing, a string of obscenities from the Chiswick camp next door echoed around the Deluca room.

Jake's mouth shut automatically, stunned by the ferocity of Tony's *pep* talk. He was ranting about the Deluca touchdown. How Chiswick's strategy was to keep their opponents off the board altogether and how badly they'd fucked up. He was screaming *failure, failure, failure*. Calling them morons. Calling them *girls*.

"Why is he yelling at them?"

Jake tuned back in to his locker room and saw the stunned looks on his players' faces as Ned, a skinny red-headed kicker, voiced the question that was obviously on all of their minds.

"They're really good," Ned said. "They're all over us."

Jake glanced at Ella standing by the door, her expression livid, then at Trish who looked deathly pale. "Yes." Jake cleared his throat. "Yes, they are. Their coach, however, is a monumental asshole."

A few of the guys laughed but Jake could see that most of them were still tuned into Tony Winchester's continued verbal abuse of his team. He couldn't blame them. It was ghoulishly, horrifyingly, compelling. Like hanging around a crash site watching the victims being cut out of their cars.

But he didn't want *Tony* in their heads.

Jake belted on a nearby locker, the sound crashing into the morbid stillness and pulling everyone's attention back to him.

"Don't listen to him," Jake said quietly. "Listen to me."

He spoke to them then, about their struggle to get here. About their spirit, their heart, their triumphs – things that Ella usually talked about. He praised their individual strengths and applauded their teamwork. And gradually the next-door rant faded and he could see by the expressions on their faces that they were only listening to him.

"Whatever happens today, you boys have made me prouder than I've ever been. Prouder even than when I won my first Super Bowl ring. And you have one thing that they..."

Jake pointed next door to where the rant continued.

"Don't have. *Respect*. For me. For Pete. For Ms. Lucas. For each other. And you have my respect too. I know how hard you've worked and it's because of you I get out of bed each morning with a spring in my step. It's because of you my life has a purpose again. After the way my career ended, I didn't want to be back in the limelight, but you've shown me that just because things are hard, doesn't mean you shouldn't do them. Which is why, despite what that board says, we're going to win this."

Finishing up, Jake took a moment to look at each team member and shake their hand. "Pete?" He raised an eyebrow at Pete, indicating he could take the floor, but he declined. "Ella?"

She shook her head, tears shining in her eyes. "Nothing to add, Coach."

A loud rap at the door alerted them that half time was nearly over. "Alright," Jake said. "Let's line up outside and run onto that field like we've already won."

The boys sprang to their feet, cheering and high-fiving as they filed out and waited in the tunnel for the signal to take the field. The adults stood behind them, Jake slipping his hand into Ella's and the full wattage of her you-were-so-hot-just-now smile hit him right in the groin.

The clatter of cleats alerted Jake to the presence of the Chiswick team emerging from their locker room.

"Well, well, well," a voice drawled from behind him. "If it isn't The Prince and the Pauper."

Ella flinched and Jake stiffened as they half turned. He held her hand tight in case she decided smacking Winchester's face was worth it.

Or he did.

Rosie took a step in their direction and he placed a stilling hand on her. No way was he going to get into a slanging match in front of his team and the press who had a clear view into the tunnel mouth. He forced himself to be calm and kept his voice low.

"It's been a long time, Tony."

Tony nodded. "That it has." He flicked his gaze over Trish. "Hey Trish. Still smokin', I see."

Cerberus growled a Genghis-level growl as Trish smiled contemptuously. "Still a douchebag, I see."

Clearly unrattled by Trish's insult, Tony's laugh echoed in the tunnel, enhancing his creepiness but then a figure appeared at the mouth of the tunnel. "Time to rumble," it announced.

Jake returned his attention to the team. "Let's go."

The Demons ran onto the field, followed by Chiswick. Tony stopped by Jake and together they watched their boys line up against each other. Tony's gaze flicked to the Deluca cheer squad and he smirked.

"What kind of cheerleaders are they?" he scoffed. "You can't even look up their skirts."

Jake gave Tony a hard look. "The minor kind."

It gave Jake enormous satisfaction to see Tony's jaw tighten. "You always were a morally superior prick," he spat.

"Better than being just a prick," Jake said then walked away lest the urge to beat Tony to a pulp in front of a dozen cameras became uncontrollable.

* * *

Ella's stomach looped-the-loop as the second half started. Jake's speech had been magnificent but had been resoundingly overwritten in her head by Tony's awful comments in the tunnel.

The stakes had never been clearer.

But she needn't have worried. It was as if a switch had been flicked. Chiswick looked defeated from the whistle, making simple errors and not capitalizing on a host of opportunities.

Tony ranted. The more he ranted, the worse they played.

"I've made up my mind," Trish said to Ella as they tried to ignore the tantrums of a grown man and watch the play. "I'm going to the police next week to press charges against Tony."

Ella gaped. She admired Trish's chutzpah but being outed by a journalist was very different to voluntarily putting herself out there. "I think that's amazingly brave but are you *sure*?"

"I am." She nodded. "I *need* to do this."

Trish's expression was deadly serious and Ella realized that staying on the sidelines wasn't an option for Trish anymore. It seemed like this whole Demons experience hadn't just been cathartic for her and Cam and Jake. It'd been cathartic for Trish, too.

But still...

"This many years down the track it's going to be hard to prove," she pointed out. "Even with Jake's evidence."

"It doesn't matter." Trish shook her head. "If they throw it out of court, it doesn't matter. I need to say out loud what he did to me. And anything I can do to see that Tony Winchester isn't allowed to coach minors again, I'm prepared to do."

Ella squeezed Trish's hand, in no doubt about her conviction but wanting her to be aware of any potential ripples. "It could get messy. Miranda could be affected."

Trish shrugged. "You and Cam are still here, aren't you?"

Ella smiled. Yes, they were. And no doubt better for having all their dirty linen hung out to dry.

A cheer exploded from behind her and Rosie leaped to her feet, yanking Ella with her as Deluca ran in their third touchdown. Trish rose too and they all hugged and cheered. When Ned quickly converted it for two points – his third conversion in a row – the cheer became a roar and Ella grinned as a puce-faced Tony Winchester went apoplectic.

Karma, baby.

Five minutes later, however, the high they'd been riding took a sudden nosedive. A collective gasp rang around the field at a sickening tackle perpetrated on Ned by two of Chiswick's defensive tackles. The referee blew his whistle as Ned lay crunched in a heap on the ground.

Simon flew to his feet. "They've targeted him."

Jake and Pete were running onto the field, followed by a stretcher bearer and a medic. Ella twisted her head to locate Ned's parents already making their way down, their faces anxious. She turned in time to see Tony Winchester smiling and patting the shoulder of one of the Chiswick boys who'd been responsible for the dangerous tackle.

A minute later, Ned was on his feet but very groggy, being supported by the medic and Jake. The referee blew his whistle for a penalty, but Ella knew that Tony Winchester's mission had been accomplished – they'd taken out Deluca's best kicker.

The medics took Ned into the locker room, followed by his worried parents. "Is he okay?" Ella asked as Jake joined her and play resumed.

Jake gave a stiff nod. "A little concussed. They'll take him to hospital, probably keep him under observation overnight."

Tactically it was the worst thing Tony Winchester could have sanctioned, because now the Demons were just plain *mad* and they played the remaining fifteen minutes like they'd been born with their boots on. With one minute to go, the Demons were in an unassailable position.

Ella and Rosie had tears streaming down their faces as the whistle sounded and Ella laughed as the cameras caught Tony Winchester mid-tantrum, stomping off the field. The Deluca supporters went crazy, running onto the field, Ella included. Often, she hung back waiting for the excited throngs to have their time congratulating the team and the coach before she joined the fray.

Not today.

Ella fought tooth and nail to get to Jake and Cameron in the scrum of well-wishers. Jake had done it. She'd asked him to annihilate Tony Winchester and he had. And with Trish's second salvo, the man was going to be utterly destroyed.

"Let me through," Ella called, being jostled from side to side. Cam was further away and swamped – Jake was closer and she had him firmly in her sights. "Let me pass."

Spotting Ella, he surged through the throng, grinning at her as she flung herself into his arms. "Let me be the first to kiss the coach," she yelled over the hubbub.

"I hate to disillusion you," Pete said. "You ain't the first."

"Oh, yeah?" Ella pulled Jake's head down for a thoroughly X-rated smacker.

Pete laughed. "Okay, you're the first to kiss him like *that*."

"So, Jake, does it feel good to beat your old nemesis?"

Ella frowned at the familiar voice yelling to be heard over the top of the noise. Half turning in Jake's arms, she met John Wilmott's shrewd gaze. Her lips flattened.

"I thought that was you?" Jake said.

Wilmott laughed. "I think you know who I'm talking about."

Jake paused for a beat as if he was carefully considering his answer. "It felt un-fucking unbelievable."

The reporter laughed again. "Can I quote you?"

"I'd be amazed if you didn't."

* * *

Later that night, Ella lay in Jake's arms in a post-coital drowse that was better than drugs. "That was exceptionally good," she murmured, stroking her fingers down his arm.

"Honey," he said, a smile in his voice, "winning-game sex is my forté."

Ella laughed. "You're pretty damn cocky, you know that?"

"But you like it."

She did. She really did. She hadn't thought of Pythagoras once the entire time he'd been back in her life.

And what a ride that had been.

Her hand stilled, reveling in the warm, solid muscle beneath her palm. "Thank you, Jake. For everything."

Shifting, Jake rolled up onto his side, his gaze locking with hers. "Thank *you*. You have no idea how much I owe you."

Ella's chest filled with the deepest, happiest, most contented sigh to have ever been sighed. "Lucky for you," she said, walking her fingers up his arm, "I have a payment plan."

"I like the sound of that," he murmured.

Ella smiled as he nuzzled her neck, her eyelids drifting shut. She hadn't meant *that* but it wasn't a bad idea. His tongue flicked across her skin, fritzing out her brain cells and she angled it a little further, enjoying the sensations pebbling her nipples and stirring again between her legs.

But first, business.

"I want to make the Demons a permanent part of Deluca High life," she said breathily as a wave of goosebumps stippled her skin. "We're about to get a chunk of money from a Community Foundation to develop the football program and I want you to be the coach. Pete too if he's interested."

His lips, pressed to the pulse at the base of her throat, stilled. Raising his head, his eyes met hers. "Well, look at you, Little Miss Football." His mouth curved into a smug smile. "You've certainly changed your tune."

Ella blushed. She *had* been rather denigrating about the value of sport in the beginning. "I may not have been football's best advocate, but I'd be foolish if I couldn't see the change its spawned in the school. If it keeps the kids coming to Deluca and getting them an education, then I'm all for it."

Jake blinked. "You're serious." He rolled onto his back and stared at the ceiling.

Ella rolled on top of him, bracketing her arms either side of his head as she found and held his gaze. "The boys respect and look up to you. And that speech you gave today is all I need to know about your coaching style."

"I never seriously thought about coaching, before Deluca," he murmured. "Trish is always banging on about it but I've always just dismissed it out of hand."

"Then you've missed your calling."

"High school football," he said, his voice low as if he was turning the idea over in his head.

As a teacher, Ella knew when to push and when to let things ruminate. Lowering her mouth, she pressed kisses along the scruff of his jawline and nuzzled his ear.

"Is this persuasion?"

She smiled against his skin. "Incentive."

"I suppose the pay's lousy?"

Ella had no doubt Jake could earn serious money coaching for a professional team. She could offer him only peanuts in comparison. But how much damn money did he need?

"Yup. But" – she undulated her body suggestively – "the perks are excellent."

He chuckled as he grabbed her ass, holding her flush against him. "What about the bar?"

Lifting her head, she looked down into the face of the man she had probably loved most of her life – even if she hadn't been aware of it.

"That's not you, Jake. You only bought it because it was something you knew. You're *not* your father."

The silence built around them, her heart thudding hard in her chest while she waited for the verdict. "Well?" she prompted after several *long ass* beats. She couldn't take another second of his silence. "What do you say, Coach?"

Still he didn't speak, just looked into her eyes like he was looking into her soul. Then suddenly, in one swift movement, she was flat on her back, his body pressing hers into the mattress.

"I say" – his mouth hovered over hers – "drop and give me fifty."

Her laughter was cut off by the hard press of his mouth. He could have whatever he wanted, this man of hers.

Forever and always.

ACKNOWLEDGEMENTS

Before I get on to the acknowledgements a few things about the book. For those of you not aware, Inverboro is an entirely fictional city that I set on the shores of Lake Michigan in Wisconsin. Trently is an entirely fictional small town in Kansas. I also made up the NFL team names – both the Sentries and the Founders are complete figments of my imagination.

Isn't fiction wonderful?

And now onto the thank yous!

Firstly a big thank you to everyone at Boldwood Publishing for giving this book a new lease of life. You have all welcomed me so warmly into the family and it's been an absolute delight getting to know the team. Special thanks to my editor, Megan Haslam, who I've worked with for many years now. It was so nice to follow her on her new adventure with Boldwood.

Thanks to the fab Amanda Ashby for letting me pick her brains when I was considering my publishing options.

Thanks to my agent Jill Marsal from Marsal Lyon for her guidance and calming aura.

Thanks also to my wonderful fan group the Amy Andrews All Stars. They are not only my cheer squad but my brains trust when I need help with a story-related issue especially when checking regional lingo from all around the world!

Thanks to Gigi for her beta reading and super big thanks to Kate Halma for casting her eagle eye over the book looking for US/NFL references. Any errors are my own or there for deliberate creative effect. Thanks to Penni Askew for putting me in touch.

Special sparkly thanks to my author pals who hold my hand when I need it and pop the champagne corks when there's something to celebrate. Ally

Blake, Clare Connelly, Jennifer St George, Pippa Roscoe, Rachael Stewart and Rachel Bailey. These women truly understand the ups and downs of a career author and I'm so glad to have them in my corner. Thank you, my lovelies, you are all awesome.

Thanks also to the three other musketeers in my life. My bestie Leah who's been with me since I was thirteen and always thinks I look fabulous in whatever outfit I'm wearing even when it isn't so. Every woman needs that kind of cheerleader in their life. My sister, Ros, who knew me first and loves me in a way that only a sister can. She carries my heart, And, my husband Mark, who's been loving me and making me laugh for thirty-seven years. I am truly blessed.

ABOUT THE AUTHOR

Amy Andrews is an award-winning, USA Today best-selling, Australian author of over ninety contemporary romances.

Sign up to Amy Andrews' mailing list for news, competitions and updates on future books.

Follow Amy on social media here:

facebook.com/AmyAndrewsAuthor

x.com/AmyAndrewsbooks

instagram.com/amyandrewsbooks

tiktok.com/@amyandrewsbooks

LOVE NOTES

LOVE IN EVERY CHAPTER

WHERE ALL YOUR ROMANCE
DREAMS COME TRUE!

THE HOME OF BESTSELLING
ROMANCE AND WOMEN'S
FICTION

 WARNING:
MAY CONTAIN SPICE

SIGN UP TO OUR
NEWSLETTER

https://bit.ly/Lovenotesnews

Boldwood

Boldwood Books is an award-winning fiction publishing company seeking out the best stories from around the world.

Find out more at www.boldwoodbooks.com

Join our reader community for brilliant books, competitions and offers!

Follow us
@BoldwoodBooks
@TheBoldBookClub

Sign up to our weekly deals newsletter

https://bit.ly/BoldwoodBNewsletter